George F. Chambers

The Church and State Handy-Book

of arguments, facts, and statistics suited to the times

George F. Chambers

The Church and State Handy-Book
of arguments, facts, and statistics suited to the times

ISBN/EAN: 9783337345136

Printed in Europe, USA, Canada, Australia, Japan

Cover: Foto ©Andreas Hilbeck / pixelio.de

More available books at **www.hansebooks.com**

The

Church - and - State Handy - Book

Of Arguments, Facts, and Statistics
Suited to the Times.

Compiled by

George F. Chambers, F.R.A.S.

Of the Inner Temple.

"If the trumpet give an uncertain sound, who shall prepare himself to the battle?"
1 Cor. xiv. 8.

London:
William Macintosh
Paternoster Row.

1866.

Price One Shilling.

Inscribed

Preface.

THE design of the present work may be thus expressed:—
To furnish the Church-and-State politician, in a conveniently
small compass, with a fund of information, Scriptural,
argumentative, historical, and statistical, calculated to be
useful to him in fulfilling his public duties in matters ecclesiastical
or semi-ecclesiastical. The subjects dealt with range themselves
substantially under three heads:—

1. The observance of the Lord's Day.
2. Dissenting aggressions on the Established Church.
3. Roman Catholicism as an element in British politics.

Under the first head I have discussed the Sunday question, from a
purely Biblical stand-point; and, subordinately, in the light thrown
upon it by the authoritative standards of the Church of England, and
practical experience.

Under the second head I have constructed an elementary frame-
work of Scriptural argument in favour of the union of Church and
State, following up the same with a large mass of material calculated
to be of practical value at the present moment, when such gigantic
efforts are being made by organised bands of schismatics to uproot
the Church establishment. To illustrate this, let me quote the
announced intention of the "Rev." Joseph Parker, D.D., an able
supporter of the Liberation Society's principles at Manchester:—

"*I have resolved to visit every principal town in the kingdom, so far as
pastoral duties will permit, and deliver the lectures which I am now concluding. I have resolved to publish a considerable number of tracts, short,
pointed and explicit, on Nonconformist questions, exposing the heresy of the
Prayer-Book, the sacerdotalism of the Church, the illogical effusions of the
Clergy, and the abominations of religious establishments. I propose to give
these tracts away at every Church Congress, at every Church Missionary
Meeting, on the highways, in railway carriages, from house to house, at the
seaside, at home, abroad, everywhere, following the bane with the antidote,
chasing the enemy from den to den, until death shall arrest my labours.*"

The third head is treated of in as similar a manner with the foregoing as the different character of the subject will admit. I have

sought to put together with the utmost brevity some suggestive lines of Scriptural argument, appending to these some reflections suited to a period like the present, when Popery is making such dangerous inroads into Church and State in England; for the prophetical notes is claimed only the merit of terseness, so far as I am concerned; of tolerable certainty, so far as *the two main conclusions* are concerned.

A few miscellanea conclude the volume.

To the many friends, known and unknown, in all parts of England who have aided or encouraged the present work in its various stages, I can only here offer general, but none the less sincere, thanks. It has been a great and real satisfaction to find my efforts in the cause of England's Church so widely appreciated.

Finally, it may be stated that into this work are incorporated the *Sussex Tracts for Churchmen*, for the most part long since out of print.

G. F. C.

JUNIOR CARLTON CLUB,
LONDON: *Easter* 1866.

Contents.

Book I.

The Sunday Question.

It may be safely asserted that few questions have drawn forth such displays of artful sophistry as a substitute for solid argument as that which is now to be examined.

I propose to deal with—

(1). The perpetual obligation of the Sabbath [*i.e.* in the strict Hebrew sense of a weekly day of rest].

(2). The secular advantages provable to arise from it.

(3). Some practical hints and suggestions.

The first assertion to be disproved is that *the Sabbath is a Jewish Institution, and therefore not binding on Christians.* It will be convenient here to group together some texts for review :—

Genesis ii. 3.—"And God blessed the seventh day, and sanctified it: because that in it He had rested from all His work, which God created and made."

Exodus xx. 8-11.—"Remember the Sabbath day, to keep it holy. Six days shalt thou labour, and do all thy work: but the seventh day is the Sabbath of the Lord thy God: in it thou shalt not do any work, thou, nor thy son, nor thy daughter, thy manservant, nor thy maidservant, nor thy cattle, nor thy stranger that is within thy gates: for in six days the Lord made heaven and earth, the sea, and all that in them is, and rested the seventh day: wherefore the Lord blessed the Sabbath day, and hallowed it."

Exodus xxiii. 12.—"Six days shalt thou do thy work, and on the seventh day thou shalt rest: that thine ox and thine ass may rest, and the son of thy handmaid, and the stranger may be refreshed." *

In ascribing a Jewish or Mosaic origin to the Sabbath, our opponents are in duty bound to produce testimony of its actual institution by Moses or some of his contemporaries. This they fail to do, and (assuming ignorance for the present), whoever did institute it, one thing is *quite certain*, that Moses *did not*. (*Ex.* xx. 1.)

The 16th chapter of Exodus contains a clear intimation that it was known long before the occurrence of the event which forms the main topic of that chapter. One month after their departure from Egypt, the children of Israel began to fear that they should want food, and murmured against Moses and Aaron (ver. 2). Thereupon the Lord told Moses that He would give them bread from heaven, which they should collect day by

---

* It is worthy of note that the parallel passage, *Deut.* v. 14, has an addendum—"In it thou shalt not do any work, &c., that thy manservant and thy maidservant may rest as well as thou." Let us then understand that we are to apply the obligation not alone to ourselves, as regards our own acts, but also to our dealings with our servants and dependents.

day, but that on the sixth day they were to prepare a double portion, for which order no reason is assigned. As soon as it fell for the first time they were further commanded to let none remain till the morning ; some, disobeying the command, found that it became putrid. When the sixth day arrived each man gathered two portions instead of one, which fact the elders reported to Moses and Aaron. Now why did the elders act thus ? It has been supposed that the arrangement about the sixth day was not yet communicated to the people ; if so, why did they gather the double portion of their own accord ? It could only have been because they *knew* the next day to be the Sabbath ; and therefore its non-Mosaic origin is settled. But in all probability the special instruction *was* made known ; if so, some other explanation must be found for the elders coming to Moses ; and it must have been this. They did not come to say that the people had transgressed, but to obtain an assurance that the surplus manna should not become putrid by being kept the second day, as had previously happened, and thus leave them without food. Moses's answer, according to the Authorised Version, was, "This is that which the Lord hath said. To-morrow is the rest of the Holy Sabbath unto the Lord ; bake that ye will bake to-day, and seethe that ye will seethe ; and that which remaineth over, lay up for you to be kept until the morning." But the A. V. is obscure, there being a critical reason why "This is that which the Lord hath said" must relate to what precedes—*i.e.* the report of the elders, and not to what follows, *i.e.* the mention of the Sabbath, as the A. V. would lead us to infer. Moses's answer is therefore equivalent to this : ' what has thus been done is what the Lord intended, to-morrow *being* His Holy Sabbath. Prepare the manna, and what you do not want to-day put by for to-morrow ; it became putrid on the former occasion, because you attempted to keep it against the Lord's instructions, but *now* He has bid you keep it : trust Him, and all will be well.' And having laid by the surplus, when the next morning came it was still good, and (paraphrasing) Moses bade them eat, ' for to-day *being* the Lord's Sabbath ye will find none in the field ; and so, for the future, ye shall gather it for six days ; but on the seventh, which is as you know, the Sabbath, you will find none.' It is evident throughout that the Sabbath is not spoken of as *something new and unheard of*, but as a thing *already familiar* to the people, and this paraphrase is scrupulously in accordance with the meaning of the original. When some went out to gather on the seventh day, but found none, they were thus rebuked : " See for that the Lord *hath given* you the Sabbath, therefore he giveth you on the sixth day the bread of two days " (ver. 29). It is an outrageous violation of the plain reasonable meaning of words to attempt to twist such expressions as these into intimations of the institution of a *new custom*.

But subsequent events confirm *our* supposition in a striking manner. Not many weeks afterwards, the Ten Commandments are given from Sinai, and the Fourth is ushered in alone of all the number with the solemn prefix, REMEMBER. What possible necessity could there have been for this, if the custom was of such recent date as we are asked to believe it was ? It could not have been forgotten in so short a space of time, especially when its origin was associated (*in this view of the matter*) with the miraculous manna.

Most unquestionably the " Remember " is simply intended to *remind* the Israelites of some *old* ordinance (to the intent that they might still keep it up), and not to embody in their code a recently instituted one. But a reason is assigned (*Ex.* xx. 11) which applies to all the world and not to one nation; which being the case, the logical inference is that the command is likewise *universal* and not *limited.* We read, "six days shalt *thou* labour, ... but the seventh . . . . is the Sabbath of the Lord, . . . *for* in six days the Lord made heaven and earth, &c., and rested the seventh day, *wherefore* the Lord blessed [*not the seventh but*] the Sabbath day and hallowed it." If the ground of the observance of the Sabbath depends, as we are told it does, on the circumstances attending the creation of the world, then it follows that its obligation extends to the whole human race, and not to a solitary nation. Had there been two distinct races placed on the earth at that epoch, an obligation laid on one would not have been binding on the other without an express intimation; but as there was only one race, whereof the Jews arose in after time, a *general* obligation cannot be held binding on them alone, in the absence of a special reason. Proving, as I conceive I have done,* that the obligation was not specifically Jewish, but *general*, it is therefore binding on all men, consequently on Christians now, inasmuch as it has never been abrogated. We are justified then in saying that we must go further back than *Ex.* xx. or xvi. for the origin of the Sabbath, and once agreeing to this we must go all the way back to *Gen.* ii., where we find the original reason for the sanctification of the seventh day, of which reason *Ex.* xx. 11 merely contains a repetition.

Whether the creation "days" were periods of 24 hours, which we understand by the word "day," or were simply equal periods of time, the absolute duration of which is undefined and undefinable, is of little moment. "It is obvious that *the principle involved is the observance of a day of rest unto God following six days allotted to labour*; that the stress is laid on that, not on the seventh day of the week, and that according to the strictest letter of the Commandment, by the usage of the Hebrew, which therein resembles other languages which have a definite article, *no more is really commanded than that.*" A candid appreciation of this is requisite to meet such taunts as are directed to the fact that we observe the first and not the seventh day of the week.

The history of Cain and Abel affords internal evidence that a weekly day of rest, appropriated to purposes of worship, was in their time in force. Jordan has placed this in a remarkably clear light, "The very fact of their coming together, and that for the purpose of worship, would of itself lead to the supposition that the time must have been a stated one, and well recognised by both; for otherwise we cannot conceive what could have induced the jealous Cain to unite with the pious Abel in the worship of Jehovah. Had there not been a special day set apart for worship, we should rather have expected Cain to avoid that which Abel chose, from hatred and envy of him. It is, however, plainly implied that there was a certain known time at which they both together worshipped God. The expression denoting this is rendered in the text of the Bible, 'in process of time it came to pass,' but in the margin, 'at the end of days it came to pass.' Now, this latter is not only preferable, as a construction of the original, but it directly points to that day which was 'the end of days,' the last, that is, of the seven." (Jordan, *Christian Sabbath*, p. 37.)

It may further be remarked that the narrative of the deluge, and Noah's proceedings in reference thereto, abound with so many allusions to

* The argument is Riley's, popularised.

periods of seven days as unmistakeably to prove that something special and peculiar attached to them. In Jordan's work (C. S. pp. 24–31) will be found a full argument on this matter, identifying different days of the week, and showing that with the seventh was invariably connected something involving *rest or cessation.*

Let us now investigate the particular day to meet the difficulty about the seventh day. A misapprehension often exists here. *The fourth Commandment does not enjoin the observance of the seventh day of the week.* What it does enjoin is *six days for work and then a Sabbath, a day of rest to be devoted to God.*

Some parallel passages are required to illustrate this. In *Judges* xix. 4, 5, 8, "He abode with him *three* days, . . . and it came to pass on the *fourth* day," &c., "and he arose early in the morning on the *fifth day*," &c. These are not the fourth and fifth days of the week, but the fourth and fifth with reference to the previous three. In *Ex.* xxii. 30, "*Seven* days it shall be with his dam ; on *the eighth* day thou shalt give it me." Here the eighth day is not the first day of the week, but the eighth day from the animal's birth, unless we choose to believe that all the young of oxen and sheep were born on the same day of the week ! a too palpable absurdity. Again, in *Josh.* vi. 3, 4, "Thus shalt thou do *six* days, . . . and *the seventh* day ye shall compass the city seven times." There is no reason whatever for assuming that the *seventh* day has any other than the obvious meaning of the seventh after they began to compass the city, or that it has any respect to a particular day *of the week.*

Now wherever *Sabbath*—i.e. the day of *rest* (the simple meaning of the original word)—is spoken of as the *seventh* day, it is almost always, if not always, with reference to the six previous days of labour ; and now we are brought back, without any straining or perversion of words, to repeat that the sanctification of *one* day in *seven* is the *principle.*

It is worth while just to mention the fact that for geographical reasons it is absolutely impossible for any two nations under different meridians to observe precisely the same period for Sunday. Sunday evening with us is Monday morning with our brothers and sisters in India.

We have now to inquire into the particular day of the week adopted as the day of rest under the Christian dispensation, and what indications there are of its having been settled by Divine authority.

Justin Martyr, in his *Apologia prima pro Christianis*, written in the middle of the second century A.D., gives us an exact account of the observance of the said first day of the week, for public prayer and reading of the Scriptures, &c., which had clearly become an established custom ; and it is not too much to say that a custom of this kind could not have become thus general in the Church, at this very early period, unless it had received the sanction of the Apostles, the last of whom, St. John, had only died within the recollection of the generation then living : receiving the sanction of the Apostles, it must be held to have received the sanction of Him who sent them. Other leading Fathers of the Church, Eusebius, Ignatius, Origen, &c., acquaint us with facts and make statements of their own, all of similar import.[*] But indications are not wanting that at a much earlier period the first day of the week had some peculiarity attaching to it. In I. *Cor.* xvi. 2, St. Paul charges the Corinthians, "Upon the first day of the week let every one of you lay by him in store as God hath prospered him."

---

[*] For an extended series of these, see Baylee, *Hist. Sabb.*, p. 97, *et seq.*

(59 A.D.) Now, though there is no actual mention of a religious observance, it will at least be granted that the selection of this day for an almsgiving purpose is noticeable. In *Acts* xx. 7, *et seq.*, is narrated St. Paul's visit to Troas and his preaching to the Church there, the members of which were gathered together "upon the first day of the week," evidently according to their usual custom (the peculiar wording in v. 7, "when the disciples came together," may reasonably be held to point to a *custom* of so doing). St. Paul abode there one week; whence it is clear, there were no motives of haste impelling the selection of the first day, if it were not a common thing : the seventh day, too, is entirely unnoticed, It may be assumed further, that the recognised sanctity of the first day was the cause of the apostle postponing his departure till the second day.

On these two passages a recent writer has the following observations : "'As God hath prospered him' is a remark that proceeds on the assumption that a day was recognised as that on which trading was discontinued ; and that on the eve of that day they were in a position to ascertain the state of their pecuniary circumstances. As it is the first day of the week of which these things are spoken, it is evident that *up to it* business continued. The previous seventh day was, therefore, an ordinary day of work, and *as a Sabbath day,* was no longer in existence. The glimpse we had at Troas [see *ante*] of the first day, as the only day of public worship, is here again afforded, with the additional disclosure that it was also a day of exemption from worldly occupations."—(M. Hill, *Sabbath made for Man,* p. 121.)

On presumptive evidence we are safe in asserting that the observance of the first day of the week as the Christian Sabbath is of Apostolic authority. Can we do more than this ? Is there any trace of Christ Himself authorising a first-day Christian Sabbath as a substitution for the seventh-day Jewish one ? I believe that there is such a trace. From various passages (*St. Luke* iv. 16, &c.) we find that it was our Saviour's " custom " to attend the synagogue worship on the seventh day, the then Sabbath ; but it pleased Him to select the first day for that great event —His resurrection from the dead ; and when He rose on that day He went to meet His disciples, and it is further noticeable that passing over the next seventh day, He met them the second time on the first day of the week following His resurrection (*St. John* xx. 26), and finally it was on the first day of another week, the Day of Pentecost, (*Acts* ii. 1), that the great outpouring of the Holy Ghost took place. Without insisting unduly on all these coincidences, it is at least certain that by Christ Himself, when freed from all Jewish associations, a preference was given to the first day of the week, for which no reason is assigned, and, unless our view be adopted, no reason is assignable. The revelation made to St. John took place on what was called the Lord's Day (*Rev.* i. 10). (For proof that the day so called was the first day of the week, see Elliot, *Horæ Apocalypticæ,* iv. 566.)*

The foregoing points, imperfectly strung together it may be, through a desire for brevity, will have prepared the reader for the following deductions, which may be asserted with the fullest confidence :—

---

* The expression in the original is ἐν τῇ κυριακῇ ἡμέρᾳ : it would otherwise have been ἐν τῇ ἡμέρᾳ τοῦ κυρίου, in the day of the Lord (genitive), which means the day of the Lord's coming.

1. *A weekly Sabbath, or day of rest, was not specially a Jewish institution.*
2. *It dates from the origin of the human race.*
3. *When instituted it was binding on the whole human race.*
4. *Never having been abrogated, it is still binding.*
5. *The substitution of the first day for the seventh, as a Sabbath day, has been accepted by the Church from the earliest period, and there is good reason for believing it to be in harmony with Christ's will, though no express intimation is extant.*

6. *Every text of Holy Scripture relating to it is still in essence to be attended to by Christians.*

With these before us, it will scarcely be necessary to do much more than simply quote the subsequent passages of the Bible bearing generally on the observance of the Lord's day. We learn from different intimations in the Pentateuch that the extreme penalty of death was affixed to the violation of most of the Commandments. We are to regard this as merely a (divinely appointed) municipal provision, in no respect affecting the thing forbidden itself: for the mitigation of the penalty attaching to (say) the 3rd Commandment no more legalises blasphemy amongst Christians than the mitigation in respect of the 4th Commandment makes the principle of Sabbath observance an indifferent matter. It is well to insist upon the moral aspect of the Decalogue: if one Commandment is to be rejected, why not two, why not three, why not all?

Exodus xxxiv. 21.—"Six days shalt thou work, but on the seventh day thou shalt rest: in earing time and in harvest thou shalt rest."
Nehemiah x. 29-31.—"We entered into a curse and into an oath, to walk in God's law. . . . and that . . . if the people of the land bring ware or any victuals on the Sabbath day to sell, we would not buy it of them on the Sabbath, or on the holy day."

Let us imitate the good determination of the Jews of old. Sunday trading prevails in the present day, in the large towns of England, to a fearful extent. The, usually alleged, necessity might in all cases be got rid of by a little foresight on the part of the buyers, more especially if *all* the employers of labour would pay their workpeople's wages on some other day than Saturday. It is only fair to say that a vast proportion of the sellers are opposed to keeping their shops open, and would heartily welcome a rigorous enforcement of the existing law (29 Car. II. cap. 2). Great difficulties lie in the way of a trader voluntarily closing wherever there is much competition. Compulsory legislation alone will prove a lasting remedy. Saturday half holidays also, indirectly, tend greatly to promote Sunday observance. The number of beer-shops, "gin-palaces," &c., open on Sunday is a fruitful cause of evil. Strong repressive measures are imperatively called for.

Isaiah lvi. 2.—"Blessed is the man . . . that keepeth the Sabbath from polluting it."
Isaiah lviii. 13, 14.—"If thou turn away thy foot from the Sabbath, from doing thy pleasure on My holy day; and call the Sabbath a delight, the holy of the Lord, honourable; and shalt honour Him, not doing thine own ways, nor finding thine own pleasure, nor speaking thine own words: then shalt thou delight thyself in the Lord; and I will cause thee to ride upon the high places of the earth."
Jeremiah xvii. 21.—"Thus saith the Lord; Take heed to yourselves, and bear no burden on the Sabbath day."
Jeremiah xvii. 27.—"But if ye will not hearken unto Me to hallow the Sabbath day, and not to bear a burden, even entering in at the gates of Jerusalem on the Sabbath day; then will I kindle a fire in the gates thereof, and it shall devour the palaces of Jerusalem, and it shall not be quenched."

Mark the severity of the punishment! The existing Sunday railway traffic, Post-Office labour, and newspapers, are a disgrace to the English nation. In the matter of the newspapers, it would seem as if a breach of the Divine commandment were ostentatiously made; for, though dated for Sunday, it is well known that the vast proportion of them are printed and published on the Saturday, and many even on the Friday.

St. Matthew xii. 12.—" Wherefore it is lawful to do well on the Sabbath days."

Examples will be found in *St. Luke* xiii. 14; *St. John* v. 9; and ix. 14.

St. Matthew xii. 1.—"At that time Jesus went on the Sabbath day through the corn; and his disciples were an hungred, and began to pluck the ears of corn, and to eat."

St. Luke xiii. 15.—"Doth not each one of you on the Sabbath loose his ox or his ass from the stall, and lead him away to watering?"

Works of domestic *necessity* may be performed on Sunday, but NOT works of *luxury* or *amusement*. Sunday bands, concerts, holiday parties of all kinds, &c., cannot be too strongly condemned, not only on religious, but on social grounds.

I may here conveniently draw attention to a most flagrant breach of the Statute Law of England weekly perpetrated in London and elsewhere, in reference to tea gardens, and places of public resort. A good legal authority writes as follows:—" The 21 Geo. III. cap. 49, was passed to restrain a practice very prevalent at the time in London and Westminster: it enacts, that if a house, room, or *place*, be opened upon Sunday *for any public entertainment*, or for debating upon any subject, to which persons are admitted by money or *tickets*, the keepers of it shall forfeit 200*l.* to any person who will prosecute, the manager or president 100*l.*, and the receiver of the money or tickets 50*l.*, and every person *printing* an advertisement of such meeting forfeit 50*l.*"—(Wade, *Cabinet Lawyer*, p. 458. 18th ed.) The law thus confers ample power, and it is greatly to be wished that some spirited Englishmen would come forward and demand its enforcement. The Cremorne Gardens are perhaps the best known of these illegally opened places of resort, but there are many others in and around London. The managers indicate their knowledge that they are doing wrong, and at the same time their ignorance of the precise provision of this Act, by advertising that admission is only by *tickets*, and the advertisements appear in all kinds of newspapers, the printers of which could all be convicted, I think, without difficulty.

St. Mark ii. 27-8.—"And Jesus said unto them, The Sabbath was made for man, and not man for the Sabbath: therefore the Son of Man is Lord also of the Sabbath."

It is requisite to pause to make a comment on this text, because the opponents of Sunday observance invariably use it as an argument that man is *superior* to the Sabbath, in other words is *entitled* to use it or misuse it as he chooses. That such a meaning is sought to be drawn from it, is of itself good proof that our opponents feel their weakness, and akin to this is their utterly unwarrantable idea that Christ by these words intimated his wish to abolish the Sabbath altogether. Besides, how is Christ's remark (*St. Matt.* v. 17) that He came not " to destroy the law or the prophets . . . but to fulfil " to be met and accounted for? Our opponents who desire to claim the Bible as on their side are bound to answer this question. Again, when asked by a rich man (*St. Mark* x. 17), " What shall I do that I may inherit eternal life? " our Lord said, " *Thou knowest the Commandments;* " and He puts it beyond doubt that He refers to the decalogue by reciting five of them. None of the commandments belonging to the first table are mentioned, but no one will venture to assert that by this omission He intended to exclude say the 2nd; and if the 2nd is to stand good why not the 4th?

Some documentary evidence as to the practical results arising from the due observance of Sunday, whether voluntary, or brought about by legislation, will now be adduced, beginning with a statement that has stood the test of well nigh 200 years :—

SIR MATTHEW HALE'S OPINION.—" I have found by a strict and diligent observation, that a due observation of the duties of this day hath ever joined to it a blessing upon the rest of my time; and the week that hath been so begun hath been blessed and prosperous to me : and on the other side, when I had been negligent of the duties of this day, the rest of the week hath been unsuccessful and unhappy to my own secular employment; and this I do not write lightly or inconsiderately, but upon a long and sound observation and experience."

The debates in Parliament upon Mr. Somes's Public Houses Bill had the effect of drawing forth such an immense mass of evidence as to the good result from past legislation, &c., that it is very difficult to know what to take and what to reject, my space being limited.

Scotland is under the provisions of a total Sunday Closing Act, known as " Forbes Mackenzie's " :—

In seventeen of the chief towns of Scotland, containing together about a million of inhabitants, the number of cases of drunkenness alone, or of drunkenness and crime combined, on Sundays, amounted, during the three years before the Forbes Mackenzie Act came into operation, to 11471; whilst, during the three first years in which public-houses were closed on Sundays, cases of the same description amounted, in the aggregate, only to 4299.

The daily average number of prisoners confined in the Edinburgh and Glasgow prisons during the three years before the passing of the Act was 1221, while the daily average number during the three years subsequent to the passing of the Act was 864.

The total number of cases of drunkenness taken charge of by the Edinburgh police in 1853, the year before the passing of the Act, and in 1861, was as follows—

In 1853	9730
In 1861	6656

Number of cases on Sunday—

In 1853	1305
In 1861	858

Number of cases on Saturdays, Sundays and Mondays—

In 1853	4420
In 1861	2918

Number of cases between 8 A.M. on the Sunday mornings and 8 A.M. on the Monday mornings—

In 1853	648
In 1861	205

" He is something more than a bold man who, with such facts before him, will dare to say that the Forbes Mackenzie Act has demoralised Scotland—has been else than a blessing to the country."

On the other hand, drunkenness seems to have greatly increased during the last few years in England, where drinking in public-houses is permitted for many hours on the Sunday. It appears from the police reports, that in 1856 there were apprehended in Manchester, from 10 A.M. on the Saturdays to 10 A.M. on the Mondays, in the whole year, 417 drunken persons; in the year 1862 the aggregate number of drunken persons apprehended on those days was 1824. A larger proportion of these apprehensions occurred on the Sunday, and till 10 A.M. on Monday, than on the Saturday. The total number of cases before the Manchester magistrates for drunkenness in 1862 was 3373; of these cases, 1824 had reference to the Saturdays and Sundays, the remaining 1549 to the other five days of the week; so that the whole number for the Saturdays in the year may be taken at 912, that for the Sundays at 912, and the aggregate for each of the other days at 310. The following is a table of public-house and beer-house offences for 1862:—

	Number of Houses	Total Reported	Offences	
			Week Days	Sundays
Gross total of public-houses in Manchester	482	59	13	46
Gross total of beer-houses . . .	1792	595	136	459

The foregoing is from a most valuable and excellent address issued by the "Derbyshire Lord's Day Society."

Can any rational being dare to say that the time has not arrived for renewed restrictive legislation for England? (for Manchester is a fair type of large towns generally). Every police magistrate in the exercise of his judicial functions knows the intimate connection subsisting between licentiousness and Sunday-opened beershops.

Overwhelming testimony exists as to the good, or the harm felt by human (and animal) beings, according as they are permitted to enjoy the Sabbath day's rest or not.*

Dr. FARRE's opinion, given before a Select Committee of the House of Commons in 1832, has obtained a wide circulation. He says:—"All men, of whatever class, who must necessarily be occupied six days in the week, should abstain on the seventh, and in the course of life would assuredly gain by giving to their bodies the repose, and to their minds the change of ideas, suited to the day for which it was appointed by unerring wisdom. I have frequently observed the premature death of medical men from continual exertion. I have advised the clergyman, in lieu of his Sabbath, to rest one day in the week: it forms a continual prescription of mine. I have seen many destroyed by their duties on that day, and to preserve others I have frequently suspended them for a season from the discharge of those duties. The working of the mind in one continued strain of thought is destructive of life in the most distinguished class of society, and senators themselves stand in need of reform in that particular. I have observed many of them destroyed by neglecting this economy of

---

* A large number of citations on this point will be found in Gilfillan's valuable work.

life." (*Report of Committee on Sabbath Observance*, p. 119.) The celebrated Wilberforce also made this remark about several Parliamentary contemporaries. (Venn, in Scott's *Discourse on Wilberforce*, p. 32, note.)

Dr. CARPENTER, in 1852, wrote:—" My own experience is very strong as to the importance of the complete rest and change of thought once in the week."

In 1853, in petitioning Parliament against the opening of the Crystal Palace on Sunday, 641 London medical men said:—" Your petitioners, from their acquaintance with the labouring classes, and with the laws which regulate the human economy, are convinced that a seventh day of rest, instituted by God, and coeval with the existence of man, is essential to the bodily health and mental vigour of men in every station of life."— (*Association Medical Journal*, vol. i. p. 554. June 24, 1853.)

Sir DAVID WILKIE once said :—" Those artists who wrought on Sunday were soon disqualified from working at all."—(*The Sabbath at Home and Abroad*, p. 117.)

THE EDITOR OF THE "*Standard*" some years ago recorded his experience in these words :—" We never knew a man work seven days a week who did not kill himself or kill his mind."

Sir WILLIAM BLACKSTONE, Lord Chief Justice of England, speaks with authority :—" The keeping of one day in seven holy as a time of relaxation and refreshment, as well as for public worship, is of admirable service to a state, considered merely as a civil institution. It humanises by the help of conversation and society the manners of the lower classes, which would otherwise degenerate into a sordid ferocity and savage selfishness of spirit. It enables the industrious workman to pursue his occupation in the ensuing week with health and cheerfulness ; it imprints on the minds of the people that sense of their duty to God, so necessary to make them good citizens, but which yet would be worn out and defaced by an unremitting continuance of labour without any stated times of recalling them to the worship of their Maker."—(*Commentaries*, vol. iv. p. 63.)

Elsewhere Sir William says :—" A corruption of morals usually follows a profanation of the Sabbath."

The COUNT DE MONTALEMBERT, a Frenchman, and a Romanist besides, declares:—" Il n'y a pas de religion sans culte, et il n'y a pas de culte sans dimanche.'

Lord MACAULAY may fairly be regarded as a witness not likely to be over-biassed on our side. What said the noble lord?—If the Sunday had not been observed as a day of rest, but the axe, the spade, the anvil, and the loom, had been at work every day during the last three centuries, I have not the smallest doubt that we should have been at this moment a poorer people, and a less civilised people than we are. Of course I do not mean that a man will not produce more in a week by working seven days than by working six days. But *I very much doubt* whether at the end of the year he will generally have produced more by working seven days a week than by working six days a week, and *I firmly believe* that at the end of twenty years he will have produced *less* by working seven days a week than by working six days a week.—(*Speeches*, pp. 450–1.)

WILBERFORCE " well remembers that during the war, when it was proposed to work all Sunday in one of the Royal manufactories for a continuance, not for an occasional service, it was found that the workmen who obtained Government consent to abstain from working on Sundays executed in a few months more work than the others."—(*Life*, vol. i. p.

275.) The American and French Governments have testified to the same effect.

Commercial undertakings in England tell the same tale.

Mr. Bagnall, a large iron master, discontinued Sunday work in 1839, and two years after he stated to a Select Committee of the House of Lords:—" We have made rather more iron since we stopped on Sundays than we did before." After a seven years' trial, this gentleman wrote:—" We have made a larger quantity of iron than ever, and gone on in all our six iron works much more free from accidents and interruptions than during any preceding seven years of our lives."—(Rev. J. T. Baylee's *Facts and Statistics*, pp. 88-9.)

Dr. Livingstone, the African traveller, writes:—" On returning from Moamba to the Sindi we found our luggage had gone on, and as the chronometer was with it we had to follow it up on Sunday; we all felt sorely the want of the Sabbath through the following week. Apart from any divine command, a periodical day of repose is absolutely necessary for the human frame."—(*The Zambesi*, p. 311.)

Mr. Bianconi, the celebrated Irish coach proprietor, read a paper before the British Association for the Advancement of Science in 1843. He stated that he found by experience that it was preferable to work a horse eight miles every week day than six miles all days of the week, including Sunday, besides obtaining an absolutely greater mileage of 48 against 42. Proofs of the accuracy of this opinion could be multiplied to any extent. Not long since a London cab-driver, whose master owned twenty-four horses, told me that they had given up all Sunday work, because it was more profitable to work six days than seven, the horses remaining longer fit for work, and the men the same. No London cab-rider dare contradict the assertion that during the last ten years an immense improvement has taken place in the bearing of the London cabmen and the condition of their vehicles and horses, in consequence of the extensive adoption of the six-day license. For the omnibus men, no six-day license *yet* exists, and can a worse set of men be found belonging to any public conveyances? Let an intelligent traveller compare the servants of the Great Northern and London and North Western Railways, on which Sunday labour is brought to a minimum, with those of the Great Eastern, Great Western, and London and Brighton, where Sunday desecration, nurtured and forced in every possible way, has attained (as regards *England*) a maximum. Can there be a moment's hesitation as to which set of men present the superior character as regards civility, *physique*, &c.; and, I add in all confidence, *can there be a doubt as to the cause?*

Now for a few words to a section of Churchpeople who pride themselves on their attachment to, and veneration for, the Church of England and her Prayer Book.

In her XIIIth Canon, the Church says:—

" All manner of persons within the Church of England shall from henceforth celebrate and keep the Lord's Day, commonly called Sunday, and all other Holydays, according to God's will and pleasure, and the Order of the Church of England prescribed in that behalf; that is, in hearing the Word of God read and taught; in private and public prayers; in acknowledging their offences to God, and amendment of the same; in reconciling themselves charitably to their neighbours, where displeasure hath been; in oftentimes receiving the Communion of the Body and

Blood of Christ; in visiting the poor and sick, using all godly and sober conversation."

And in her Prayer Book she sets before her members the 4th commandment every time the Communion Service is read. Now, if these circumstances mean one thing more than another, they mean that *the Church of England recognises and lends the sanction of her authority to the perpetual obligation of a strict observance of Sunday as a day of religious occupations, and abstinence from everything secular and worldly.* [*]

Now a section of Churchpeople declaim very eloquently and vigorously against a "Puritanical observance of the Sabbath" as if the old Puritans desired to advocate any novelties in this matter. Sunday is the common property of the whole human race, and not of any one branch of the Catholic Church, or of any one sect; it belongs to all, and therefore to associate it with any one set of persons indicates a want of acquaintance with the true bearings of the question. To reject the strict observance of Sunday because Puritans happened to obtain celebrity for supporting it, would be as great an absurdity as to reject Episcopacy because Rome supports it. How reprehensible then and unchurchlike is the conduct of "High" Churchmen who advocate museums, parties, and secular holiday-making as desirable *finales* to attendance at Church *once a day* in the morning. I once heard a clergyman at the West-end of London, the Rev. E. S., preach a sermon to this effect, and could only make the consoling reflection that there were not many such misguided men in the ministry of the Church of England. The Rev. W. R. has recently received from his *Bishop* a valuable preferment at the East-end of London. This individual boasted before a committee of the House of Commons, in 1860, that frequently during the summer, when he could afford it, he took parties of his parishioners down to Hampton Court on Sunday afternoons!

In favouring strong restrictions on Sunday desecration, I desire them to be applied to all classes alike: to the rich no less than the poor. A vast weight of responsibility rests with the former. So long as they ride out in their carriages on Sundays in the parks, &c., and the Royal Family have military bands to amuse them, doubtless our work will be hampered. The analogy sometimes drawn by artful secularists between the poor man's public-house and the rich man's club is a very lame one. The frequenter of the beershop visits that place to drink, either by himself or with friends. The London Clubs, or the majority of them, are *necessities* to a great portion of their members; some of them providing beds are hotels, except in name; others are virtually such, by being places of resort for breakfasts, dinners and suppers, for their members, who are never absent from them except for their actual beds. For all this, the condition of club servants, and in fact of all domestic servants, might be much ameliorated if their superiors would forbear from unnecessarily claiming their services.

The closing of the parks to *carriages* and musicians would be an achievement well worth considerable exertion to obtain. I hope some day to see an agitation to that end successfully carried out.

---

[*] Further illustrations of what is stated in the text will be found in the VIIth Article and the XXth Homily.

SUGGESTIONS FOR PROMOTING THE DUE OBSERVANCE OF SUNDAY, ADDRESSED TO EVERYBODY.

1. Never post letters on Saturday, unless for delivery by some local post on the same day; never write or post them on Sunday, except in cases of *real* necessity.

2. Arrange, if possible, that letters *requiring answers* shall not reach their destinations on Saturday; and thus hold out any inducement for replies to be sent by the Sunday post.

3. Never on Sundays pay worldly visits, make up accounts, &c., or plan schemes for the ensuing week.

4. Avoid unnecessary cooking on Sunday; be content with a cold dinner, &c. &c.

[There are many little ways in which heads of families may lessen the work of their domestics which cannot be particularised here.]

5. Always *walk* to Church, unless sickness or infirmity imperatively necessitates your riding: in which case go early, that your servants be not kept away.

[The bad habit of running after " popular preachers " causes much needless Sunday labour to be forced on those who are not their own masters by those who are. An omnibus driver some years ago spoke in the following strong terms to a clergyman who was riding by his side on a week-day and conversing with him on the subject: " Sir, there is not a man living that would delight to spend his Sabbath with his family more than I should and go to Church on Sunday, but it is you religious people that prevent me. Upon this line my master finds the omnibus pay better on the Sunday than on any other day of the week, and why is it? Simply because people make use of me to drive them to their churches and chapels."]

6. When hiring cabs in London, be particular to give the preference to those having five-figure numbers (*e.g.* 10,487): such have six-day licences, that is to say, they do not work at all on Sunday. It is a good plan to tell the driver why you select him.

[Christian members of Vestries, Town Councils, Local Commissions, and Boards, may do much service by promoting the adoption of analogous regulations.]

7. Never go pleasure-taking on Sunday: no good will come of it: probably much harm.

[Remember Clayton Tunnel on Sunday, August 25, 1861, when 100 Sabbath-breakers suffered, defying God.]

8. On Saturday night put aside all newspapers, &c., that there be no temptation given to any to read them on the following day.

9. On no account buy anything of a tradesman who keeps his shop open on a Sunday, but expostulate with him, as opportunity offers.

10. Follow the various admonitions of the Bible, quoted in these pages.

11. Help with your time and money, those who are labouring to put down Sunday desecration. The Lord's Day Observance Society (office, 20 John Street, Adelphi, W.C.) is well worthy the support of every Christian Englishman.

12. And finally let each, under whose notice these suggestions may fall, endeavour to persuade his friends to adopt them. Much good may thus be done.

B

APPENDIX TO BOOK I.

IMPORTANT TESTIMONY AGAINST SUNDAY EXCURSION TRAINS.

The following is selected from a leading article in *Herapath's Railway Journal* (Jan. 10, 1863), one of the most important organs of the railway press in this country:

"It is a fact that the best paying railway companies in this country, excepting one, set their faces against Sunday excursions.

"All things considered, it is doubtful whether Sunday excursion trains 'pay.' . . . . We say, let the matter be inquired into, and let it be ascertained whether excursion trains on the Sunday are profitable or unprofitable. If they do not pay, there can be no reason, human or divine, for keeping up a practice which is viewed as undoubtedly ' wrong ' by some of the best amongst us. If excursions trains do pay, it might be a question whether they should be continued in the teeth of the adverse opinions of those who ought to be the best judges of what is morally right.

"We have heard it said, ' What can the poor labourer do if the Sunday excursion train is taken off; labouring all the week long, the luxury of a run into the country will be foreign to him, if he can't take it on Sunday?' This is not the language of a poor labourer himself. What *does* he *do* when he prefers a short run on the common road to a long one on a railway, spending the whole day out? He goes on Monday, as a matter of choice; but some of the railway companies tempt him to a railway trip on Sunday, and, perhaps, by their arrangements, compel him to prefer Sunday to Monday for the health-inspiring run, if performed by rail. Necessary Sunday trains may be all very well, but the present question is, whether the professed pleasure ones, which induce the multitude to travel by fares monstrously low, should be continued. The Bishops are dead against them on high grounds. On the lower grounds of commercial advantage to the companies themselves, the result of an investigation would probably be a recommendation to discontinue them.

"Excursion trains must add to the work of the railway officials, who are generally in the six days worked up to the full extent of their powers of endurance. We should, therefore, think that the abandonment of the Sunday excursion train would be hailed with joy by many a pointsman, guard, engine-driver, ticket-taker, porter, and money-taker, and that the efficiency of these hands and heads would be all the greater for a relaxation from business usually accorded to people in this country.

"Forced Sunday work, as great as on ordinary days, and which is diametrically opposed in character to that commonly performed during the day of rest in this country, is hardly calculated to attract to the service of railways the best class of servants."

SUNDAY BATTLES.

" The late terrible struggle at Pittsburg adds another to the long list of Sunday battles. The facts are so clear in this and numerous other conflicts, and the results have been so uniform and decisive, that comment is not only warranted but demanded, alike by philosophy, patriotism, and piety. The general statement cannot be gainsaid, that the more important movements of the national forces, in the early stages of the present war, were made on Sunday, and that they were undeniable failures. Patterson's column was constantly notorious for its manœuvring on Sunday, and for little else. Big Bethel, Bull Run, and Ball's Bluff were the great blunders and defeats of attacking armies on Sunday. All these engagements, excepting Ball's Bluff, under the now-imprisoned General Stone, preceded General M'Clellan's noble Sabbath order. Thenceforward the rebels have made the Sunday assaults, with invariable loss of the battles thus waged. Mill Spring opened their career of Sunday fighting, which closes with Pittsburg. The battle of Winchester was begun on Sunday morning. The first of these battles cost the rebels Kentucky ; the second, the valley of Virginia; and the third, the Mississippi Valley. The Merrimac, too, after its destructive Saturday's raid, ran a muck against the Monitor on Sunday, and has spent a month in repairing damages. Add to these facts, that most of the generals commanding, whose names figure as assailants in these battles, were slain in them, or are in disgrace on account of them, and there is food for reflection in these bits of history. What has become of our General Pierce, of Big Bethel memory? What of General Stone? Where are Zollicoffer and Sydney Johnston? In short, since we have ceased the business of Sunday fighting, and the rebels took it up, we have had only victories to record, and they only defeats and surrenders. Fort Donnelson and Island No. 10 were our Sunday morning benison on week-day prowess. Nor are these isolated historical facts. History is full of them, The British forces assailed us on Lake Champlain and at New Orleans on Sunday, and were defeated. We assailed them at Quebec; our army was repulsed, and its leader slain. We began the battle of Monmouth, and had the worst of it. Napoleon began the battle of Waterloo, and lost his army and his empire. The battle of Blenheim, which has been repeatedly cited by the *Herald*, with its usual accuracy, as a successful Sunday battle, was not fought on Sunday, but began on Wednesday. We content ourselves with the simple collation of these suggestive facts. Let them go to swell that mighty volume of testimony to the supremacy and stability of a law as old as Creation, which claims quite another use of one-seventh part of time than the work of willing human butchery."—(*New York Times*, April 11, 1862.)

THE FORBES MACKENZIE ACT OF SCOTLAND.

In 1859 the enemies of the Lord's Day influenced the Government to appoint a Royal Commission to inquire into the operations of this celebrated enactment. The result was satisfactory in a remarkable degree, much to the chagrin of the agitators. No less than 749 witnesses were examined, and the Commissioners report as follows :
" The improvement in large towns has been most remarkable. Whereas formerly on Sunday mornings numbers of persons in every stage of intoxication were seen issuing from the public houses, to the great annoyance of the respectable portion of the population on their way to church, the streets are now quiet and orderly, and few cases of drunkenness are seen. The evidence of the police authorities proved that, while there has been a considerable diminution in the number of cases of drunkenness and disorder since the passing of the Act 16 and 17 Vict. cap. 67, the change has been more marked on Sunday than on any other day of the week. Employers of labour, and workmen themselves, were unanimous in testifying to the great improvement that had taken place in the regularity of attendance at work on Monday morning ; *and many publicans examined before us expressed themselves as grateful for the existing law, regarding the cessation of business on Sunday as a boon of which they would not willingly be deprived.*"

A RAILWAY MANAGER'S OPINION.

" Combe Wood, Bonchurch, Isle of Wight, Oct. 29, 1861.

" My dear Sir,—In answer to your enquiries, and your desire to have my opinion in regard to Sunday excursion trains, gathered from my eighteen years' experience as General Manager of the L. and N.-W. Railway, I can only say that during that time no excursion trains ever ran on Sunday ; and I am satisfied that while the interests of the proprietors did not suffer, the discipline and character of the company were promoted. I have had a large experience of excursion traffic, and was always very favourable to its development ; but I believe no company ultimately benefits by working its system to the extent of seven days a week, and that by a well-arranged system of Saturday trains, returning on Monday, an equal pecuniary return, at a much less cost, is produced. Putting the question, therefore, on the lowest ground of argument, I have no hesitation in saying, that a railway company consults its true interests in restraining Sunday work within as narrow limits as possible. The Scotch railways, as a whole, pay better than the English ones, and there the work on Sunday is reduced to a minimum.
" Yours very truly,

" Rev. H. V. Elliot, Brighton."   " M. Huish.

One of the numerous evils connected, *but not inseparably*, with the railway system, is the undue haste with which contractors press forward the completion of new works, especially under circumstances mainly brought about by want of due energy and foresight at the outset. A consequence of this is very obvious—Sunday Labour. Miss Marsh, discussing this matter, makes the following very practical suggestion : " If each proprietor of land through whose ground the railway passes would not sell it without making a stipulation that the working man should have his seventh day's rest secured, he would bring down a blessing on both souls and bodies, and would find that the Lord of the Sabbath would repay him sevenfold into his bosom. And if this became an integral part of railway contracts, the contractors would bestir themselves at first to secure a large number of men, and so 'take time by the forelock.' "—(*English Hearts and Hands*, p. 350.)

I understand that a gentleman in Kent, now deceased, always made the insertion of certain clauses limiting the number of trains to stop on Sundays at stations on his property a *sine quâ non* to Railway Bills receiving his assent as a landowner. This must be characterised as an excellent plan.

SUNDAY SLAVERY ON RAILWAYS.

A meeting of the signal and switch-men employed upon the various metropolitan railways was held in London on Nov. 8, 1865. There was a very large attendance. Mr. Irving, of the Brighton line, took the chair. He said that the meeting had been called by a committee of men employed upon the Brighton and South Eastern lines, for the purpose of establishing a society, by means of which it was hoped they would obtain an amelioration of *the many grievances under which they laboured, the principal of which were long hours and short pay. If the public became fully alive to the dangers they were always exposed to while travelling by railway, consequent upon the overworking of the signalmen, he felt sure they would support the men in their present efforts.* Mr. Brown, of the South Eastern, said he had been a signalman for 26 years, 16 of which he had served on the Brighton line. For several years his wages were 24s. a week, with 36 trains a day to look after; but the latter portion of his time he had no less than 300 trains daily to look to, and he then obtained a rise of 1s. per week. He was compelled to be in his signalbox 12 and 14 hours at a time, and *to get* his meals while attending to his duties. Mr. Emery said he had been a signalman on the London, Chatham, and Dover line for 6 years, and his hours of labour were 12 on each of the 6 days of the week, and 18 *on Sundays* (shame). During the 6 years he had been off duty but 3 days. His wages were 26s. per week. Mr. Masters said he was a signalman at the West London Railway, sometimes working 12 hours every day for 6 days, and 18 *on Sundays.* His wages were 26s. per week, and when he asked for more money he was told he might leave it if he didn't like it. *He was compelled to snatch his food in the best way he could, there being no time allowed for meals.* If railway companies consulted their own interests they would work their signalmen less hours, and not have to pay so much compensation money for accidents. Mr. Pitcher, signalman at Stewart's Lane Junction, on the London, Chatham, and Dover line, stated he had been on duty 48 *hours at one time,* and he had then only obtained 5 hours' rest before going upon duty again (shame). *Several other signalmen made similar statements.*

SUNDAY LABOUR IN THE POST OFFICE.

In connection with the observations on p. 17, something further may be said. *There is no delivery of letters on Sundays* in London or the district 12 miles round, in Newcastle-on-Tyne, Gateshead, and many smaller English towns, and in nearly the whole of Scotland, representing a population of upwards of 4,000,000. *It is desired to extend a similar measure of relief to all the letter-carriers of the United Kingdom.*

The *British Postal Guide* for January 1866 contains the following official notices:— (1) "Any person can have his letters, &c. retained in the Post Office on Sundays by addressing to the Postmaster a written request, duly signed, to that effect." (2) "If the persons who receive six-sevenths of the Sunday correspondence of any rural district sign a memorial to the Postmaster-General in favour of the discontinuance of the Sunday post, the Sunday deliveries will be stopped."

Persons desirous of helping the letter-carriers in their efforts to secure Sunday rest cannot do better than assist in circulating *Sunday Postal Delivery: an Appeal for Provincial Postmen.* (Suter and Alexander, 32 Cheapside, E.C. 6d. per 100.) An overwhelming majority of letter-receivers are willing to give to the postman his Sunday's rest, if the matter is only brought home to them. A carrier, who applied for 500 of these papers, stated in his letter, "I am one of those unfortunate fellows that has as much work to do on Sundays as any other day." The papers were supplied, and a few weeks afterwards he wrote as follows:—"I am getting on first rate; nearly done Sunday work. I have got nearly all the people in my district to sign those papers, and I think in about another week or two my Sunday work will be stopped altogether. I have got somewhere about between 300 or 400 people that have signed, and I do not think that there will be more than 7 or 8 people stand out." This man, whose walk was *nineteen* miles a day, is now quite free from Sunday work, and besides the higher reasons for congratulation, is saved 1000 miles of walking a year.

A correspondent, writing from a town where the above handbill has been extensively circulated, says:—"Many of the postmen find their Sunday morning's work much lightened. I heard of one man who had done last Sunday by a little after 7 in the morning; another who only had 9 letters, I believe, to take out; and another told me that he left something like 200 letters in the office."

Book II.

The Church of England tested by Holy Scripture.

Part I.—ITS OUTWARD ORDER.

The following passages are cited to show that the spirit and tenour of Holy Scripture have been followed by the Church in her rites and ceremonies. It is not contended that single texts of Scripture, especially those taken from the Old Testament, do of themselves authorise the customs of the Church; but it is something to know, that, in arranging her services and ceremonial, the Church has followed, as near as may be, those general principles of Divine worship which alone received the sanction and were under the special direction of Almighty God in old time; and in most instances were adopted by express Divine command.

1.—*The Edifices of the Church.*

Exodus xxix. 44.—" I will sanctify the tabernacle of the congregation, and the altar: I will sanctify also both Aaron and his sons, to minister to Me in the priest's office."

Deuteronomy xii. 13-14.—" Take heed to thyself that thou offer not thy burnt-offerings in every place that thou seest: but in the place that the Lord shall choose in one of thy tribes."

Exodus xl. 34.—" Then a cloud covered the tent of the congregation, and the glory of the Lord filled the tabernacle."

I Kings viii.—The dedication of Solomon's temple.

Ezra vi. 16-17.—The dedication of the second temple.

I. Corinthians xi. 22.—" What! have ye not houses to eat and to drink in? or despise ye the Church of God?"

Some think little or nothing of the consecration of churches, and that any buildings will do for public worship. I venture, however, to believe that systematic public worship in any but a consecrated edifice, *is wholly unwarranted by Scripture.* If not, why in the instances referred to above were so many ceremonies gone through in the dedication of the several edifices to the public service of God? Those who *argue* against such evidence can only *repudiate* this Old Testament authority, as Dissenters do in Church-and-State matters. The Church of England in requiring her churches and churchyards to be consecrated, follows the usage of the Christian Church from time immemorial, and, as we learn above, of the

Jewish Church also. That no particular reference is made in the New Testament to the consecration of buildings for Christian worship, is explained by the well-known fact that the persecution to which the Church was subjected in the early days of Christianity, and for some time subsequent to the closing of the New Testament canon, prevented the erection of such structures; but the last of the above quotations clearly shows that a distinction was contemplated even in Apostolic times between Churches and ordinary houses.

I. *Kings* vi.; II. *Chronicles* iii., iv.

A minute description is given in these chapters of the temple built by Solomon. From the description handed down to us, Solomon's temple must have been a structure of great beauty and magnificence. So the churches we build for God's worship should be constructed of the very best materials at our command, and as beautiful and costly as our resources will allow. If we erect magnificent dwelling-houses or buildings for secular purposes, how much more ought we to erect magnificent buildings for God. " The king [David] said . . . See now, I dwell in an *house of cedar, but the ark* of God dwelleth within curtains." (II. *Sam.* vii. 2.)

2.—*The Ministers of the Church.*

Hebrews v. 1–4.—" For every high priest taken from among men is *ordained* for men in things pertaining to God . . . . and *no man taketh this honour unto himself,* but he that is called of God, as was Aaron."

Acts vi. 6.—" Whom they set before the apostles: and when they had prayed, they [the apostles] *laid their hands on them.*" [St. Stephen and others, candidates for the ministerial office.]

Acts xiii. 3.—" And when they had fasted and prayed, and *laid their hands on them,* they sent them away."

I. *Timothy* iv. 14.—" Neglect not the gift that is in thee, which was given thee by prophecy, *with the laying on of the hands of the presbytery.*"

II. *Timothy* i. 6.—" Wherefore I put thee in remembrance that thou stir up the gift of God *which is in thee by the putting on of hands.*"

Acts xiv. 23.—" And when they had *ordained* them elders in every church," &c.

I. *Corinthians* xii. 28–29.—" And God hath set some in the church, first apostles, secondarily prophets, thirdly teachers . . . . Are all apostles? Are all prophets? Are all teachers?" See also *Ephesians* iv. 11.

Titus i. 5.—" For this cause left I [Paul] thee [Titus] in Crete, that thou shouldest set in order the things that are wanting, and *ordain elders in every city,* as I had appointed thee."

Jeremiah xxiii. 21.—" God said, ' I have not sent these prophets, yet they ran.'"

Romans x. 15.—" And how shall they preach *except they be sent?*"

These verses bring under our notice the commission to confer the power to minister, first as deacons, secondly as priests, and thirdly as bishops, transmitted by our Saviour, through the apostles, to (*inter alios*) the bishops of the early British Church, founded independent of Rome, in the second century * of the Christian era, and handed down by them

---

* About the year 190 A.D., Lucius, a British king, endowed the Church richly, founded Archbishoprics and Bishoprics, and built seven new churches. York and London were of the number of the sees then founded. If a certain statement of St. Clement's (in his *Epistola ad Corinthos,* sect. 7) be interpreted literally, it follows that the British Church was founded by St. Paul himself; and Archbishop Usher and others take this view of the matter. This Epistle was written in or about the year 98 A.D.

through their successors to the existing bishops of the Churches of England, Scotland, Ireland, the Colonies, and America.

Dissenters, in general, ridicule this ordinance, and many of them flatly violate St. Paul's warning, inasmuch as they do take this honour to themselves, by *pretending* that they can, of themselves, legitimately become Ministers of the Gospel, in the special sense of the word.

The Church rightly set herself against such irregular proceedings by requiring every candidate for holy functions to be carefully trained, before he undergoes the laying on of hands; in other words, before he is *ordained* (*Heb.* v. 1). In the case of Dissenters, even if their preachers do receive preliminary training, as is now sometimes the case, they set at nought the Apostolic institution of the laying on of the hands of a bishop. Bishop Horne has some powerful remarks on this subject, which will be found under II. *Chron.* xxvi. 19, in D'Oyly and Mant's *Commentary.*

The verse cited last draws our attention to the fact that even under the Jewish dispensation unauthorised teachers intruded themselves into holy functions; and the cases of Korah (*Num.* xvi. 3), Saul (I. *Sam.* xiii. 9), and Jeroboam (I. *Kings* xii. 31), may be mentioned as striking illustrations of the light in which self-appointed spiritual guides are regarded by the Lord of Hosts.

Romans xv. 20.—" Yea, so have I strived to preach the Gospel, not where Christ was named, *lest I should build upon another man's foundation.*"

Is this a scruple which ever affects the mind of a Dissenting teacher? I fear not.

Exodus xxviii. 39-43.—The priests are all to be robed in fine linen "when they come unto the tabernacle of the congregation, or when they come near unto the altar to minister in the holy place."

Whence the Church of England, following also the practice of the Christian Church from the earliest ages, appoints her priests to wear white linen surplices, as representing the purity and innocence wherewith GOD's ministers ought to be clothed.

Durand (an old Church writer of the 13th century) remarks on the girdle of the ephod spoken of in verse 9 of the following chapter (*Ex.* xxix.); that as the garments used by the Jewish priests were girt *tight* about them to signify the *bondage* of the law, so the *looseness* of the surplices worn by the Christian priests points to the *freedom* of the Gospel.

II. *Chronicles* v. 12.—"The Levites, which were the singers . . . . being arrayed in white linen . . . . stood at the east end of the altar."

The Church of England, copying the custom named in this verse, has the clearest authority for permitting singers (*i.e.* choristers) to be clothed in white surplices, and to be placed at the eastern end of the church in which they sing (*i.e.* in the chancel).

I. *Chronicles* xv. 16.—"And David spake to the chief of the Levites to appoint their brethren to be the singers with instruments of music, psalteries and harps and cymbals."

Instruments of music for use in public worship can hardly deserve the opprobrious epithets applied to them by many Dissenters; seeing that they have once been sanctioned by God.

3.—*The Public Worship of the Church.*

St. Matthew xxi. 13.—" My house shall be called the house of PRAYER."

Many make preaching of more importance than prayer in public worship. The Church, in providing for both, but giving the higher place to the latter, only adopts this strongly expressed wish of our Lord.

Acts xvi. 13.—"And on the Sabbath we went out of the city by a river-side, where PRAYER was wont to be made."

Zechariah viii. 21.—"And the inhabitants of one city shall go to another, saying, Let us go speedily to PRAY before the Lord."

II. *Chronicles* vii. 15.—"Now Mine eyes shall be open, and Mine ears attent unto the PRAYER that is made in this place." [The temple.]

From these and other passages, where a stated place of worship is referred to, we are warranted in assuming that preaching was intended to be *subordinate* to praise and prayer, as *our Church makes it.* If reference should be made on the other side to our Saviour's open air preaching, I should simply say that that does not apply here, as He was acting as a missionary and not the duly appointed minister of any one town or synagogue. It is worthy of mention that the Church has copied faithfully the ancient procedure as it is laid down in those few instances when preaching *is* referred to, *e.g. St. Luke* iv. 17 ; *Acts* xiii. 14. The Jews had particular portions of Scripture for particular days, as has the Church. Some few Dissenters even have expressed regret that they have no formal calendar of Christian Seasons, and it seems not improbable that something of the kind may come into use among them along with set forms of prayer. Signs of their yearning after the ritual of the Church are numerous just now. Gothic architecture, organs, the weekly offertory, surplices, white neck-ties, &c., all tell the same tale.

Hebrews xiii. 9.—"Be not carried about with divers and strange doctrines. For it is a good thing that the heart be established."

I. *Corinthians* xiv. 40.—" Let all things be done decently and in order."

St. Luke xi. 1-2.—" One of His disciples said unto Him, Lord, teach us to pray, as John also taught his disciples. And He said unto them, When ye pray, say, Our Father," &c.

St. Matthew xxvi. 44.—" And He [Jesus] . . . . prayed the third time, *saying the same words.*"

II. *Timothy* i. 13.—" Hold fast the *form* of sound words."

The Church of England sets before all her members, as her guide and theirs, Holy Scripture and her Liturgy, or Book of Common Prayer. A settled form of prayer is authorised, having been used, by our Saviour, and was previously used by the Jewish Church ; and that the Christian Church in all ages has had forms, confirms their value as means by which, with one mind and one mouth, the faithful can worship GOD in a decent and orderly manner. The "form of sound words " is thought to allude to some creed which the Early Christians were in the habit of reciting in their public assemblies. Extemporaneous prayer (if desirable at times for private use) in public worship has been weighed in the balances and found wanting. Amongst others, Mr. J. A. James, the late well-known dissenting preacher at Birmingham, has often lamented to his co-religionists the dulness of many of their public prayers, and any frequenter of " Revival " and Prayer-meetings would, or at least *could*, doubtless, say the same. Mr. James remarks :—" *Unfortunately*, for the interest of our prayer-meetings, the brethren who lead our devotions are *so outrageously long and dull.*" "We are often prayed into a good frame, and then prayed out again." "It is also *to be regretted that the prayers are so much alike* in the *arrangement* of the parts."—(*Christian Fellowship*, p. 56, 6th edition.)

Exodus xxix. 38-39.—A morning and evening sacrifice and service, daily throughout the year, is enjoined by God.

Acts iii. 1.—"Now Peter and John went up together into the temple, at the hour of prayer, being the ninth hour." [3 P.M.]

In this latter verse we have the authority of two of the leading apostles for the practice of attending daily public worship, and the observance of special hours of prayer. Surely, then, that which is founded upon Divine authority, and confirmed by Apostolic practice, ought not to be disregarded or disapproved of by any who " call themselves Christians."

Romans xiv. 5.—"One man esteemeth one day above another: another esteemeth every day alike. Let every man be fully persuaded in his own mind."

This verse affords an opportunity of saying a few words on the subject of Saints' Day Commemorations. The Church of England in reforming herself and revising her Liturgy 300 years ago, thought fit to abolish all commemorations which did not relate to Christians celebrated in the canon of the New Testament ; by this means she avoided the superstitions of Rome, and confined herself to Primitive Apostolic usage, for we have direct historical evidence to show that the Early Christians were in the habit of holding special religious services on the anniversaries of the deaths of the apostles and martyrs.—(Tertullian, *De Coronâ Militis*, cap. 3. 198 A.D.)

Saints' day commemorations are to be regarded as " things lawful, but not essential," and those who dislike them should always act up to the spirit of St. Paul's remarks in the 5th and 6th verses of *Romans* xiv.— (See Hooker, *Eccl. Pol.* Bk. V. ch. lxx. § 8.)

I. *Corinthians* ix. 14.—"Even so hath the Lord ordained that they which preach the Gospel should live of the Gospel."

Galatians vi. 6.—"Let him that is taught in the word communicate unto him that teacheth in all good things."

The Apostle here strongly censures stinginess towards the clergy. How many wealthy professing Churchmen seem to have no sense of their duty, and the responsibility their wealth confers. Though they have perhaps thousands a year, yet they seem to feel that they have done all that is required of them when they have laid down the standard sum of 1*l.* 1*s.* per annum.

I. *Corinthians* xvi. 2.—"Upon the first day of the week let every one of you lay by him in store as God hath prospered him."

St. Paul here recommends a weekly collection. The practice obtains in some churches, might it not be extended to all ? As a matter of fact, it is a most successful plan for inducing congregational benevolence, yet many oppose it, thinking more of their purses and their own ease, than of their Church's invitation to alms-giving. This should not be. Great care should, however, be taken to avoid all semblance of constraint on the part of the collectors. On the example set forth in *St. Matt.* vi. 4, *bags* are much preferable to plates or basins.

Galatians vi. 9–10.—" And let us not be weary in well doing: for in due season we shall reap, if we faint not. As we have therefore opportunity, let us do good unto all men, *especially unto them who are of the household of faith."*

In distributing alms, or conferring benefits, we are to give the *preference* to those ' who are of the household of faith.'

St. Matthew xxviii. 19.—" Go ye therefore and teach all nations, baptizing them in the name of the Father, and of the Son, and of the Holy Ghost."

Here we have the institution of the first of those two sacraments which is declared in our Church Catechism to be " generally necessary to salvation." A large body of sectaries repudiate infant baptism as an absurdity.[*] They are deaf to all argument drawn from analogy, precedent, or tradition, and declare it, to suit their own whims, to be a malpractice. Baptism in the Christian Church, is simply a graft upon the Jewish rite of circumcision, performed when the child was eight days old. If a *change* was to have been introduced in the Christian dispensation, the former method of initiation into the Jewish covenant at infancy being superseded by an adult initiation into the Christian, it is morally certain that the new procedure would have been explicitly enjoined in the New Testament. It may further be remarked that if Anti-pædobaptists can satisfy their own minds that " all nations" only means all grown up people, then a more barefaced perversion of the plain and literal meaning of words can scarcely be conceived. A similar perversion, not in this case of words only, occurs in those cases in which whole households were baptized ; we are gratuitously asked to presume that there were no children in these households. The positive testimony of contemporary Church historians that the baptism of infants was actually practised in the times of the Apostles, ought to settle the question. But these new-fangled folks, carrying the very proper right of private judgment to a most extreme limit, set themselves up as popes, and defy all constituted authority and teaching.

Acts viii. 14–17.—" Now when the Apostles which were at Jerusalem heard that Samaria had received the word of God, they sent unto them Peter and John : who, when they were come down, prayed for them, that they might receive the Holy Ghost : (for as yet he was fallen upon none of them : only they were baptized in the name of the Lord Jesus.) Then laid they their hands on them, and they received the Holy Ghost."

Acts xix. 5–6.—" When they heard this, they were baptized in the name of the Lord Jesus. And when Paul had laid his hands upon them, the Holy Ghost came on them."

These verses set forth the Church's rite of confirmation, which is undoubtedly of Apostolic origin, though railed at by Dissenters.[†] Those who administer it have ever been held the chief pastors and governors of the Church. Thus in this instance, when Samaria had received the word of God, and had been baptized by Philip, a deacon or inferior minister, Peter and John were sent to administer confirmation to them. And so it has always been administered by the hands of bishops, the successors of the Apostles, as is well known and attested through all ages of the Church. The persons to whom it is administered are all baptized persons, competently instructed in the principles of religion. Persons must first be made members of the Church before they can receive the blessings promised and bestowed on it ; and thus it will be seen that confirmation is a

---

[*] Some excellent remarks on this subject will be found in the Rev. J. C. Ryle's *Expository Thoughts on St. Mark*, p. 205, in reference to *St. Mark* x. 14.

[†] It may surprise many of these to be told that *Calvin* upheld Confirmation as well as Infant Baptism and Baptismal Regeneration (*Comm. Epist. Hebr.*).

most proper and becoming rite to follow the introduction to the Christian covenant, of which baptism is the first step.—(*Hole.*)

This Section may appropriately be concluded with a few remarks on objections frequently made against certain phrases which occur in the Book of Common Prayer.

1. In the CREED OF ST. ATHANASIUS.—" Whosoever will be saved : before all things it is necessary that he hold the Catholic Faith. Which Faith except every one do keep whole and undefiled : without doubt he shall perish everlastingly. . . . . This is the Catholic Faith : which except a man believe faithfully, he cannot be saved."

The objection made to these "damnatory clauses," as they are called, is a lamentable instance of the latitudinarian spirit of the age, by which things considered by the Church to be essential to salvation are sought to be quietly set aside to conciliate opponents. If the Catholic faith is now to be regarded as an old-fashioned figment quite out of date in these " Liberal" days of " Progress," then let Churchmen be plainly told so ; let us be asked to declare at once that ' Whosoever will be saved, before all things it is quite *superfluous and immaterial* that he believe the Catholic faith'—then we shall know what we are about.

2. In the office of PUBLIC BAPTISM.—" Seeing now, dearly beloved brethren, that this child is *regenerate*." *

This objection arises chiefly from the counfounding together "conversion" and "regeneration," as words expressing the same meaning, which is not the case.† Conversion is a change of feeling wrought in the faculties, a turning to God after a life of sin. Regeneration is a change of state or condition wrought by external (in this case Divine) agency.

3. In the office of the SOLEMNIZATION OF MATRIMONY.—" With my body, I thee worship."

The objection to the word worship simply proceeds from ignorance. To worship here means to honour. The word is still used in this sense in the phrase " His Worship the Mayor," and which means no more than " His Honour," or " His Excellency the Mayor." In I. *Chron.* xxix. 20, we find " and all the congregation bowed down their heads and worshipped the Lord and the King" [Solomon]. It is scarcely necessary to point out that " worship " *must* bear some other meaning than the most usual one.

4. In the office for the VISITATION OF THE SICK.—" I absolve thee from all thy sins."

The meaning of these words directed to be used by the Visiting Priest,

---

* Compare the answer to Question 5 on the Sacraments, in the Church Catechism. " Being by nature born in sin, and the children of wrath, we are *hereby* [*i. e.* by the act of baptism] made the children of grace." The passage in *Acts* ii. 38.—" Repent and be baptized . . . . for the remission of sins, and ye shall receive the gift of the Holy Ghost." And again, *Acts* xxii. 16.—" Arise, and be baptized, and wash away thy sins," clearly intimate that some connexion subsists between the act of baptism and the remission of sins. Compare I. *St. Peter* iii. 21. Wesley's views on this point I shall quote under another head. For an irrefragable argument on the main question, see Sadler's *Church Doctrine*, p. 41, *et seq.*
† See Dr. Nicholl's excellent remarks cited by Bishop Mant, in *Notes to the Book of Common Prayer.*

is obvious to every candid mind when read with the context. "By Christ's authority committed to me, I absolve thee from all thy sins, in the name of the Father," &c. Our Church does not direct her priests to say, 'in *my own* name and of *my own* power, I absolve thee from thy sins,' but simply 'if thou be truly penitent, I am empowered to declare (and I hereby do declare) to thee that Christ does remit thy sins, having commissioned me to be the person through whom that remission is to be audibly conveyed.'

5. In the BURIAL SERVICE.—"In sure and certain hope of the resurrection to eternal life."

Possibly this passage might advantageously be *verbally* revised, but a little patient scrutiny will show that the words will *not* bear the sense frequently put upon them. It is not said that 'we commit his body to the ground . . . . . in sure and certain hope of *his* resurrection to eternal life, through our Lord Jesus Christ; who shall change *his* vile body,' &c., but "in sure and certain hope of *the* resurrection . . . who shall change *our* vile body," &c. The difference is most essential; there is clearly no impropriety in saying that the resurrection is certain, or that the Christian's vile body will be changed. It is no shame on the compilers of our Liturgy or on their apologists, to confess that their language is not always so intelligible to the unlearned as it might be. I think, however, that it may safely be said that few works stand *less* in need of revision than the Prayer Book of the English Church.

PART II.—CHURCH AND STATE.

VERY early in the Bible do we find the principle of the union of Church and State showing itself, even as far back as B.C. *cir.* 1913.

Genesis xiv. 18-20.—"And Melchizedek, King of Salem, brought forth bread and wine; and he was the Priest of the most high God. . . . And [Abraham] gave him tithes of all" [the spoils].

In Melchizedek were united the headship of the Church and the headship of the State—the priestly office and the kingly. Moreover we find that the Priesthood was supported by tithes, exactly as the Clergy of the Church of England are now maintained. St. Paul distinctly declares (*Heb.* vii. 14, *et seq.*) that the new Priesthood of Christ was after [*i.e.* according to] the order of Melchizedek, *i.e.* an established order. If Melchizedek's Priesthood was consistent with Christianity, and of course it was, then an Established Priesthood, such as we have in England, must of necessity be similarly consistent. It should also be noted that this provision for the support of an established Faith had nothing Jewish about it; it preceded the Jewish or Mosaic polity by 422 years.

Genesis xxviii. 22.—Jacob makes a vow to choose the Lord for his God, and adds, "of all that thou shalt give me, I will surely give the tenth unto Thee."

Taken in connection with other passages, this clearly goes to show the existence of a settled order of priests, "and a settled and no doubt Divinely-appointed payment for their support."—(*Essays on the Church*, p. 21.) In

Lev. xxvii. 30, we find tithes spoken of in connection with the Church of the Mosaic dispensation.

Job xxxi. 26-8.—Job mentions that if by any waywardness he were led to worship the Sun or the Moon, "*this also were an iniquity to be punished by the judge*: for I should have denied the God that is above." *cir.* 1520 B.C.

Here we have a very ancient example of the power of the State to interfere in religious matters.

Exodus xxviii. ; *Numbers* xviii., &c. &c.

In these chapters we find an account of how Moses (the chief earthly Governor of the Israelites) by God's special commands set apart Aaron and his family, and the tribe of Levi generally, to be the priests of the nation ; in other words, how God, by the hand of Moses, constituted the Jewish State-Church. *cir.* 1491 B.C.

My limits prevent me examining in detail the nature of this constitution, but amongst other things we find that the priests were distributed over the country to act as ministers (*Josh.* xxi.). They were not left to depend for subsistence upon the voluntary offerings of the people, but had an adequate and definite provision of tithes secured to them by law (*Num.* xviii. 21) ; they were, in fact, an endowed Ministry,—their endowments secured to them by the civil power. In every one of these respects is the Established Church of England an imitation, a fac-simile of the ancient Jewish Church.

Unquestionably, then, the Jewish Church was a *State-Church*, and, what is more, was made so by God Himself. "Dissenters themselves are compelled to allow this [Wardlaw, &c.] ; the evidence is too strong to admit of a denial. What then do they do ? They affirm that the whole Mosaic dispensation was merely typical, or else that the union of Church and State in Israel was an exceptional case. But these assertions will not help them much. If the State-Church in Israel was, as they say, a typical Church, there must be an anti-type corresponding to it. Will our Dissenting friends be bold enough to tell us that a *State*-Church in ancient times typified an *anti-State* Church in modern times ; that when God instituted the *union* of Church and State, in the days of old, He did it to typify the *separation* of Church and State in these latter days ? As well might they affirm that monarchy is the type of a republic, a marriage typical of divorce. Surely common sense tells us, that if the union of Church and State in Moses' days be typical at all, it is typical of the union of Church and State in the days of the Gospel of Christ." (Eddowes, *Lecture on Church and State,* p. 8.)

The second assertion which Dissenters make, viz. : that the Jewish Church was an exceptional case, it being a Theocratic Institution, may be easily disposed of. I will admit that it was an exceptional case ; but for how long ? only for 395 years, till *cir.* 1095 B.C., when the Israelites demanded a king, that they might be like the other nations of the earth (I. *Sam.* viii. 5). The direct Theocracy terminated ; the exceptional case, therefore, ceased to exist. But did the State-Church system cease to exist ? By no means. 154 years subsequently the pious king Jehoshaphat sent through the country priests to lead the people and princes (*i.e.* civil authorities), to back them up (II. *Chron.* xvii. 7-8). Here is an instance of what Dissenters would call a most unjustifiable interference of the Government with the religious concerns of the people, yet

God approved of it. (See context.) In verse 10, we have the result: "and the fear of the Lord fell upon all the kingdoms . . . round about Judah."

For building his temple Solomon obtained labourers by a "levy," (I. *Kings* v. 13. Marg. " a tribute of men." Did any body ever hear of a government raising a *voluntary* tribute ?) The Church in her Church-rates only levies money or goods ; but Solomon under God's authority, went far beyond this, and levied even *men* to aid in erecting his great Cathedral at Jerusalem. Had there been a " Liberation" Society in those days, here would have been capital for the Jewish Mialls and Fosters to mount the platform with ! All the building arrangements were on a scale that proves them to have been paid for out of the National Treasury. (But earlier than this we meet with a compulsory levy of money for the support of Public Worship. *Ex.* xxxviii. 26.)

Other examples of kingly interference with religious matters in the sovereign's official capacity occur in II. *Chron.* xxxi. 20–1 ; xxxiv. 33 and xxxv. 1, *et seq.* In the first of these especially is the Divine approval expressed in the most unequivocal language :—"And thus did Hezekiah throughout all Judah, and wrought that which was good and right and truth before the Lord his God. And in every work that he began in the service of the House of God, and in the law, and in the Commandments, to seek his God, he did it with all his heart, and prospered." In v. 12 we have an allusion to tithes. In II. *Chron.* xxxiv. 8 we are told that Josiah sent the *Governor of the city,* and the Recorder "to repair the House of the Lord his God." Again, the civil power "interfering" in religious matters.

By far the most remarkable case, however, is that of the building of the second Temple at Jerusalem, under the auspices of Cyrus and Darius. We have the express authority of the prophet Isaiah that the former heathen monarch in initiating this great work, did it at God's special bidding (*Is.* xliv. 28), and that consequently the result met with His ap-proval, in spite of the money which procured it having come out of the pockets of the Persian tax-payers. In *Ezra* vi. 8, we find an account of the decree made by Darius confirmatory of that issued by his predecessor Cyrus. " I make a decree what ye shall do to the elders of these Jews for the building of the House of God : that of the King's goods even of the tribute beyond the river, forthwith expenses be given unto these men." The things necessary for performing the service were included (v. 9.), and the whole proceedings strongly suggest an analogy to the principle and application of Church-rates. Severe penalties were to be inflicted on any who disobeyed the royal edict. (v. 11.)

Nehemiah ix. 34–5 is a rather remarkable passage. It contains a peculiar expression as to the cause of the calamities which had befalle Israel. " Our kings, our princes, our priests, our fathers . . . . have not served Thee in *their kingdoms.*" 'Have not adequately employed their official influence in God's behalf, and, behold the consequences,' as we may paraphrase it.

II. *Samuel* xxiii.—" He that ruleth over men must be just, ruling in the fear of God." *Psalm* ii. 10.—" Be wise now therefore, O ye kings : be instructed, ye judges of the earth. Serve the Lord with fear."

Clearly *as rulers, as kings, as judges,* not as individuals. Else why so pointed a way of putting it ? Note the spirit which appears in *Psalm* lxviii. 29-31 ; lxxii. 10, 11 ; lxxix. 6; cxxxviii. 4. All point to one general fact : that the national acknowledgment of God was a *desideratum* uppermost in the minds of the writers.

Isaiah xlix. 23.—" Kings shall be [the] nursing fathers and their Queens [the] nursing mothers" [of the Church.]

Isaiah lx. 12.—" *Nation* and *kingdom* that will not serve Thee shall perish ; yea, those nations shall be utterly wasted."

The more ingenious than candid Wardlaw persists in asserting that it would be as *individuals* that kings and nations would patronise Christianity, but is this a fair interpretation of words ? Can there be any doubt that "nation and kingdom" means nation and kingdom in its *corporate* position, and not the individuals forming the nations ?

Ezekiel xliii.-xlv.

Is a passage which contains "the lineaments, too clearly traced to be mistaken, of an extensive national establishment." (*Essays on the Church*, p. 25.) Gill and Matthew Henry, the two eminent Dissenting commentators, who lived before Liberation Societies were dreamt of, refer this prediction to some bright era of the Gospel Church, but the great modern anti-State Church writer, Dr. Wardlaw, with characteristic good sense (for his side), says—*nothing.*

Jonah iii. 6-10.

National proclamation of a fast. National religious observance by civil authority (Hearken, O ye Dissenters !) " and God saw their works " . . . and said he would not do unto them the threatened evil.

Zechariah ii. 11.

" Another instance of the common mode of expression throughout the Hebrew Scriptures, in which *kings* and *nations* are constantly spoken of as capable of, and responsible for, the knowledge and worship of God." (*Essays on the Church*, p. 26.)

To sum up. Some or other kind of State religion has existed in *every nation* of ancient or modern times with but very, very few exceptions. Egypt, Persia, Greece, Carthage, Regal, Republican, and Imperial Rome, Druidical Britain, and a multitude of states and empires, bear me out. No matter whether that religion were Jewish, Pagan, Mahomedan, or Christian ; in all cases there was a State-united creed. If all nations, in all ages of the world, have deemed a national religion a necessary adjunct to secular government, are English Dissenters for their own caprice and ends to be quietly permitted to overturn that branch of Christ's Holy Catholic Church, which has for well nigh 1300 years been established in these realms, to the great spiritual and temporal blessing of the Anglo-Saxon race ?

As this concludes my considerations based on the Old Testament, it may now be proper to advert to the fact that *Dissenters, for Church and State arguments, wholly repudiate the Old Testament Scriptures*, on the convenient plea that for matters of this kind, they are altogether superseded by the New. It is scarcely necessary to point out the reason, namely that the Old Testament so unmistakeably witnesses against them, that they are driven at once to say, ' We do not acknowledge your jurisdiction,' a manœuvre more efficacious than honest.

I am altogether at a loss to see how schismatics who argue thus, can get over St. Paul's remark, "Whatsoever things were written aforetime were written for our *learning*." (*Rom.* xv. 4.) How can this be reconciled with their practice of regarding the O. T. as so much writing, the importance of which has passed away, and which is therefore now only of interest to the *Biblical Antiquarian*? This is, in real fact, how we are asked to regard this portion of the Sacred Volume by these anti-State-Church men. N.B [*i.e.* Note *well.*]—"*All* Scripture is given by inspiration of *God.*" (II. *Tim.* iii. 16.)

Turning then to the New Testament, a Voluntary will tell you that he defies you to show any authority for a State-Church. Now, though in special terms this may not be *easy*, yet we can adduce numerous instances in which a State religion comes under the direct notice of our Saviour and His Apostles without receiving *a word of condemnation*, a fact from which (taken in connexion with remarks elsewhere in the Bible) we must reasonably infer that His approval was intended to be given to the State-Church *principle.*

St. Luke ii. 21.—" And when eight days were accomplished for the circumcising of the child, His name was called Jesus."

Thus early in our Saviour's earthly career was He suffered to conform to the established religion of the land in which He was born. Can we believe that this conformity would have been permitted by His Heavenly Father, if He had wished National Churches henceforth to be set at nought?

St. Luke iv. 15.—" And He taught in their synagogues, being glorified of all."

St. John vii. 14.—" Now about the midst of the feast Jesus went up into the temple, and taught."

See also *St. Matt.* xii. 9; xxvi. 55; *St. Mark* iii. 1; *St. Luke* iv. 16; vi. 6; xiii. 10; xxii. 53; *St. John* viii. 2; xviii. 20. These references unequivocally show one important fact, viz. that Christ was *constantly* in the habit of attending and preaching in the Jewish synagogues and temple, and thus tacitly giving His sanction to the national religion as such.

St. Matthew xxvi. 19-20.—" And the disciples did as Jesus had appointed them; and they made ready the Passover. Now when the even was come, He sat down with the twelve."

Here we have another instance of our Lord's conformity to the Jewish religion, notwithstanding its essential difference from that which He himself had inaugurated.

St. Matthew viii. 4.—After cleansing a leper, " Jesus saith unto him . . . go thy way, shew thyself to the priest, and offer the gift that Moses commanded, for a testimony unto them."

Another instance of reverential respect for the ordinances of the Established Church when there was, humanly speaking, little call for it.

St. Matthew xxiii. 23.—" Ye pay tithe of mint and anise and cummin, and have omitted the weightier matters of the law."

Christ here inferentially sanctions the payment of tithe to the Jewish priesthood (and the Christian clergy); though He complains of other important matters which the Pharisees had omitted to do.

Hebrews vii. **8.**—"And here men that die receive tithes."

St. Paul also in this passage speaks of tithes in such a manner as (by implication) to sanction their payment.

Hebrews vii. **5.**—"Verily they that are of the sons of Levi, who receive the office of the priesthood, have a commandment to take tithes of the people according to the law, that is, of their brethren."

I merely cite this as a peculiarly explicit statement of facts affecting the Jewish State-Church, and to point out that throughout the entire New Testament not a syllable can be found warranting the supposition that this precedent was to be superseded and cast off under the New, that is to say the Christian, Dispensation. Surely such silence is in the highest degree significant.

But, after all, is it impossible to find in the New Testament a distinct assertion of the right of the Apostles to the same kind of public support as that enjoyed by their Jewish predecessors? I think not.

St. Paul says:—

I. *Corinthians* ix. **13-14.**—"Do ye not know that they which minister about holy things live of the things of the temple? and they which wait at the altar are partakers with the altar? Even so hath the Lord ordained that they which preach the Gospel should live of the Gospel."

But how were the priests who ministered in the temple and at the altar supported under the law? Why, by tithes and legally secured compulsory offerings. "Even so," says the Apostle, *i.e.*, in an exactly similar manner, "hath the Lord ordained that they who preach the Gospel should live of the Gospel," *i.e.*, by tithes and legally secured compulsory offerings. It is impossible to draw any other conclusion; and when Europe became Christian, the right was universally conceded, and was never questioned during hundreds of years—not in fact till the present century, and then only by insignificant minorities in a few States.

St. Matthew xxiii. **1-3.**—"Then spake Jesus . . . saying, The scribes and the Pharisees sit in Moses' seat: all therefore whatsoever they bid you observe, that observe and do."

Here our Saviour most explicitly calls upon his hearers to attend to the instruction of the established priesthood; possibly having in his mind the precept in *Mal.* ii. 7.

———————

The pages of Holy Writ teem with practical maxims having reference to questions of public concern. I cite disconnectedly the following, as rich in matter for reflection on the part of the Christian citizen, and all more or less involved in the subject of Church and State:—

Exodus xxii. **28.**—"Thou shalt not revile the judges [marg.], nor curse the ruler of thy people."

Proverbs xxiv. **21.**—"My son, fear thou the Lord and the king: *and meddle not with them that are given to change*."

Ecclesiastes viii. **2.**—"I counsel thee to keep the king's commandment, and that in regard of the oath of God."

Ecclesiastes x. **20.**—"Curse not the king, no not in thy thought; and curse not the rich in thy bedchamber."

I. *Samuel* xxvi. **9.**—"And David said to Abishai, Destroy him not: for who can stretch forth his hand against the Lord's anointed, and be guiltless?"

Happily, in our highly favoured Christian land such a precept as this might seem almost superfluous; but though there are not, however, amongst us any actual regicides, there are sympathisers with regicides in abundance. Many Englishmen would shrink from taking up arms (for the text includes this) against Queen Victoria, who see no impropriety in recommending and helping others to take up arms against *their* lawful sovereigns, or in fêting them when they have done so. The Garibaldi demonstration which occurred in April 1864 was a striking illustration of the way in which some people will stultify themselves and their principles of half a century's growth, for a transient and trivial object. Wherein does Garibaldi differ from Guy Fawkes, Titus Oates, Thistlewood, or O'Connell, viewed as a patriot? Surely Guy Fawkes, if not as successful, was at least as conscientious as the Italian buccaneer named above.

Romans xiii. 1-2.—"*Let every soul be subject unto the higher powers. For there is no power but of God: the powers that be are ordained of God. Whosoever therefore resisteth the power, resisteth the ordinance of God, and they that resist shall receive to themselves damnation.*" See also the succeeding verses.

Romans xiii. 7.—"*Render therefore to all their dues; tribute to whom tribute is due; custom to whom custom; fear to whom fear; honour to whom honour.*"

I. *Thessalonians* v. 12-13.—"And we beseech you, brethren, to know them which labour among you, and are over you in the Lord, and admonish you: and to esteem them very highly in love for their work's sake. And be at peace among yourselves."

Titus iii. 1-2.—"Put them in mind to be subject to principalities and powers, to obey magistrates, to be ready to every good work, to speak evil of no man, to be no brawlers, but gentle, showing all meekness unto all men."

Hebrews xiii. 7.—"Remember them which have the rule over you, who have spoken unto you the word of God."

Hebrews xiii. 17.—"Obey them that have the rule over you, and submit yourselves; for they watch for your souls, as they that must give account, that they may do it with joy, and not with grief."

I. *St. Peter* ii. 13-14.—"Submit yourselves to every ordinance of man for the Lord's sake; whether it be to the king, as supreme, or unto governors, as unto them that are sent by him."

I. *St. Peter* ii. 17.—"Honour all men. Love the brotherhood. Fear God. Honour the king."

I. *Timothy* ii. 1-2.—"I exhort therefore, that, first of all, supplications, prayers, intercessions, and giving of thanks, be made for all men; for kings, and for all that are in authority; that we may lead a quiet and peaceable life in all godliness and honesty."

St. Matthew xxii. 21.—"Render therefore unto Cæsar the things which are Cæsar's; and unto God, the things that are God's."

St. Matthew xvii. 24-7.—"And when they were come to Capernaum, they that received the tribute money [*in orig. didrachma* = 1s. 3d.] came to Peter, and said, Doth not your master pay tribute? He saith, Yes." Then in reply to a question by the Apostles, Jesus said, "Lest we should offend them, go thou to the sea, and cast an hook, and take up the fish that first cometh up; and when thou hast opened his mouth, thou shalt find a piece of money [*in orig. stater* = 2s. 6d.]: that take, and give unto them for me and thee."

This passage affords, in general terms, a practical comment on the one taken from the 22nd chapter, quoted immediately before; but a more minute examination of it discloses a singular circumstance. The sum paid for each person, in our money, would be equivalent to 1s. 3d.; now the marginal note suggests that this was the half-shekel annually levied from every grown-up Jew for the maintenance of divine service (*Ex.* xxx. 13), and the Dissenting commentators, Gill and Matthew Henry, admit that such was doubtless the case. It is worthy of remark, as indicating *the systematic dishonesty of Dissent*, that in *some* of the modern editions of Matthew Henry's *Commentary*, his remarks in favour of Dissenters paying Church Taxes ARE WHOLLY SUPPRESSED. They will be given under another head.

Here, then, we have a positive instance of our Lord paying, without hesitation, CHURCH-RATE towards maintaining services which, though He conformed to them, had nevertheless imbibed corruptions of which He could not possibly have approved.

Dissenters frequently refuse to pay Church-rates, Easter Dues, and other " tribute, to whom tribute is due," on the convenient plea of " conscience." Now I would never speak ill of a *really* conscientious man in anything, but I do ask, in all good faith, *what Divine command do Dissenters more plainly and more obviously disobey than this?* I defy them to explain away, even by the most refined sophistries, such passages as have been quoted above.

II. *St. Peter* ii. 10.—" Them that walk after the flesh in the lust of uncleanness, and despise government. *Presumptuous are they, self-willed, they are not afraid to speak evil of dignities."*

How graphically these words describe a large body of the Dissenters of the present day, including some well known as writers and preachers, we shall presently see.

Acts xxiii. 5.—" Then said Paul, I wist not, brethren, that he was the high priest; for it is written, Thou shalt not speak evil of the ruler of thy people."

Here we have another notable instance of St. Paul's respect for the dignitaries of the Church. Oh that Dissenting ministers, who preach so much about Christian doctrine, would recommend to their brethren and congregations Christian and apostolic *practice.* They should study more than they do *St. Matt.* vii. 3, and *Rom.* ii. 21.

To proceed a little. If we examine the BIBLE (our only guide), not only do we not find there any justification of Dissent, or the sin of schism, but we find schismatics (" Dissenters ")* *denounced in the most unqualified language* by the "great Apostle of the Gentiles :"—

Romans xvi. 17-18.—" Now I beseech you, brethren, *mark them which cause divisions* and offences contrary to the doctrine which ye have learned; and *avoid them.* For they that are such serve not our Lord Jesus Christ, but their own belly ; and by good words and fair speeches deceive the hearts of the simple."

I. *Corinthians* i. 10.—" Now I beseech you, brethen, by the name of our Lord Jesus Christ, that ye all speak the same thing, *and that there be no divisions* [schisms *in orig.*] *among you.*"

I. *Corinthians* iii. 3-4.—"For whereas there is among you envying, and strife, and divisions, are ye not carnal, and walk as men ? *For while one saith, I am of Paul ; and another, I am of Apollos; are ye not carnal?"*

II. *Timothy* iv. 3.—" For the time will come when they will not endure sound doctrine ; *but after their own lusts shall they heap to themselves teachers, having itching ears."*

Most faithfully does St. Paul pourtray and condemn in these verses, schism. Even in his time, he had to deprecate persons calling themselves (as we should say) " Paulites," "Apollosites." So also would he condemn

---

* " The distinction between Dissent and Schism seems to have been lost among us ; schismatics being now universally called Dissenters. Dissent is properly a differing in opinion ; Schism is a separation from the communion of the Church." (From an excellent Tract, *The Church of England before the Reformation,* S. P. C. K. 243.) Dissent, in the accurate definition of the word, is not necessarily unreasonable or noxious. What is popularly called Dissent, being really Schism, *why not call it by its right name?*

the Irvingites, the Glassites, the Calvinists, and all the other 'ites and 'ists of the present day. Such is the vicious, inherently vicious, nature of Dissent, that even when a body of persons secede from the Church, and form themselves into a separate community, the new community holds together but a short time. Thus, the " Baptists," originally a single sect, have constantly fallen out amongst themselves. We have now the " General (Unitarian) Baptists," " General (New-Connexion) Baptists," "Particular Baptists,' "Seventh-day Baptists,' "Scotch Baptists," &c., all sects of a sect; a fact (and many others might be adduced) showing the inevitable tendencies of Dissent. " They heap to themselves teachers." This was true in 66 A.D.; it is still true in 1866 A.D.

I now pass to the last book in the Canon of the New Testament—the Book of Revelation.

Revelation xxi. 24.—" And the nations of them which are saved shall walk in the light of it [New Jerusalem], and the *Kings* of the earth do bring their glory and honour unto it."
Revelation xii. 10.

A song of praise. Gill and Henry both refer the occasion of this song to the extirpation of Paganism by Constantine, and the Saints returning thanks for the Emperor's patronage of Christianity; " and thus, in the latest portion of Divine Revelation, as in the earliest, we find that which modern Dissenting writers unreservedly repudiate,—to wit, nationality, and Government responsibility in matters of religion."—(*Essays on the Church*, p. 28.)

To the CHURCHMAN who reads these pages I would say, Seek to become mindful of those privileges you possess in being a member of such a SCRIPTURAL CHURCH as is that branch of the Holy Catholic Church which is established in England; use your influence in defending her; and avail yourself of opportunities, whenever they arise, of pointing out their errors to any who may have seceded from her.

To the DISSENTER (if haply my remarks should come under the notice of any one such) I would say, " Search the Scriptures," and see for yourself that these things *are so.* Ponder over calmly (in the spirit of *Ps.* cxxxiii. 1) the statements herein set before you; cease to oppose yourself any longer to the whole tenour of the word of God; rejoin that Church from which you have so unjustifiably seceded, and again become a partaker of those Holy Sacraments and privileges of which you deprived yourself by one fatal step, and we Churchmen will *gladly welcome* you again into our ranks.

JOHN WESLEY ON CHURCH MATTERS.

John Wesley's real relations with the Established Church are painfully misapprehended in the present day alike by Churchmen and Dissenters: by the former he is not unfrequently looked upon as a schismatic, and in all respects as a man of a most objectionable stamp; and by the latter as a great apostle of Dissent in its widest acceptation.

I will now cite a few passages from Wesley's works indicative of the writer's real ideas on Church matters, for few seem acquainted with them. Comments of my own seem for the most part scarcely requisite :—

" Are we not unawares, by little and little, gliding into a separation from the Church? Oh, use every means to prevent this ! 1. Exhort all our people *to keep close to the Church* and the Sacrament. 2. Warn them *against niceness of hearing*, a prevailing evil ! 3. Warn them also against despising the prayers of the Church. 4. Against *calling our Society* the Church. 5. Against calling our preachers *ministers*—our houses *meeting-houses.** . . . 6. *Do not license them as Dissenters.* . . . *We are not Dissenters* in the only sense which our law acknowledges—namely, those who renounce the service of the Church. *We do not*, we dare not separate from it. *We are not seceders,* nor do we bear any resemblance to them. We set out upon quite opposite principles. The seceders laid the foundation of their work in judging and condemning others; we laid the foundation of our work in judging and condemning ourselves, . . . and never let us make light of going to Church, either by word or deed. Remember Mr. Hook, a very eminent and zealous Papist, when I asked him ' Sir, what do you do for public worship here, where you have no Romish worship?' he answered, 'Sir, I am so fully convinced it is the duty of every man to worship God in public, that I go to church every Sunday. If I cannot have such worship as I would, I will have such worship as I can.' But some may say, "Our (Methodist) worship is public worship.' Yes, *but not such as supersedes the Church Service.*'

Quest. 46.—A Methodist inquires, " Nay, but is it not our duty to separate from the Church, considering both the wickedness of the clergy and the people ? "

Answer by Wesley.—" *We conceive not.* 1. Because both the priests and the people were fully as wicked in the Jewish Church, and yet it was not the duty of the Holy Israelites to separate from them. 2. Neither did our Lord command his disciples to separate from them. He rather commanded the contrary. 3. Hence it is clear *that* could not be the meaning of St. Paul's words ' Come ye out from among them, and be ye separate.' "

(*Minutes of Conversations* between John Wesley and others. 16mo. London. pp. 29–31. No date, but apparently about 1780.) [It is not unworthy of note that the preceding disappeared in the edition of 1797, published 6 years after Wesley's death, as reprinted in 1850!!!]

" My brother and I closed the conference by a solemn declaration of our purpose *never to separate from the Church.*"—(*Minutes of Conference,* Aug. 25, 1756.)

" What may be reasonably believed to be God's design in raising up the preachers called Methodists? Not to form any new sect, but to reform the nation, particularly the Church, and to spread scriptural holiness through the land."—(*Works,* 8vo. London, 1831, vol. xxiii.)

Under date of 1787, Jan. 2, Wesley writes :—" I went on to Deptford, but it seemed I was got into a den of lions. Most of the leading men of the Society were mad for separating from the Church. I endeavoured to reason with them in vain; they had neither sense nor good manners left. At length, after meeting the whole Society, I told them, ' *If you are resolved, you may have your service in church hours ; but remember, from that time you will see my face no more.*' This struck deep, and from that time I have heard no more of separating from the Church."—(*Last Journal,* p. 26.)

" I never had any design of separating from the Church. I have no such design now. I do not believe Methodists in general design it when I am no more seen. I do, and will do, all that is in my power to prevent such an event. I declare once more, that I live and die a member of the Church of England, and that none who regard my judgment or advice will separate from it."—December 1789.

At Athlone :—" I was among those who both feared and loved God, but to this day they have not recovered the loss which they sustained when they left off going to church. It is true they have long since been convinced of their mistake ; yet the fruit of it still remains ; so that there are very few who retain that vigour of spirit which they before enjoyed."—(*Works,* vol. iii. p. 283.)

In the year 1758, John Wesley drew up " Reasons against a Separation from the Church of England." These are classed under three heads; they are too lengthy to be given here, and would suffer by abridgment. They will be found in his *Works,* vol. xiii. pp. 193–9. In a postscript, Charles

---

* The term applied in law, Acts of Parliament, &c., to the places of worship belonging to those who have seceded from the Church. How careful the good man was to avoid all appearance of evil—the slightest appearance of encouraging secession from the Established Church.

Wesley writes, " I think myself bound in duty to add my testimony to my brothers.' His twelve reasons against our ever separating from the Church of England are mine also. I subscribe to them with all my heart; only with regard to the first, *I am quite clear* that it is *neither expedient nor lawful* for me to separate, and I never had the least inclination or temptation to do so. My affection for the Church is as strong as ever, and I clearly see my calling, which is to live and die in her communion. This, therefore, I am determined to do, the Lord being my helper."—(*Ibid.* p. 199.)

"I hope this may suffice to show any fair and candid inquirer that it is very possible to be united to Christ and the Church of England at the same time ; that we need not separate from the Church in order to preserve our allegiance to Christ."—(*Works,* vol. x. p. 505.)

"I believe there is no liturgy in the world, either in ancient or modern language, which breathes more of a solid, scriptural, rational piety than the Common Prayer of the Church of England ; and though the main of it was compiled considerably more than 200 years ago, yet is the language of it not only pure, but strong and elegant in the highest degree." —(*Works,* vol. xiv. p. 317.)

"Having had an opportunity of seeing several of the Churches abroad, and having deeply considered several sorts of Dissenters at home, I am fully convinced that our own Church, with all her blemishes, is nearer the Scriptural plan than any other in Europe." —(Letter from J. W. to Sir H. Trelawny : *Works,* vol. xiii.)

"I hold all the doctrines of the Church of England. I love her Liturgy, I approve her plan of discipline, and only wish it could be put in execution.'—(Sermon in *Arminian Magazine,* 1790.)

"We believe it would not be right for us to administer either baptism or the Lord's Supper, *unless we had a commission to do so from those Bishops whom we apprehend to be in succession from the Apostles.*

"We believe that there is and always was in every Christian Church an outward priesthood ordained by Jesus Christ, and an outward sacrifice offered therein by men authorised to act as ambassadors for Christ and stewards of the mysteries of God."

"We believe that the threefold order of ministers is not only authorised by its apostolic institution, but also by the written Word."—(Journal : *Works,* vol. ii. p. 329, ed. of 1809.)

Addressing lay preachers—and all are lay preachers who are not ordained by a Bishop—as to their desire to administer sacraments, Wesley says, "You believe it to be a duty: I BELIEVE IT TO BE A SIN."

Godfathers and Godmothers—

"Are highly expedient; for when they are prudently chosen, they may be of unspeakable use to the persons baptized, and a great relief and comfort to the parents of them."— (*Works,* vol. x. p. 507.)

BAPTISMAL REGENERATION.

"By baptism we who were 'by nature children of wrath' are made the children of God; and this regeneration, which our Church in so many places ascribes to baptism, is more than barely being admitted into the Church, though commonly connected therewith ; being 'grafted into the body of Christ's Church we are made the children of God by adoption and grace.' This is grounded on the plain words of our Lord, 'Except a man be born again of water and of the spirit, he cannot enter into the kingdom of God.' (John iii. 5.) By water, then, as a means, the water of baptism, we are regenerated or born again, whence it is also called by the Apostle 'the washing of regeneration.' Our Church, therefore, ascribes no greater virtue to baptism than Christ himself has done. Nor does she ascribe it to the outward washing, but to the inward grace, which, added together, makes it a sacrament. Herein a principle of grace is infused, which will not be wholly taken away unless we quench the Holy Spirit of God by long outward wickedness."—(*Works,* vol. x. p. 191, 8vo., London, 1830.)

The foregoing opinions, taken from many more similar ones, ought to suffice for showing what Wesley used to think, and I fully believe they there are plenty of his followers who will say "ditto." Indeed some of these have already boldly come forward and proclaimed their desire to uphold the Church as established in England.

Having cited thus much from Wesley, I add the following general testimonies by prominent Dissenters:—

JOHN OWEN, D.D. (Independent.)

"Some think if you [members of Parliament] are well settled, you ought not, as rulers of the nation, to put forth your power for the interest of Christ. The Lord keep your hearts from that apprehension!"

"If it comes to this, that you shall say you have nothing to do with religion, *as rulers of the nation,* God will quickly manifest that *he hath nothing to do with you* as rulers of the nation. Certainly, it is incumbent on you to take care that the faith which you have received, which was once delivered to the Saints, in all necessary concernments of it may be *protected, preserved,* and *propagated* to and among the people which God hath set you over . . . if you will justify yourselves as fathers or rulers of your country, *you will find this to be incumbent on you.*"—(Sermon on "*Christ's Kingdom and the Magistrates' Power,*" preached before Parliament.)

JOHN FLAVEL (Presbyterian).

"What is the duty of political fathers or magistrates to their political children's subjects? It is to rule and govern the people over whom God hath set them, with wisdom, *carefully providing for their souls, in every place in their dominions.*"—(*Assembly's Catechism.*)

MATTHEW HENRY.

"Church duties legally imposed are to be paid notwithstanding Church corruptions. If Christ pay tribute, who can pretend to an exemption?"—(*Commentary: St. Matt.* xvii. 24-7.)

"It is the duty of rulers to take care of religion, and to see that the duties of it be regularly and carefully performed by those under their charge, and that *nothing be wanting that is requisite thereto.*"

"Let us much more give God praise for the *national establishment of our religion;* . . . that the Reformation was in our land a *national* act; that Christianity, thus purified, *is supported by good and wholesome laws, and is twisted in with the very constitution of our Government.*"

JOHN HOWE,

Anticipating a bright future for the Christian Religion, looked to see this prosperity brought about, "*First by means of the kings and potentates of the earth.* . . . Think whether this will not do much to the making of a happy State as to the interest of religion in the world."

PHILIP DODDRIDGE.

"Ministers of all denominations claim our prayers, and peculiarly those of Established Churches. . . . Nor ought we to forget those more learned and pious men whom our governors may from time to time think fit to raise to exalted stations amongst the Clergy. . . . By their pious and zealous endeavours an Establishment will flourish, and separate interests decrease."—(Sermon on *Deut.* xxiii. 9.)

RICHARD BAXTER,

Addressing civil rulers, says:—"Let none persuade you that you are such terrestrial animals that have nothing to do with the heavenly concernments of your subjects. . . . You must bend the force of all your government to the saving of people's souls."—(*Christian Directory, Works,* vol. vi. p. 14., 8vo., London, 1830.

It is not a little significant that some Dissenters who are Voluntaries in England are State-Churchmen abroad. Does not this go far to show that jealousy is at the root of much of their hostility to the Church? Thus, the directors of the Independent "London Missionary Society" once wrote to the sovereign of a Polynesian State, "advising HIM *to banish the national idol*, and to attend to the instructions of the Missionaries." (Ellis, *Polynesian Researches*, vol. ii. p. 528.) In Ceylon the Missionary waited, in the first instance, on the *Governor* to ask advice where he (the Missionary) had better go. The Governor offered, and the Independent Missionary accepted, 50 dollars a month, and he was promised further assistance ! ! !

More recently the "Rev." W. Tyerman and G. Bennet, Esq., visited the South Sea Islands, and confess having "had a long interview with the King (of Hawaii), in which *we urged the propriety of publicly adopting Christianity as the religion of his dominions ! ! !*" (*Travels*, vol. i. p. 439.) In referring to New Holland, these same Independent gentlemen remark (very properly, *we Churchmen say*,) that "It is *deeply to be lamented that Protestant Governments take so little care to convey the knowledge of the true religion* wherever they carry their arms, their commerce, or their arts in colonisation."

"Rev." WILLIAM KIRKUS, LL.B. (Independent).

Mr. Kirkus is the Head Master of a large Dissenting school at Hackney.

"There is no book, excepting the Bible, from which I have derived so much benefit as from the Book of Common Prayer. It seems to me, perhaps, the very gravest of the misfortunes almost inseparable from my position as a Dissenter, that I am unable to make constant use of it in public worship. Yet perhaps this misfortune should hardly be called *inseparable* from the position of a Dissenter. The Book of Common Prayer belongs to every Englishman. It is still the test of orthodoxy; and has done more than any other book to preserve the majority of sober-minded men from infidelity on the one hand, and fanaticism on the other.'—(Preface to *Miscellaneous Essays*. 1863.)

APPENDIX TO PART II.

CHURCHMEN may be interested to know how the Dissenters meet our arguments drawn from the Bible. Dr. Wardlaw, one of their ablest champions, offers I. *Cor.* ix. 11 and 14; *Gal.* vi. 6; I. *Thess.* v. 12-13; and *St. John* xviii. 36—"My kingdom is not of this world." *Our* argument is drawn from a wide range of God's Word, Genesis to Revelation: in time it reaches over 1550 years: and it is met by five passages all written within 25 years, to say nothing of the fact that only one of the five has even the outward appearance of having anything to do with the question. "My kingdom is not of this world" simply indicates that at the time when Christ spoke, circumstances were adverse to the Church in matters temporal. Our Saviour elsewhere said, that "the Son of man had not where to lay his head." St. Paul laboured in "hunger and thirst, in cold and nakedness." Surely anti-State-Churchmen do not mean to say that *this* kind of existence is the proper normal one for ministers of the Gospel ! No; it is like the "My kingdom, &c."—a plain statement of the then subsisting facts. These five passages (and the other four have nothing on earth to do with Church and State) are all that Dissenters urge against the coincident testimony of the Old and New Testament scriptures all but universally accepted by the Church and the Sects alike, down to the year 1830.

The climax of Dr. Wardlaw's argument [?] is reached when he tells us (*Lectures*) that *his* doctrine is concealed in the adverb "now;" but "NOW is my kingdom not from hence." The accomplished essayist pertinently remarks:—"Think of a doctrine, which Dr. Wardlaw represents as of immense importance, lying hidden in the Greek adverb νῦν! A scriptural argument, which at last shrinks into the compass of a subordinate word of three letters! The thing is too absurd. It has only to be named to be at once appreciated."—(*Essays*, p. 33.)

The question of Church and State, argued from the New Testament, is simply this: Our Saviour came into the world and found a State Church ; He recognised and supported it ; and He left it as He found it. Every analogy warrants us, nay, compels us, to believe that His silence was designed; that had He intended to dispense with State Churches, *He would have said so.*

Book III.

A Warning to Churchmen.

The following quotations are put forth for the purpose of showing Churchmen heretofore ignorant of, or indifferent to, the aggressions of the *Political* Dissenters, the nature of the fierce attacks to which the Established Church is now being subjected. The struggle before us is one of CHURCH or NO CHURCH: it will be a desperate one, and we must all be stirring; high and low, rich and poor, Tory and Whig, ought all to join in UNION IN THE CAUSE OF CHURCH DEFENCE.

It cannot, however, be too explicitly and too plainly understood by the country, that not we, but the Dissenters, commenced the conflict; we were content to allow them civil and religious toleration, and, in the fond hope of securing peace and harmony, we accorded them a great deal too much of both. Our good nature has been shamefully abused: let us then arouse ourselves, ere it be too late, to defend our beloved Church, not the creature of yesterday, but the progressively-developed institution of 1600 years' standing.

Religious Dissent is all but engulphed in Democratic Dissent; Dissent is for the most part no longer synonymous with spiritually-minded religion, but with REVOLUTION. The last 30 years have seen the great bulk of English Dissenters (more particularly the Antipædobaptists and the Independents) transformed into a mob of intriguing political agitators, bound together by no one tie but that of " envy, hatred, malice, and all " possible " uncharitableness " towards the Church of England.

Fellow-Churchmen, read the following pages, and see for yourselves whether my statements are not borne out by facts.

THE LIBERATION SOCIETY.

The mainsprings of the present onslaughts on the Temporalities of the Church of England are located, as is well known, in an obscure building in Serjeants' Inn, Fleet Street, London, the offices of a powerful organisation of disaffected schismatics, martyrs (as they fancy themselves to be) to the persecuting spirit of the Church, known all over the country as " The Society for the Liberation of Religion from State Patronage and Control," though originally termed, at its formation in 1845, "The British Anti-State-Church Association,"—an appellation far more telling than the Jesuitical one it has since adopted.

Its objects, as stated in its published prospectus, are:—

"The abrogation of all laws and usages which inflict disability, or confer privilege, on ecclesiastical grounds, upon any subject of the realm."

"The discontinuance of all payments from the Consolidated Fund, and of all Parliamentary grants and compulsory exactions, for religious purposes."

"THE APPLICATION TO SECULAR USES, after an equitable satisfaction of existing interests, of ALL national property now held in trust by the united Church of England and Ireland, the Presbyterian Church of Scotland, and, concurrently with it, the liberation of those Churches from all State control."

My limits forbid me entering into a detailed account of the Society's machinery, and how it is worked: I must therefore rest content with a short statement. Its income is about 4000*l.* a year, which sum is spent in sending lecturers through the country; in distributing Anti-Church tracts and handbills, particularly in parishes likely to be the scene of Church Rate contests; in promoting the presentation of Anti-Church petitions to Parliament; in publishing a monthly journal called *The Liberator*, for the dissemination of Anti-Church news; and, in fact, in defraying all the obvious expenses incidental to the conduct of a widely based POLITICAL organisation having ramifications in all parts of England, and subscribers of some kind in almost every village.

Besides *The Liberator*, several Metropolitan and Provincial Newspapers are, to a greater or less extent, "inspired" by the Society, amongst which the *Nonconformist*, the *Morning Star*, the *Daily News*, and the *Leeds Mercury* may be named.

The following measures, introduced into Parliament at various times within the last few years, may, with strict truth, be stated to have been more or less the work of, or slyly abetted by, *or to have found their chief supporters in*, those who are also the chief supporters of the Liberation Society:—

1. Abolition of the Irish "Ministers' Money." [Carried.]
2. Abolition of Jewish Disabilities. [Carried.]
3. Abolition of the English "Regium Donum." [Carried.]
4. Abolition of Church Rates.
5. Abolition of the Irish "Regium Donum."
6. Endowed Schools Bill. (Mr. Dillwyn.)
7. Trustees of Charities Bill. (Mr. Dillwyn.)
8. Qualification for Offices Bill. (Mr. Hadfield.)
9. Nonconformists' Burials Bill. (Sir S. M. Peto.)
10. Liberty of Religious Worship Bill. (Mr. Locke King.)
11. Opposition to the Religious Worship Census. [Carried.]
12. Abolition of the Edinburgh Annuity Tax.
13. Legalisation of Marriage with a deceased Wife's Sister.
14. Oaths and Affirmations Bill. (Sir J. Trelawney.)
15. Abolition of the Bible Printing Patent.
16. Clergy Relief Bill. (Mr. Bouverie.)
17. Oxford Tests Abolition Bill. (Mr. Coleridge.)
18. Fellows of Colleges Declaration Bill. (Mr. Bouverie.)

A short exposition of the present demands of the Dissenters may be useful to those who do not pay much attention to the proceedings in Parliament:—

4. Everybody knows what Church Rates are, and what their abolition means.

5. The *Regium Donum* is an allowance of about 30,000*l.* a year paid to certain Dissenting Preachers in Ireland out of the public funds.

6. The Court of Chancery has decided that, unless there is a special provision to the contrary in the trust deed, "religious teaching" in an endowed school must be held to mean the teaching of the Church of England, as the religion alone recognised by the law. Mr. Dillwyn wishes to annul this decision, and to throw open to Dissenters all endowed schools not *explicitly* tied to the Church of England, and so to alienate from Churchmen endowments left by Churchmen for Church Education purposes. By a conciliatory Bill passed in 1859, Dissenters' children are admitted to schools whose trust deeds are *not* explicit, without being *forced* to receive instruction in Church doctrines ; but this good-natured concession will not satisfy the Liberation Society.

7. This Bill is intimately connected with the preceding. Under the existing law, Dissenters are ineligible to act as trustees to Church charities. Mr. Dillwyn claims a share in the administration of such charities.

8. Persons accepting certain public offices are required to declare that they will not use their official influence to subvert the Established Church. Mr. Hadfield proposes to permit them so to use their influence if they choose.

9. This Bill is to legalise funeral services in churchyards by *anybody*. If passed, it would go further to degrade the Church to the position of a sect than any measure ever introduced by the Dissenters.

10. Under the existing law, no Clergyman can conduct a public service in any parish without the consent of the Incumbent. Mr. Locke King wishes to abolish this very proper provision.

12. The Annuity Tax provides for the maintenance of certain Presbyterian Preachers at Edinburgh. The North-of-the-Tweed Radicals apply the same epithets to it that their Southern brethren do to Church Rates.

13. Explains itself.

14. Is a Bill for the abolition of all oaths, and the substitution of a simple declaration on the part of a witness that he will speak the truth. This is emphatically the Atheist's Bill.

15. The only persons licensed to print the Holy Scriptures in England and Wales are the Queen's Printers and the two Universities. As this arrangement savours of "State interference with religion," the Dissenters tried in 1860 to get it abolished, but failed.

16. This Bill, as originally brought forward, enacted that by a sixpenny declaration a clergyman might throw off his Orders, and become, to all intents and purposes, a layman, thus controverting, by the authority of Parliament, a well-known maxim held by the Church in all ages. A select committee, however, removed some of the most objectionable features of this Bill ; but even thus diluted, the Bill was happily rejected on the third reading.

17 and 18 are Bills to throw open University Degrees and Fellowships, and consequently the Government of the Universities, to *all comers*.

The Society has also a "Parliamentary Sub-Committee," whose duties consist in carrying on a system of "touting" of Members of Parliament, to induce them to vote for the Society's Bills, followed (if the attempt fails, *which formerly it seldom did*) by threats of the displeasure of their constituents, and possible loss of their seats, if the Society's influence can bring about that result, which occasionally it can, as at Huddersfield in 1859.

THE ALLIANCE BETWEEN DISSENT AND POPERY.

The following letter from the Secretary of the Irish National Association (a *semi-Fenian* league) reveals two or three interesting facts. It appeared in various newspapers during the General Election of 1865:—

"DEAR SIR,—Mr. Carvell Williams, Secretary of the Liberation Society, asks me what we are doing at the canvass for the coming elections. He says the Liberation Society got 13,000*l.* out of the 25,000*l.* *required to extend their working. They sent down the Rev.* Mr. Conder, a *Nonconformist minister*, to harangue the electors of the Isle of Wight in favour of Sir J. Simeon, a [*Roman*] *Catholic.* I think the Liberation people will carry Simeon's election.—Yours, &c.,

"J. O'N. DAUNT."

And so they did, to their eternal infamy. The Wesleyans alone, I believe, protested against the compact between Rome and Geneva to trample down the Church of England, represented by the Protestant candidate, Sir C. Locock, Bt.

THE BI-CENTENARY MOVEMENT.

What *was avowedly* proposed may be learnt from many sources; but that a *bonâ fide* religious commemoration of the expulsion, by-the-by, of *Dissenting* Ministers from the *Church's* benefices was intended is now proved unmistakeably to be false. (See *post*, Book X.)

"The Liberation Society *is deeply interested* in the proceedings to which Nonconformists are looking forward, but there are good reasons why it should not organise any special movement. . . . . The plain truth is, let the occasion be improved in any way, and the Church Establishment IS SURE TO SUFFER DAMAGE."—*Liberator*, Feb. 1862, p. 26.

Under cover of a religious demonstration, the Dissenters expected to be able to do a little Church revilement business; the proceedings of 1662 were not *the* end, but the means to *an* end widely different.

The schismatics charged our clergy with—

"*Frightful demoralisation of conscience*," which was said to be "produced by a solemn subscription to tests which the inner man repudiates," with "*clerical insincerity*, bred and nourished by the reluctant constraint which the Clergy take upon themselves in obedience to the Act of Uniformity;" with "*official self-consciousness*;" with "*official sophistry*;" with "*self-inflating hallucinations*," &c. &c.—*Nonconformist* Newspaper, Feb. 12, 1862.

"How is it that they [the Evangelical Clergy] do not see—for we must suppose they do not—that their position is irreconcilable with some of the most ordinary principles of public morality?" "The fact which we would everywhere proclaim is this, that the Act of Uniformity shuts men up to this alternative—PERJURY or SECESSION."—*The Ipswich Bi-Centenary Committee* (in one of their Tracts).

"*Are the Evangelical Clergy, in the matter of subscription, dishonest and untruthful?* . . . . *Yes, the Evangelical Clergy are guilty of unfaithfulness, and they know it.*"— *Patriot* Newspaper, April 1862.

Hundreds of pages might be made up, of reprints from the various journals and magazines of the Sects, published during 1862-3, all conched in the bitter, unchristian style of the above; but no good purpose would be served by further quotations. The malignant fury of the Dissenters is now sufficiently established all over England. The plague was rife among them, and, outside the Wesleyan body, comparatively few were hostile to the movement. Here and there a Dissenter ventured to expostulate with his fellows on their violence, and he was quickly put down: *e. g.*, at a "Congregational Conference" on February 1, 1862, the "Rev." J. Stoughton suggested that "this is not the occasion when they should bring forward, as the basis of their proceedings, the principles and practice of the Anti-State-Church Association." Whereupon the "Rev." J. G. Rogers jumped up and said that "in Lancashire it was felt that it was *more important* to bring out the principles of the Liberation Society *than anything else."*

DISSENTING SUNDAY-SCHOOL TEACHERS.

The connection between these and what I am now discussing may not at first sight be obvious, but it soon will become so. Some years ago there was published, at the office of the Liberation Society, an *Address to Teachers of Dissenting Schools*, by the "Rev." William Forster.

After reminding the teachers how powerful their influence is in forming the minds of those under their control, the pamphlet proceeded to urge them to exercise it in antagonism to the Church. Thus:—

" The tone of feeling in the next generation is to be given, to a very great extent, by your culture."—p. 12.

" And if you engraft into their minds the deep conviction that every State-Church is anti-Christian in its foundation, constitution, policy, spirit, and working, then will you awaken a sentiment which will strengthen, swell, and spread, until it has swept every State-Church, as a secular institution, from the statute-book of this kingdom."—p. 12.

Then, referring to the Church, we were told:—

" The immense funds which it swallows up, the servile spirit which it generates, the sympathy which it extends to all illiberal institutions, the impediment which it places before the course of just legislation, the barrier which it opposes to the intellectual and social progress of the people, call upon all patriots and philanthropists to labour for its downfall."—p. 13.

" But all these evils are reduced to insignificance compared with the spiritual mischief which it works on the souls of men—a mischief deep as hell and durable as eternity. Now, Dissenters are the only individuals who have the remedy for this prodigious evil. 'They are the salt of the land.' "—p. 13.

Then as to Dissent:—

" Before your scholars can enter into the reasons of Dissent, you must tell them it is right and true. It is in this way you give them your own notions about God, their souls, sin, Christ, the Holy Scriptures, and other religious topics. They believe what you affirm or deny of these things, not because you have proved your propositions, but on your bare word."—p. 18.

" All the first ideas of a child respecting religious objects come to it through its faith in man. All infant education goes upon this principle of communicating knowledge. We mention this fact in order to induce you to act on it in inculcating Dissent. Speak of it as something in accordance with the will of God. Let your scholars feel that you consider separation from State-Churches as highly pleasing to Christ. Tell them that national establishments of religion are sinful, are wrong in themselves, and in all their workings. If you do this, you will produce a deep faith in Dissent; you will connect it in their earliest associations with the true and honourable; you will knead it into their inmost moral nature."—p. 18.

These extracts speak for themselves; but I would venture to remark, that their importance chiefly consists in the fact that such sentiments may be inculcated on Sundays to children who during the week attend the Church school and get a good education at our expense, and that those whose minds are to be "deeply convinced" of the anti-Christian character of the national Church, are a class who in after-life are liable to be greatly influenced by their early teaching. I should like to see prevail generally the rule which many Church school managers lay down, that they will take into their day schools none who do not also attend their Sunday schools.

Pass we on now to the publicly declared sentiments of some of the Members and Friends of the Liberation Society.

MR. EDWARD MIALL (Independent).

Mr. Miall was formerly Preacher at an Independent Meeting-house at Ware, and afterwards of one at Leicester; M.P. for Rochdale, 1852–7; and proprietor of the *Nonconformist* Newspaper. I place him first, not only on account of the peculiar bitterness with which he has for many years past assailed the Church of England, but because he is usually considered by his party as their leader-in-chief. My quotations are from the *Nonconformist's Sketch Book*, 8vo. London, 1842; but the author's *British Churches in relation to the British People*, should also be consulted.

"The time for trifling has gone by. The Establishment, *a life-destroying upas*, deeply rooted in our soil, undisturbed, drinks up fresh vigour. It sprouts again. It puts forth fresh branches. It sheds its noxious seeds in our colonies. If there be evil in it, that evil is daily becoming confirmed, augmented, perpetuated. The *curse* is going down to our posterity, abroad to our emigrants, aggravated in its intensity. For our part, we are resolved to wash our hands of the guilt. In the name of myriads, victims of AN IMPIOUS PRETENCE—when they lean upon it, fatally deluded; when they discern its hollowness, rendered infidels for life—in the name of unborn generations, of the untold millions that shall one day populate the distant dependencies of Britain—in the name of Christianity, misrepresented, disgraced, downcast, trodden under foot by aristocratic legislation, we charge the body of Dissenting Ministers with unfaithfulness to sacred principles, evasion of a noble mission, and seeming recklessness of all the mighty interests at issue."—*Sketch Book*, p. 16.

"A State Church! Have they never pondered upon the practical meaning of that word? Have they never looked into that dark, polluted, inner chamber of which it is the door? Have they never caught a glimpse of the loathsome things that live, and crawl, and gender there?"—*Ibid.* p. 16.

The Church is an "ABOMINATION," to be swept away; it is "the most fitting refuge for wealthy worldliness."—*Ibid.* p. 20.

"We believe that Dissenting Ministers have swerved into dishonesty" [no doubt about it].—*Ibid.* p. 20.

The Established Church is "an admitted evil—an evil of FRIGHTFUL MAGNITUDE."... The Church of England is "an image carved with marvellous cunning, tricked out in solemn vestments, a part woven by human fancy, a part stolen from the chest of truth —an image, we repeat, an outside semblance, a counterfeit . . . . empty, without heart, destitute of any well-spring of vitality . . . . Kings, nobles, and bishops, under the sanction and on behalf of their Church, perpetuate a thousand enormities, violate every maxim of religion, degrade, insult, harass, imprison—regard neither justice nor mercy in their pursuit of pelf."—*Ibid.* p. 27.

"To shatter this image, and give the dust of it to the four winds of heaven . . . . is *the sacred mission of Protestant Dissenting Ministers*."—*Ibid.* p. 29.

The Church of England is "*a great aristocratic imposture—a disgusting pretence*, the hollowness of which may be easily exposed—a falsehood cloaked in truth, which levies fearful imposts, produces bitter dissensions, stands in the way of all national progress, engenders infidelity to a most alarming extent, misrepresents and dishonours true religion."—*Ibid.* p. 34.

"Racks, thumb-screws, and bootikins—the sword and the faggot—squabbles for money —scrambles for place—a population escaping from brutal superstition, only to rush into the bosom of daring and profligate infidelity; these are the results and the trophies of coercion—of a State Church."—*Ibid.* p. 39.

"Are there not vested interests planted in every square mile of the country [*i.e.* Parish Clergy] *to nip and extinguish Christianity in earnest?*"—*Ibid.* p. 41.

The presence of Bishops in the Upper House of Parliament answers "no earthly purpose but to keep alive bigotry and embitter strife."—*Ibid.* p. 58.

"The resumption [*i.e.* robbery] for civil purposes of all funds now devoted by the State to the maintenance of the Church—the abolition of all privileges connected with the profession of an authorised creed—and the repeal of all statutes empowering the magistrate to interpose his aid in religious affairs, is what we mean by the separation of Church and State."—*Ibid.* p. 60.

"15,000 Clergy . . . stationed at convenient intervals over the length and breadth of the land, and thus coming in contact with society at all points—could mechanism more fatal to religion [?], or more serviceable to the interests of the upper class, be framed and put together?"—*Ibid.* p. 68.

"Whatever religion is mixed up with it [the Church of England] is there by accident, is frowned on as intrusive, is not only not necessary to the system, but, in so far as it is consistent, is antagonistic to it."—*Ibid.* p. 70.

The Church of England "*desecrates religion*, and obstructs popular freedom. . . . It becomes every lover of his country, as well as every Christian, to denounce it. No man can be regarded as a sound-hearted patriot who advocates the maintenance of a State-Church."—*Ibid.* p. 70.

The English Clergy are "men who of necessity are inimical to all reform, abettors of every abuse, united, organised, and therefore formidable opponents of progressive improvement."—*Ibid.* p. 72.

The English Establishment "obstructs general improvement, cripples intelligence, stunts the national mind, and keeps people fools in order that they may be slaves."—*Ibid.* p. 72.

"The selfishness, ambition, intolerance, and hypocrisy" of the English Clergy. "What deeds of darkness have been too foul, what malignant attacks upon the rights of man have been too infernal, to be perpetrated" by them? . . . "In what page of our national records are we to look for the disinterestedness, the liberality, or the gentleness of the Clergy? . . . They have been invariably the deadliest foes of liberty, civil and religious. Despotism and tyranny always found in them the ready tools to enslave the people. . . . Their hatred of improvement, their scorching intolerance, remain just what they were, modified only by the spirit of the age. . . . *The education of the people owes nothing to them* [?]. They checked it as long as decency would forbid, and when nothing could effectually stay its progress, they advertised and puffed off an article of their own, steeped in the bigotry of their religious system. . . . The body [of them] has been a political curse. They have uniformly stood in the way of their country's improvement."—*Ibid.* p. 75.

"Democracy is a reality—a State-Church is a mere conventionalism; reason animates the one—the other can only live in the absence of reason; the former is a sincerity, a vital, glowing, earnest sincerity—the other a semblance only, a form, a disguise, a falsehood, having designs which it dares not avow, and avowing designs which it never had."—*Ibid.* p. 118.

"Could we but trace the history of our Establishment [in England], and mark its influence upon the national character, we should find that against deep, intelligent, self-denying piety, it has always set its face as a flint" [!!!]—*Ibid.* p. 185.

"In the eye of a State-Church, immorality and licentiousness are trifles" [!!!]—*Ibid.* p. 185.

"As a spiritual institution, we are warranted in pronouncing the Church of England to be at once *a blunder, a failure, and a hoax*" [!!!]—*Ibid.* p. 212.

"*The separation of Church and State, as it is their* [the Dissenters'] *real object, so in our judgment it is their proper, their right noble mission.*"—*Ibid.* p. 270.

"The useful reforms she [the Church of England] obstructs—the vicious principles, both social and political, to which she gives her sanction . . . the debasing influence she exerts upon the religion of all parties and sects . . . render her a PUBLIC NUISANCE, the speedy removal of which interests every class of people in this country."—*Ibid.* p. 278.

"Upon all national Churches is enstamped, in deep and indelible characters, the mark of the beast."—*Ibid.* p. 280.

"Homage the most indirect paid to the State-Church is, in essence, the recognition of falsehood and the worship of a lie!"—*Ibid.* p. 280.

The "Rev." Thomas BINNEY (Independent).

Mr. Binney is the Preacher at the Weigh-house Meeting-house, Fish Street Hill, London.

"It is with me, I confess, a matter of deep, serious, religious conviction, that the Established Church is a GREAT NATIONAL EVIL; that it is an obstacle to the progress of truth and godliness in this land; that IT DESTROYS MORE SOULS THAN IT SAVES; and that therefore its end is most devoutly to be wished for by every lover of God and man. Right or wrong, this is my belief."—*Address delivered on laying the first stone of the New King's Weigh-house Meeting-house*, 1834, p. 52.

"I wish to assent to the principle that the Churches are the property of the whole nation, *including the Dissenters* . . . I believe the time will come when the nation and not a sect will have the use of them."—*Speech at the Anti-Church Rate Conference, Freemasons' Hall*, Feb. 12, 1861.

Mr. John BRIGHT (Quaker).

It is needless to say that Mr. Bright is the well-known Peace-at-any-price M.P. In Church matters, however, he is for *War-at-any-price*.

"The Dissenters regard this matter [Church Rates] as a matter of supremacy. It is not as matter of twopence in the pound that they regard it. . . . But it is really a question of supremacy, and of supremacy, too, on the part of a great establishment which is as much political as religious, against which their forefathers have fought, *and against which they are still obliged to contend*. . . . Anything which binds them to a subjugation to your Church, gives it a supremacy, or enables it especially to exact money from them, *is a thing to which it is impossible for them in any way to assent*."—*Speech on the Second Reading of the Church Rates Abolition Bill*, Feb. 27, 1861.

The " Rev." William BROCK (Antipædobaptist).

Mr. Brock is the Minister of Bloomsbury Meeting-house, London, and is well known to most persons as the biographer of Sir H. Havelock, who held the same views.

"I have never concealed my opinions upon the question of Church and State, and am more than ever convinced that until a separation takes place there will be no peace for England religiously. All we ask for is the perfect equality of all denominations, and we shall never be satisfied with less than this."—*Speech at the Annual Meeting of the Liberation Society*, May 2, 1861.

"We would have all ecclesiastical buildings [Churches, &c.] recognised as belonging to the State. We would have all ecclesiastical lands come gradually into the actual possession of the State. We would have all property represented by the word tithe revert to the use of the State, either by the ordinary process of redemption, or by some such other equitable arrangement as the Legislature may devise."—*Lecture at the Norwich Religious Liberty Society*, Feb. 9, 1847.

Mr. George Joseph COCKERELL (Independent).

Mr. Cockerell is a large Coal Merchant at Cornhill, London; and was Sheriff of London in 1861-2. In politics he is an ultra-Radical.

"I do not believe in just stopping short at the matter of Church Rates"—*i.e.* we must go on much farther.—*Speech at the Annual Meeting of the Liberation Society*, May 2, 1861.

The " Rev." J. CROMPTON.

Mr. Crompton is a Dissenting Preacher, but I have been unable to ascertain any particulars relating to him.

"As an order, the existence of the English Clergy, on their present footing, is AN EVIL (and has been so through history) OF A GIGANTIC NATURE. . . They are, and have been, the greatest obstacles of progress and improvement the country possesses."—*Lecture at the Norwich Religious Liberty Society*, Feb. 23, 1847.

The " Rev." R. W. DALE (Independent).

Mr. Dale is the Preacher at the Carr's Lane Meeting-house, Birmingham, having succeeded the late Mr. J. A. James.

The Pilgrim Fathers " denied the Church of England to be a true Church at all, though there were very many excellent Christian persons in it; AND TO THAT DENIAL I FIRMLY HOLD."—*Lecture on the Pilgrim Fathers.* 16mo. London, 1854, p. 13.

MR. JOHN FOSTER.

Mr. Foster was a distinguished anti-Churchman of the last generation. The Editor of the *Christian Witness* says that he "will be generally accepted by the Dissenters of England as an advocate worthy of their cause."

"Making religion a part of the State, is anti-Christian in theory and noxious in practice."—Quoted in *The Christian Witness*, Feb. 1847, p. 76.

"A fearful mass and variety of evils, consistently, and for the most part necessarily, result from the very nature of an Established Church, and are not accidental and separable; and therefore the thing is radically and fundamentally bad, and pernicious to religion."—*Ibid.* p. 78.

The English Clergy are "multitudes of authorised teachers, who *teach not the Gospel.*"—*Ibid.* p. 78.

The Church of England "we judge to be ANTI-CHRISTIAN, UNSCRIPTURAL, and CORRUPT."—*Ibid.* p. 80.

The "Rev." JOHN HOWARD HINTON (Antipædobaptist).

Mr. Hinton is the Preacher to the congregation Meeting at Devonshire Square, Bishopsgate, London.

"I have been a soldier in this battle [Abolition of Church Rates] from my youth, and I am in better hope to-day than I ever have been of seeing the victory won. (Loud cheers.) And I say this, that whether Parliament chooses to give us this out of justice or not, we will have it, with them or without them. (Loud cheers.)"—*Speech at the Anti-Church Rate Conference, Freemasons' Hall,* Feb. 12, 1861.

The late "Rev." JOHN ANGELL JAMES (Independent).

The late well-known Preacher at the Carr's Lane Meeting-house, Birmingham.

The alliance of the Church of England "with the State is a great evil, and the prolific source of many others, and, as long as it remains as a system of religious instruction, must inevitably corrupt it, and render it to a considerable extent an engine of secular policy."—*Works,* Vol. xiv. p. 148, 8vo. London 1862.

Church reform, as suggested by some of her friends, "would not meet the case. It would at best only purify the stream, and leave the fountain still polluted. THE ALLIANCE OF THE CHURCH WITH THE STATE IS THE MIGHTY MISCHIEF. No provisions, however wisely ordered, nor precautions, however judiciously framed, can guard against the corruptions which must inevitably result to the Church from an Establishment. As long as this remains, the Church cannot preserve its gravity."—*Ibid.* p. 162.

The "Rev." JOHN KELLY (Independent).

Mr. Kelly is a great man at the "Congregational Union."

'The Church of England is a mode of government marked by titles and claims which Christ has expressly forbidden his servants to assume—a mode of government which, in its working, is proving itself imbecile for good, and potent *only for evil.*'—*Address, Congregational Year Book,* 1861, p. 45.

The late "Rev." GEORGE LEGGE, LL.D. (Independent).

Mr. Legge was an Independent Preacher at Leicester, and was Chairman of the "Congregational [fashionable word for Independent] Union of England and Wales," for 1859. Holding this high position in his

D

sect, and having received an unanimous vote of thanks for his address, the Union are, of course, authoritatively pledged to Mr. Legge's opinions.

"Further, there is Church-and-State-ism, or Establishment-arianism, which we [the Congregational Union] regard as at once a BLUNDER and a SIN."—*Address at Aberdare*, Sept. 13, 1859. *Congregational Year Book*, 1860, p. 42.

The Hon. and Rev. BAPTIST WRIOTHESLEY NOEL (Antipædobaptist).

Mr. Noel's antecedents are too well known to require a lengthy notice here. He is *de jure* a clergyman of the Church of England ; but in 1848, while Incumbent of St. John's Chapel, Bedford Row, he became *de facto* a schismatic, and is now Preacher at an Antipædobaptist Meeting-house in the same locality. He is of noble birth, being the brother of the Earl of Gainsborough. My quotations are from his *Essay on the Union of the Church and the State*, 2d edition, 8vo. London, 1849.

"The Union between the Church and State in any country is unprincipled, absurd, and mischievous."—*Essay*, p. 238.

The Church of England and its Clergy "are corrupted, and the Union [of Church and State] being one principal cause of their corruption, the Union is at this time one great obstacle to the progress of religion in the country."—*Ibid.* p. 543.

"It is impossible that the Establishment, under the control of worldly politicians, led by worldly prelates, and taught by worldly pastors chosen by worldly patrons, can possibly extend the empire of spiritual religion through the land."—*Ibid.* p. 545.

"The safety of the constitution demands the immediate removal of the Union of Church and State. It disfigures our constitution, distracts our social peace, revolts our sense of justice, is condemned by religion [?], and irritates millions [?] against the social system under which they live."—*Ibid.* p. 562.

A "Separation of the Church and State is the distinct tendency of the present nations of Europe, which must, sooner or later, govern the course of the rest." Mr. Noel then goes on to refer to the proceedings of the French National Convention in 1795, and the German National Assembly in 1848 (both short-lived Democratic bodies), in repudiating National religion, whose example, our author hopes, will be followed soon by Englishmen [!!!].—*Ibid.* p. 563.

The separation of Church and State "has been put to the test by a great nation across the Atlantic with extraordinary success [!!!], the events of Europe are happily hastening it on ; and may England be among the earliest of the European nations to fulfil the duty and reap the advantages."—*Ibid.* p. 571.

The late " Rev." ANDREW REED, " D.D." (Independent).

Mr. Reed was the Preacher at the Wycliffe Meeting-house, Commercial Road, and was well known in connection with the Asylum for Idiots, Redhill.

"The majority of the Clergy in the Established Church ever has exerted, and still does exert, a powerful influence against what we regard as the Religion of the Bible."—*Lecture at the Norwich Religious Liberty Society*, Feb. 23, 1847.

The " Rev." CHARLES HADDON SPURGEON (Antipædobaptist).

It is hardly necessary for me to state that this is the well-known " popular Preacher " at Newington. I am given to understand by those who have heard him, that insults to the Church and her Spiritual Rulers are constantly indulged in by him in his sermons. The quotations below are from the *Baptist Magazine*, 8vo. London, 1861.

"To Churchmen we would say, What *right* has your sect to be patronised by the State in preference to all others ? Do you not perceive that the power which has made you the State-Church can unmake you, and withdraw its golden sanctions ? Your

Church was originally fashioned by despotic will, and elected to supremacy by arbitrary power; but there are no despots now to whom you can look, no irresponsible conclaves on whom you can rely. . . . You shall rue the day in which oppression unloosed our tongues. We will expose your abuses to the very children in the street; we will teach the peasant at the plough to loathe the inconsistencies of your Prayer Book, and the pauper on the road shall know the history of your ferocious persecutions in the days of yore [!]. We will collect statistics of your Ministers, and let our citizens know how many or how few are Evangelicals; we will demand Scriptural proof for Confirmation and for Priestly Absolution; and we will never permit the nation to subside into apathy so favourable to proud pretensions. We court not the struggle, but we are ready for it if you are ambitious for the combat. We know your unhealed and unmollified wounds, and our blows will tell upon your putrefying sores. Our armoury is filled with arrows, feathered with your follies and barbed with your backslidings. Provoke not the fray. . . . . You will find it a hard matter to retrace your steps if you go astray much farther."—*B. M.* June, p. 334.

The " Rev." Thomas TOLLER (Independent).

Mr. Toller is or was a Preacher at Kettering, Northamptonshire.

"We hold that the connection of a Church with the State carries absurdity on the face of it; that all civil establishments of religion are inconsistent with the very nature of religion; a violation of the inalienable rights of men, and, therefore, contradictory to the laws and spirit of Christianity."—*Sermon* published in the *Congregational Pulpit*, October 1855, p. 201.

The " Rev." Robert VAUGHAN, "D.D." (Independent).

Mr. Vaughan is a highly influential Preacher (unattached) in London. He was for many years the Editor of the *British Quarterly Review*, and one of the few real scholars his sect can boast of; he is also one of the Honorary Secretaries of the Religious Tract Society.

"Some have been much surprised, or have affected to be so, of late, in having discovered, as they would lead us to suppose, that Dissenters are really opposed to an Established Church. Why, a Congregational [Independent] Dissenter, from the very essence of what is distinctive in his profession, must be opposed to it. If there be a State Endowment of religion, there must be State influence and control in relation to it. But it is of the very essence of our Independency to resist all such interference. We cannot forego this controversy—we dare not."—*Speech at the Meeting of the Congregational Union, at Birmingham*, October 9, 1861.

This is an authoritative denial of what, in spite of every fair proof to the contrary, many Churchmen will persist in trying to believe is possible, viz. that there can be lasting peace and harmony between Church and Dissent. Churchmen have often, ere this, been warned of the fatal delusion they were under, but all in vain. However disagreeable or unpalatable it may be to many of us, nothing short of a stern determination to crush the social and political influence of Dissent will save the Establishment, *as such.* Every Churchman who entertains a particle of self-respect either for himself or his Church, ought to cease from all dealings with political schismatics. Churchmen ought all to retire from the Bible Society, the Tract Society, the City Mission, and all "mixed" institutions; and if none already exist in connection with the Church, they should found them. The Rev. Dr. Miller, the esteemed Rector of Greenwich, set a noble example when at Birmingham, which I hope will be widely followed.

The " Rev." T. A. WHEELER (Antipædobaptist).

Mr. Wheeler is or was a Preacher at Norwich.

"A 'sectarian Clergy' appropriate annually 9,000,000*l.* sterling [!!!] of strictly national property."—*Lecture at the Norwich Religious Liberty Society,* March 2, 1847.

Notoriously a LIE.

A national Religious Establishment is "the friend and ally of arbitrary power, the foe of popular advancement, denying freedom of action to the mind, and impeding the progress of truth, and as such we look upon it as meriting our severest censure, and demanding our most persevering opposition."—*Ibid.*

" The system itself [of the Church of England] we denounce, AND ARE PREPARED FOR A WAR AGAINST IT WHICH NO TRUCE SHALL LULL, AND NOUGHT BUT ITS OVER-THROW SHALL END."—*Ibid.*

AN ANONYMOUS WRITER.

I have mislaid the reference to this paragraph, but it is rather an important one, more particularly as its sentiments were unfolded by one of the witnesses before the Lords Committee on Church Rates.—(See *post*, p. 85.)

" We demand that the NATIONAL PROPERTY [*i.e.* our Churches and Chapels] shall be used for NATIONAL PURPOSES, or leased out to its present holders at a rental which shall acknowledge NATIONAL PROPRIETORSHIP," &c.

THE " CHRISTIAN'S PENNY MAGAZINE "

Is a popular periodical " issued by the Congregational Union of England and Wales," and edited until recently by John Campbell, D.D. Its circulation, which at one time amounted to 100,000 copies per number, is now, happily, much diminished.

In the worship of the English Church, " God is defied to his face by a man daring to call himself the Minister of Christ." [?]—*C. P. M.,* Jan. 1846, p. 14.

The Bishops of the Church of England " ride in carriages, seldom preach [?], and yearly spend thousands of the public money in *pride, luxury,* and *idleness.*"—*Ibid.* March 1847, p. 76.

"The Church of England PRACTICALLY DENIES THE SUFFICIENCY OF THE HOLY SCRIPTURES."—*Ibid.* p. 76.

"The Church of England . . . IS AN ENGINE IN THE HANDS OF SATAN, TO DELUDE AND DECEIVE THE PEOPLE."—*Ibid.* p. 70.

The Archbishops, Bishops, and inferior Clergy are, " *most of them, carnal men,* enemies to a free Gospel Church and to the spread of the Gospel."—*Ibid.* p. 77.

The people who pay rates, tithes, &c., " receive nothing but insult from the lordly priesthood " of the Church of England.—*Ibid.* p. 77.

The village clergyman " is the principal opposer of the power of godliness."—*Ibid.* p. 77.

The reader has by this time been pretty well initiated into the choice language and elegant phraseology of the Dissenters ; but he will, I think, be scarcely prepared for the following example of what is neither more nor less than BLASPHEMY OF THE VILEST KIND—the production, too, not of a professed Infidel, but of a self-styled Christian. Worthy indeed is the *Christian's Penny Magazine* of standing side by side with Tom Paine's *Age of Reason,* and the many blasphemous works of Voltaire, Hone, Holyoake, and other Atheists of their stamp.

"THE RIGHT TO PLUNDER VINDICATED;

"*Being Chap. XXIX. of the Acts of the Apostles, lately added for the Upholding of Church Rates, &c.**

"VERSE 1. Now it came to pass, while Paul tarried at Corinth, that he made a rate of two-pence in the pound upon the Jews, and upon the Gentiles, and upon the Church of God : and the rate was upon this wise:

2. When the brethren came together on the first day of the week, Stephanas, which was the first fruits of Achaia, being churchwarden that same year, moved that a rate should be made of two-pence in the pound for the mitre of Paul, and for his apron, and for the wine, and for the bell-ringers, and for the organist, and for the painted window, and for the beadle, and for the grave-digger, and for the clerk.

3. So a brother whose name was Aristarchus seconded the motion.

4. And Paul the Lord Bishop of Achaia sat in the chair, in his rochet ; and the very reverend Gaius, Dean of Corinth, sat at his right hand.

5. And a man whose name was Albinus rose up straightway in the midst, and spake against the rate. . . .

6. But the brethren lifted up their voices in the vestry with one accord, and cried mightily for about the space of half an hour, Turn him out ! and they threw dust in the air, and made no small stir, stamping with their feet, and hissing; insomuch that Albinus was put to shame and held his peace.

7. And Paul the apostle took the vote, and the brethren lifted up their hands, and they made a rate. . . .

8. 9. 10. 11. And the churchwardens departed to collect the rate, and coming unto the house of one Silvanus, a Hebrew of the Hebrews, and a ruler of the synagogue, behold he refused to pay. So the brethren hasted to tell it to the saints.

13. And Paul spake, and said unto the churchwardens, and unto the beadle, Go quickly into the street which is called Straight, unto the house of the ruler of the Jews, nigh unto the gate of the city, with staves in your hands, and carry away suddenly his table, and his bed, and his silver jug, and his spoon, and the spoon of his wife, and whatsoever he hath, and bring them into the market-place, and sell them unto all that pass by, until the rate shall be paid.

14. And if he will shut up the door of his house, behold, ye shall break into it ; and if he hold fast to his table, or his bed, or his jug, or his spoon, or anything which is his, ye shall smite him with your truncheon very grievously, and carry him away to the dungeon, and give him the bread of affliction and the water of affliction for six months, until he repent.

15. So the churchwardens went their way, and they took with them a brother whose name was Phlegon, which was the beadle of the church ; and he was arrayed in scarlet apparel for glory and for beauty, and he had a cocked hat upon his head, and a staff like unto a weaver's beam in his hand.

16. 17. And they came unto the house of the ruler of the synagogue, and having entered in by violence. . . .

19. Phlegon looked up to heaven, and seized upon the table, and upon the jug of the ruler, as Paul had commanded; upon his silver spoon also, and upon the spoon of his wife, which he had given her.

20. And Silvanus held fast with his hand upon the table. Then Phlegon sighed, and took him by the beard and smote him upon the head, so that he fell upon the earth. . . .

21. Then the churchwardens and the beadle took the bed, and the table, and the jug, and the spoons of Silvanus, and they departed unto the market-place, mourning over his unbelief, and sold them unto them which passed by, and payment was made.

23. And great fear came upon the Christians, and upon the heathen, and upon the Jews, and they paid the rate of two-pence in the pound, and all men glorified the power of the Church and of the apostles.

24. And Paul gave a parish with light duty, and a living in Macedonia, unto the sons of the churchwardens: and they gave unto Phlegon, the beadle, soup for the comfort of his body, and blankets, and an allotment at Christmas, for the zeal which he showed."—*C. P. M.*, March 1848, p. 71.

I leave this disgraceful composition to my readers to make their own comments on ; I will add nothing myself beyond saying that I concur in the opinion that it " is a foul and lasting blot upon Dissent, and shows how weak and how wicked she must be when she has no better weapons than profaneness and ribaldry the most disgusting."

---

* The principal passages are given *verbatim* ; the remainder are abridged as nearly as possible in the words of the original.

BOOK IV

Church Statistics.

ANY statement of figures relating to a portion of a population is at once an index, more or less trustworthy, to the whole. Thus if, of the adult population of any given village of 100 persons, 49 were men and 51 women, the chances are very great that in an adjoining village four times the size there would be, of 400 adults, 196 men and 204 women. Applying this well-known principle of statistical science to certain numbers presented to our notice in different Government returns, &c., we are able to obtain some calculations as to the numerical strength of the Church and Sects in England and Wales, which I here tabulate :—

	The Church. Per cent.	The Sects. Per cent.
Separate Places of Worship, 1851	44'4	55'6
Attendance on Census Sunday Morning, 1851	54 6	45'4
Accommodation, 1851	57'1	42'9
Ministers of Religion, 1861	67'9	32'1
Burials	71'5	28'5
Government Grants of Money, 1864	76'2	23'8
Schools	83'0	17'0
Marriages in Places of Worship, 1863	85'5	14'5
Members of Parliament (H. C.), 1866	92'6	7'3
Mean	70'4	29'6

In connection with the Census of 1851, an attempt was made, in an unauthorised and very indirect manner, to obtain some knowledge of the relative numbers of the adherents of the Church on the one hand, and of the different Sects on the other, by counting the number of those who attended the different places of worship. By a most elaborate series of calculations, from the data afforded by these Census returns, Mr. Horace Mann (himself a Dissenter, and therefore, if anything, prejudiced *against* the Church) obtained the following results :—

			Per cent. of Population.
Churchmen		7,546,948	=42
Romanists		610,786	= 3½
Dissenters, &c. :—			
Wesleyans	2,308,953		=12'8
Independents	1,321,904		= 7'3
Antipædobaptists	979,964		= 5'4
All others	692,788		= 3'8
		5,303,609	=29½
Total worshipping population		13,461,343	=75
Remainder, non-worshipping		4,466,266	=25
		17,927,609	100

This table reveals the fact that of the *worshipping* population of England and Wales, 56 per cent. attend the services of the Established Church, and only 44 the meeting-houses of the Sects. To the remaining 25 per cent. of the population, the Church performs *missionary* work, as the Sects, by their own avowal, have nothing to do with our home heathen poor. According to Mr. Spurgeon's candid confession, there is gradually growing up amongst Dissenters a feeling of disinclination to have any-thing to do with those *who cannot pay*.

There is one thing to be noted, concerning the enumeration from which Mr. Mann's figures are derived, of considerable importance, and it is this. Sunday, March 8, 1851, the day on which it was taken, was *very generally* wet, and the Bishop of Oxford pointed out what effect this would have on the numbers. The strength of Dissent lies in the large towns, where people live for the most part in close proximity to one another, and to their places of worship. On the other hand, the strength of the Church lies in the rural districts, where population is thin, and where people live for the most part at some distance (often very considerable) from their places of worship. The consequence is of course well known to be, that in inclement weather country Churches lose a much larger proportion of their ordinary congregations than town Churches. The Census Sunday being wet, the resulting enumeration would be less unfavourable to the Sects than it would be to the Church, and so it may reasonably be doubted whether 56 per cent. does not fall short of the normal number of the Church's worshippers. A man may not mind 300 yards of wet pavement, but human nature is generally too ready to refuse a 2-mile walk through muddy lanes. I omit all reference to the probable circumstance that the Sects would be far more likely than the Church to whip up for the occasion. That a whip did take place, and a pretty vigorous one too, is proved by such facts as the following :—A Wesleyan Reformed meeting-house at Leeds, returned as accommodating 200 persons, had a morning congrega-tion of 650, an afternoon ditto of 723, and an evening ditto of 1030 ! A Wesleyan Association meeting-house in St. Marylebone, returned as ac-commodating 198 persons, had a morning congregation of 277, and an evening ditto of 336. A General Baptist meeting-house at Coventry, re-turned as accommodating 300 persons, had a congregation of 397. It can scarcely be doubted that there was much exaggeration on the part of the Sects, as instances like these can be multiplied by reference to the official returns.

On the whole, we are unquestionably warranted in assuming that the Church comprehends in its fold fully *two-thirds* of the entire population of England and Wales (Mr. Mann says 67 per cent.; Mr. Mann, it will be recollected, *was* a Dissenter). And the general fact that the Church is in some kind of a *majority* is triumphantly proved by the extraordinary vehemence with which the Dissenters agitated in 1860 against the pro-posed personal inquiry into the religious belief of every individual, in the Census of 1861. Their anxiety bordered on temporary insanity ; and Lord Palmerston, most unfortunately, after pledging himself to maintain the proposed clause, ultimately yielded to the Dissenting clamour. It would have been a crucial test, but our opponents were—*afraid*.

The following list of Parliamentary divisions during the last 13 years comprise almost all those relating to great Church questions, and a few others besides for general reference. Some of these latter extend further back. The totals, for and against, include tellers, pairs, and members shut out. The numbers in columns 7 and 8 will occasionally be found to differ from the announced figures, because members shut out are included:

ABOLITION OF OATHS IN COURTS OF JUSTICE BILL.

Date	Stage	Ayes	Noes	Total for	Total against	Majority		Total voting
						For	Agst	
COMMONS.								
1861, June 12	2nd Reading	66	136	80	151	—	71	231
1862, June 24	Leave	88	59	90	61	29	—	151
1863, March 11	2nd Reading	96	142	113	159	—	46	272

ABOLITION OF THE REGIUM DONUM (IRISH PRESBYTERIAN).

Date	Stage	Ayes	Noes	Total for	Total against	Majority		Total voting
						For	Agst	
COMMONS.								
1853, May 20	Vote	46	181	48	183	—	135	231
1854, July 6	Vote	62	149	70	157	—	87	227
1855, July 30	Vote	32	96	45	109	—	64	154
1856, April 18	Vote	60	230	62	234	—	172	396
1857, July 13	Vote	41	117	49	127	—	78	176
1858, July 12	Vote	55	165	60	170	—	110	230
1859, July 29	Vote	40	126	45	131	—	86	176
1861, July 23	Vote	18	78	20	80	—	68	100
1862, July 21	Vote	16	58	19	61	—	42	80
1863, March 26	Vote	26	53	28	55	—	27	83
1864, June 26	Vote	21	127	24	130	—	106	154

OXFORD UNIVERSITY TESTS ABOLITION BILL

Date	Stage	Ayes	Noes	Total for	Total against	Majority		Total voting
						For	Agst.	
COMMONS.								
1864, March 16	2nd Reading	211	189	228	206	22	—	434
,, June 1	Committee	236	226	281	271	10	—	552
,, July 1	3rd Reading	150	140	237	227	10	—	464
,, ,,	3rd Reading	170	170	258	257	1	—	515
,, ,,	Pass	171	173	258	260	—	2	518
1865, June 14	2nd Reading	206	190	246	230	16	—	476
1866, March 21	2nd Reading	217	103	223	109	114	—	332

LEGALISATION OF MARRIAGE WITH A DECEASED WIFE'S SISTER.

Date	Stage	Ayes	Noes	Total for	Total against	Majority For	Majority Agst	Total voting
LORDS.								
1856, April 25	2nd Reading	24	43	24	43	—	19	67
1858, July 23	2nd Reading	22	46	22	46	—	24	68
1859, March 22	2nd Reading	39	49	54	64	—	10	118
COMMONS.								
1855, March 13	Leave	87	53	138	104	34	—	242
„ May 9	2nd Reading	165	157	171	162	9	—	333
1858, March 23	Leave	105	62	154	110	44	—	264
„ May 5	2nd Reading	174	134	206	166	40	—	372
„ July 2	3rd Reading	100	70	102	72	30	—	174
1859, Feb. 8	Leave	155	85	158	87	71	—	245
„ „ 16	2nd Reading	135	77	154	96	58	—	250
„ March 3	3rd Reading	137	89	179	131	48	—	310
1861, April 17	2nd Reading	172	177	197	202	—	5	399
1862, Feb. 19	2nd Reading	144	133	146	135	11	—	281
„ March 12	Committee	116	148	146	181	—	35	327

RELIGIOUS WORSHIP BILL (Hon. P. J. Locke King).

Date	Stage	Ayes	Noes	Total for	Total against	Majority For	Majority Agst.	Total voting
COMMONS.								
1860, March 14	2nd Reading	131	168	135	172	—	37	307
1861, May 1	2nd Reading	145	191	147	193	—	46	340

TEN-POUND COUNTY FRANCHISE BILL (Hon. P. J. Locke King).

Date	Stage	Ayes	Noes	Total for	Total against	Majority For	Majority Agst.	Total voting
COMMONS.								
1858, June 10	2nd Reading	226	168	309	251	58	—	560
1861, March 13	2nd Reading	220	248	253	281	—	28	534
1864, April 13	2nd Reading	227	254	262	289	—	27	551

SIX-POUND BOROUGH FRANCHISE BILL (Mr. Baines).

Date	Stage	Ayes	Noes	Total for	Total against	Majority		Total voting
						For	Agst.	
COMMONS.								
1861, April 11	2nd Reading	193	245	238	289	—	51	527
1864, May 11	2nd Reading	216	272	243	298	—	55	541
1865, May 8	2nd Reading	214	288	247	321	—	74	568

ABOLITION OF CHURCH RATES.

Date	Stage	Ayes	Noes	Total for	Total against	Majority		Total voting
						For	Agst.	
LORDS.								
1858, July 2	2nd Reading	36	187	61	212	—	151	273
1860, June 19	2nd Reading	31	128	67	164	—	97	231
COMMONS.								
1853, May 26	Motion	172	220	182	230	—	48	412
1854, May 23	Leave	129	62	162	96	68	—	258
„ June 21	2nd Reading	182	209	211	238	—	27	449
1855, March 29	Leave	155	76	188	109	79	—	297
„ May 16	2nd Reading	217	189	252	222	30	—	474
1856, March 5	2nd Reading	221	178	251	206	45	—	457
1858, Feb. 17	2nd Reading	213	160	241	188	53	—	429
„ May 13	Clause 1	227	153	286	210	76	—	496
„ June 8	3rd Reading	266	203	295	233	62	—	528
1859, March 15	2nd Reading	242	168	284	209	75	—	493
„ July 13	2nd Reading	263	193	309	239	70	—	548
1860, Feb. 8	2nd Reading	263	234	295	266	29	—	561
„ April 27	3rd Reading	235	226	280	269	11	—	549
1861, Feb. 27	2nd Reading	281	266	305	290	15	—	595
„ June 19	3rd Reading	274	274	297	298	—	1	595
1862, May 14	2nd Reading	286	287	304	305	—	1	609
„ „	Resl. ag. Ab.	272	287	274	289	—	15	563
1863, April 29	2nd Reading	275	285	294	304	—	10	598
1866, March 7	2nd Reading	285	252	314	279	35	—	593

NONCONFORMIST BURIALS BILL (Sir S. M. Peto).

Date	Stage	Ayes	Noes	Total for	Total against	Majority		Total voting
						For	Agst.	
COMMONS								
1861, April 24	2nd Reading	155	236	171	252	—	81	423
1863, April 15	2nd Reading	96	221	120	245	—	125	365

ABOLITION OF THE MAYNOOTH GRANT.

Date	Stage	Ayes	Noes	Total for	Total against	Majority For	Majority Agst.	Total voting
LORDS.								
1853, April 18	Enqy. Com.	53	110	64	121	—	57	185
COMMONS.								
1853, May 19	Omit the vote	74	54	160	140	20	—	300
1854, July 3	Res. for vote	90	106	97	113	—	16	210
1855, July 20	Select Com.	97	76	99	78	21	—	177
1856, April 15	Leave	159	133	211	185	26	—	396
„ June 25	2nd Reading	174	164	222	216	6	—	438
1857, Feb. 19	Motion	159	167	186	194	—	8	380
„ May 21	Motion	91	125	212	246	—	34	458
1858, April 29	Motion	155	210	163	218	—	55	381
1860, Feb. 14	Motion	128	186	172	230	—	58	402
1861, June 4	Motion	114	191	137	214	—	77	351
1862, May 6	Motion	111	193	132	214	—	82	346
1863 June 2	Motion	100	198	122	219	—	97	349

THE BALLOT.

Date	Stage	Ayes	Noes	Total for	Total against	Majority For	Majority Agst.	Total voting
LORDS.								
1860, March 19	Resolution	4	39	4	39	—	35	43
COMMONS.								
1853, June 14	Leave	172	232	177	236	—	59	413
1854, June 13	Leave	157	194	173	213	—	40	386
1855, May 22	Leave	166	218	201	253	—	52	454
1856, May 20	Leave	111	151	157	195	—	38	352
1857, June 30	Leave	189	257	218	288	—	70	506
1858, June 8	Leave	197	294	223	319	—	96	542
1859, April 2	Leave	99	102	138	141	—	3	279
1860, March 20	Leave	147	254	190	297	—	107	487
1861, April 23	Leave	154	279	185	310	—	125	495
1862, May 27	Leave	85	52	195	162	33	—	357
„ July 2	2nd Reading	126	211	178	263	—	85	441
1864, June 21	Resolution	123	212	163	252	—	89	415
1865, June 16	Resolution	74	118	116	158	—	42	271

QUALIFICATION FOR OFFICES BILL.

Date	Stage	Ayes	Noes	Total for	Total against	Majority		Total voting
						For	Agst.	
Lords.		·						
1860, March 22	2nd Reading	21	44	21	44	—	23	65
1861, March 19	2nd Reading	38	49	38	49	—	11	87
1862, May 13	2nd Reading	55	88	55	88	—	33	143
1863, April 24	2nd Reading	52	69	63	80	—	17	143
1865, May 1	2nd Reading	49	72	61	84	—	23	145
Commons.								
1861, Feb. 20	2nd Reading	93	80	96	88	13	—	179
1862, Feb. 19	2nd Reading	63	64	65	58	7	—	123
„ „ 26	3rd Reading	140	127	153	140	13	—	293
1863, Feb. 18	2nd Reading	74	63	76	65	11	—	141
„ March 4	3rd Reading	175	172	223	220	3	—	443
1865, March 23	3rd Reading	130	56	135	61	74	—	196
1866, Feb. 19	2nd Reading	176	55	183	62	121	—	245

CLERGY RELIEF BILL

(Mr. E. P. Bouverie).

Date	Stage	Ayes	Noes	Total for	Total against	Majority		Total voting
						For	Agst.	
Commons. 1862, July 9	2nd Reading	88	98	101	111	—	10	212

TRUSTEES OF CHARITIES BILL

(Mr. L. L. Dillwyn).

Date	Stage	Ayes	Noes	Total for	Total against	Majority		Total voting
						For	Agst.	
Commons.								
1861, Feb. 20	2nd Reading	164	157	198	191	7	—	389
„ April 17	Committee	171	200	204	233	—	29	437

ENDOWED SCHOOLS BILL

(Mr. L. L. Dillwyn).

Date	Stage	Ayes	Noes	Total for	Total against	Majority		Total voting
						For	Agst.	
COMMONS.								
1859, July 6	2nd Reading	210	192	240	222	18	—	462
1860, March 21	2nd Reading	120	190	134	207	—	73	341

DIVISIONS ON MOTIONS OR BILLS AFFECTING THE OBSERVANCE OF SUNDAY.

Date	Subject	For Observance	Against Observ.	For	Against	Majority		Total voting
						For	Agst.	
COMMONS.								
1850, May 30	Motion, P. O.	93	68	108	80	38	—	188
„ July 9	Motion, P. O.	112	195	116	199	—	83	315
1855, March 20	Museums	235	48	245	57	188	—	302
1856, Feb. 21	Museums	376	48	382	50	332	—	432
1863, June 8	Gardens	123	107	135	119	16	—	254
„ March 17	Public Houses	141	52	143	54	89	—	197
„ June 3	Public Houses	103	278	105	282	—	177	387
1864, May 6	Public Houses	87	123	129	165	—	36	294
„ June 20	Railways	40	21	42	23	19	—	65
1865, March 22	Railways	42	39	44	41	3	—	85
1866, March 14	Railways	200	83	202	85	117	—	287

ACT OF UNIFORMITY AMENDMENT BILL

(Mr. E. P. Bouverie).

Date	Stage	Ayes	Noes	For	Against	Majority		Total voting
						For	Agst.	
COMMONS.								
1863, May 5	Leave	157	135	173	151	22	.	324
1864, July 13	2nd Reading	101	157	106	161	—	55	267

Marked * led to changes of Ministry or Dissolutions of Parliament.

Date	Subject	L.	C.	Total L.	Total C.	Majority		Total voting
						L.	C.	
LORDS.								
*1841, Aug. 24	No confidence	96	168	101	173	—	72	274
1846, May 28	Corn Bill, 2°	211	164	212	165	47	—	377
„ June 15	Corn Bill	136	102	175	142	33	—	317
„ „ 16	Corn Bill	140	107	140	107	33	—	247
1849, May 8	Navigation B.	173	163	183	173	10	—	356
„ „ 21	„	116	103	162	149	13	—	311
1850, June 17	Greece	132	169	152	189	—	37	341
1858, May 14	Vote of Cens.	158	167	158	167	—	9	325
1860, May 21	Paper Duty	104	193	139	227	—	88	366
1864, July 8	Denmark	168	177	190	199	—	9	389
COMMONS.								
1841, May 18	Sugar	281	317	301	337	—	36	638
* „ June 4	No confidence	311	312	324	325	—	1	649
* „ Aug. 27	„	269	360	273	364	—	91	637
1846, Feb. 27	Corn Bill	337	240	339	242	97	—	581
„ March 27	Corn Bill 2°	302	214	334	245	89	—	579
„ May 15	Corn Bill 3°	327	229	329	231	99	—	560
* „ June 25	IrishCoercion	219	292	222	294	—	72	516
1848, June 29	Sugar	260	245	283	268	15	—	551
1849, March 12	Navigation	266	210	269	213	56	—	482
„ April 23	Navigation 3°	275	214	296	235	61	—	531
1850, June 28	Confidence	310	264	316	267	49	—	583
1851, Feb. 13	Agric. Distress	281	267	296	282	14	—	578
*1852, Feb. 20	Militia	125	136	155	166	—	11	321
* „ Dec. 16	Budget	305	286	321	302	19	—	623
*1855, Jan. 29	Crimea	148	305	182	339	—	157	521
1856, May 1	Kars Censure	303	176	334	205	129	—	539
*1857, March 3	China	247	263	273	289	—	16	562
*1858, Feb. 19	T. M. Gibson	215	234	219	238	—	19	457
*1859, March 31	Reform	330	291	340	301	39	—	641
* „ June 10	No confidence	323	310	328	315	13	—	643
1860, June 7	Postp.Reform	269	248	308	287	21	—	595
„ Aug. 6	Rags	266	233	315	282	33	—	597
1861, May 2	Tea	299	282	322	305	17	—	627
„ „ 29	Paper	296	281	312	297	15	—	609
1864, June 17	Ashantee	233	226	287	280	7	—	567
„ July 8	Denmark	313	295	324	306	18	—	630

Book V.

A Plea for Church Extension.

THE great problem of the day is, how to meet the spiritual destitution which unfortunately prevails to so alarming an extent in all our large towns, from London downwards. In stating this, I may have to deal with those who do not believe in the existence of the deficiency we allege, so I shall commence at once with some figures and facts.

The first subject for inquiry is, in the usual order of things, what percentage of the population can go to Church *if they choose?*

Deducting young children, the sick and infirm, and those engaged in works of necessity, and those compelled to labour on Sunday for the *amusements* and *pleasures of others*, in connection with railways and other public conveyances, it has been determined by Mr. Mann, a high authority, that accommodation ought to be provided for 58 per cent. of the general population of England and Wales. Rural requirements are necessarily less than urban, in consequence of the distance of the Churches unavoidably operating to diminish the attendance. However, we shall probably be near the truth in assuming 50 per cent. as the required accommodation. Let us now see what practically exists.

I will divide England into town districts and country districts, including in the former all the places containing above 10,000 inhabitants in 1851. From the former I deduct one-third for the accommodation provided by the Meeting-houses of the Sects, and one-fifth from the latter for the same reason. It will thus appear that for town districts the Church requires Church room for 33·3 per cent., and for country districts Church room for 40 per cent. of the gross population, in order that all should possess facilities for attending her Public Worship. Now, in 1851 the position of affairs was as follows :—

	Population	Sittings	Per cent. of Pop. provided for	Deficiency Per cent.	Deficiency Absolutely.
Town districts . .	9,229,120	1,995,729	21·6	11·7	1,099,807
Country districts .	8,698,489	3,322,186	38·2	1·8	156,572

In words, then, in England, in 1851, nearly 1¼ millions of our population were utterly destitute of Church accommodation, after making every allowance for the supplies furnished by the Sects, not large in quantity (Wesleyans, 12·2 per cent. of population ; Independents, 6 per cent. ; all others much less), and very inferior in quality. It is high time for English Churchmen to look these appalling facts boldly in the face. But it may be said, " Your statistics are old ; perhaps they will not hold good now." This is true, but, unfortunately, only in a very small degree. The following table, however, does convey some cheering information :—

Increase of Population and Increase of Church Accommodation, 1801-51.

Date.	Town Districts.		Country Districts.	
	Increase of Pop. per cent.	Increase of Sittings per cent.	Increase of Pop. per cent.	Increase of Sittings per cent.
1801-11	18·1	1·2	11·7	0·4
1811-21	23·0	2·7	14·5	0·6
1821-31	22·8	8·5	10·4	1·4
1831-41	20·2	14·2	9·6	4·7
1841-51	19·3	24·2	6·3	10·7

We learn from this that down to 1841 the population was increasing much more rapidly than the Church accommodation. After 1841 the tide turned, and the sittings augmented more than the population, which so far satisfactory state of things is certainly still kept up; but it is the large arrears to be cleared off which cause the difficulty.

Between 1851 and 1861 the actual increase in the population amounted to 2,134,116. Allotting four-fifteenths to schism (*probably* it ought to be much *less*), this new population would require 784,000 sittings. As the augmentation of sittings in the 1831-41 period was only 294,000 ; as in the 1841-51 period, the augmentation was no less than 542,000 ; and seeing that in the last 10 years Church extension has been going on at a wonderful rate, it is not too much to hope that not only have the 784,000 sittings been provided, but that something considerable has been done towards wiping out the 1¼ millions deficiency with which we started in 1851. However, it will be no misrepresentation of facts, allowing a little for Mission Chapels and licensed rooms, to say that at this moment there are *one million* of our fellow-countrymen unprovided with Church accommodation, however anxious they may be to have it.

Surely, here, then, we have an incontrovertible fact, which requires our most earnest attention; and my object in penning these few lines is to urge on Churchmen the paramount duty of joining in the work of Church extension, with their money and with their personal efforts. As a general rule, a Society is the best agent for distributing funds for Church-building purposes. The management expenses are necessarily much less in amount than those of the generality of charitable institutions, and really pressing claims have a better chance of being provided for than if the distribution is left to individual effort. Of course, when Church extension operations are going on in one's own district or parish, the case is different.

Now a few words of suggestion to each reader, in harmony with the plan of letting charity *begin* at home. If you are in London, make it your business (as unquestionably it is your duty) to give an annual subscription to the London Diocesan Church Building Society (Office, 21 Regent Street). Never mind your not being able to give much ; if such is the case, think of the object and the principle : annual sums as low as five shillings will, no doubt, be thankfully received. The spiritual destitution of our great metropolis is so fearful to contemplate, that this Society has claims on the sympathy of all Englishmen, whether living in London or not. If you live in the country, probably a Church Extension Society of some kind exists in your own diocese or county ; if so, become a subscriber to it without delay. If one does not exist, or some *strong* reason indisposes you to join it, there is yet the Incorporated Church Building Society, of London, but national in its sphere of usefulness (Office, 7 Whitehall). This Institution is not nearly so well supported as it used, and deserves to be. The suppression by a non-Church-loving Government of the annual Queen's Letter, formerly read in all our Churches once a year, has materially injured the financial affairs of the Society, and contributed to lessen the circle of its acquaintances. " Out of sight, out of mind."

We require to raise funds for two objects in intimate connexion with each other—Church *Building* and Church *Endowment*. The latter is invariably most neglected, but, in a general way, and in a certain sense, of more importance than the former. If a newly-formed district were adequately endowed at the outset, the edifice would follow sooner or later to a certainty ; but the converse is not by any means always the case. People are very willing to give money when they see a tangible result (bricks and mortar) ; but money applied to the sustentation of the Clergyman does not outwardly show, proportionately to its amount.

The Rev. G. Venables has recently put forth some very sensible and practical remarks, the substance of which I now proceed to give, for they deserve careful attention.

We should resort to every legitimate way of raising funds, and not confine ourselves to the stock plan of collecting, in donations of cash down. The following may be mentioned as eligible means :—

(1.) A revival of the ancient and noble spirit of Christian liberality by which all the machinery for working a new parish is provided, in the erection of a Church, Schools, and Parsonage, with an endowment, by the private munificence of an individual, of a firm, or of a public company. Instances of this kind are happily becoming commoner every day. Landowners and millowners are gradually learning that the possession of property confers a mighty responsibility in reference to the spiritual and temporal wants of those under them. The Northern millowners particularly require to be stirred up, and glad we should be to see that it is being done.

(2.) The voluntary restoration of impropriated tithes, by those laymen who at present enjoy what belongs to God and the Church ; to whom shall be given the patronage of the new parishes endowed therewith.

(3.) A moderate rent-charge laid by owners on their estates, lands, mines, &c. Of all plans of endowment none appears to be so easy and so simple as for a freeholder to lay an annual charge on his property for the glory of God for ever. It demands but little self-denial, and the results are permanent. Six or eight proprietors in a parish, by charging their property to the amount of 40*l.* or 50*l.*, might thus secure, without great cost to themselves, a fair income for their minister, with the further satisfaction of knowing that the benefits would be secured to their parish in perpetuity.

(4.) Weekly or monthly collections *in every Church*, the proceeds to be applied in providing local endowments, or for augmenting small benefices. Supposing every Church in England and Wales were to produce weekly the paltry sum of 12*s.*, the gross sum (468,000*l.*) would suffice to endow 100 new parishes or Churches in a year ; but how very much more than 12*s.* a week would 4 Churches out of 5 produce on an average, even allowing for occasional collections for other purposes.

Such is a concise outline of the various ways, some or other of which could be resorted to by every one, to meet the pressing demand which exists for wholesale Church extension. No Churchman, be his income 50*l.* or 50,000*l.*, can, with any show of reason, refuse to join in the great work, on the ground that he cannot afford it, or does not know how to set about it; there is work for all.

Signs are not wanting that the true bearings of the Tithe Question are gradually becoming understood in quarters greatly in need of enlightenment. With all respect it may be said, that the bulk of our landowners have hitherto regarded impropriated tithes as purely secular property, standing on the same footing as houses, lands, &c. That such an estimate is entirely erroneous is clear to every thoughtful Churchman; but the thing to be done, now, is to work a change in the minds of the thoughtless titheowners themselves, to make them understand that they have no other right to possess tithe property than that conferred by force. The subject is, in a certain sense, a delicate one, and we are not desiring to press too heavily on existing titheowners, seeing that the Church property they possess came to them by inheritance, through no fault of their own. It is, however, impossible to characterise their original secularisation by Henry VIII. by any other name than that of ruthless plunder to satisfy the rapacious demands of courtiers. Their descendants are free from blame in the receiving, but certainly not in the retaining, and this is the point which should be put prominently forward.

Spiritual destitution is a subject uppermost in the minds of Churchmen just now, and the rapid multiplication of District Churches, and consequently of poor ill-paid Benefices, is working evils which already begin to make themselves felt. At the present moment, the tithes of 4000 parishes in England and Wales are alienated from the Church, and their annual value (1,500,000*l.*) is such that, if restored as they should be, we should hear no more of poor Livings (or starvings) for a long time to come, and the Church corporate, relieved from the painful anxiety of providing sustenance for her Ministers, would be able to apply herself with redoubled energy to her great work of saving souls. According to the Report of the Ecclesiastical Commissioners for 1835, there were 297 Benefices in England and Wales under 50*l.* per annum; 1629 Benefices over 50*l.*, and under 100*l.*; 1602 Benefices over 100*l.*, and under 150*l.*; and 1354 Benefices over 150*l.*, and under 200*l.* per annum: some have since had their tithes, in part, restored, and thus have secured pecuniary augmentation; but the spiritual destitution arising from the alienation of tithes is extreme; and the above figures probably understate the case now subsisting, in consequence of the increase of "districts."

Earnest-minded Churchmen in want of work can render no greater service than by agitating for the restoration of impropriated tithes by seeking to influence friends and relations who are titheowners. The work once done is done for ever. So there is this incentive for action, that everything will be going forward, no repetition of exertions (for the same case) being requisite, as happens in connection with many other good efforts.

The commutation of tithes effected in 1837 has, undoubtedly, worked well on the whole; but we may congratulate ourselves on the fact, that the desired abolition of the word tithe has failed. Legislators, influenced little by friendly feeling towards the Church, sought to introduce the word rent-charge, but without success. "We are all aware that by the legislation of modern times, tithes *eo nomine* are said to be extinguished by commutation, in spite of Ethelwolf's decree that they should be '*incommutabiles*,' having been at length discovered to be a vexatious impediment to the improvement of land, and an inconvenient lien held by the Church upon the produce of the soil; and it was at that time hoped ere long that the very name of tithe should be blotted out of our vocabulary and abolished throughout the country.   But such is the conservative force of practical religious tradition, that though the *thing* is said to be commuted, the *name* remains fixed in the mind and language of the people of England.   No farmer is at the pains of calling the customary payment he makes to the Clergyman of his parish *rent-charge* —he calls it, as his father did before him, *tithe*.   Nay, you may see the *thing* itself still.   Go into the fields in harvest time, and watch the reapers : you will find *ten sheaves still placed together in one shock*, for the convenience of satisfying the ancient claim of one sheaf in ten for tithe—a silent witness, unconsciously borne year after year, by the English peasant, to the ancient portion due to God.'

There is an association at work for promoting the restoration of tithes, which is far less well supported than it should be.   It is called the Tithe Redemption Trust (Secretary, Rev. W. W. Malet, 7 Whitehall), and it aims at furnishing grants of money for purchasing tithes and defraying the necessary expenses.

The parochial system, handed down to us from Saxon times, is by far the best and most effectual means of meeting spiritual destitution.   Money spent in developing it, and at the same time in increasing the Episcopate, will be well spent.   "We want and we must have an increase in the number of our parishes, and we must also have a large increase in our Episcopate.   The Bishops are not sufficiently numerous to do all that is wanted of them, and hence they are too often unpopular," and get charged with neglect of diocesan duties, a complaint which is often perfectly well-founded, but in no sense due to voluntary neglect.

Let those laymen, who are constantly finding fault with Bishops and Clergy for not doing all that they might do, see whether no responsibility rests on *their* own shoulders.   More Bishops and more Clergy, and more endowments to support them (which the laity are the proper persons, in the main, to furnish), will be the only effectual remedy for Pastoral neglect, the existence of which, in many large towns, it would be affectation to deny.

When Henry VIII. came to the throne there were 22 Sees for a population of about 4½ millions, giving one Bishop, on an average, charge of 200,000 souls.   During that monarch's reign, 6 new Sees were actually created, and 4 more proposed.   One of these was soon afterwards suppressed, and the number remained at 27 till recently.   Coincidently with the ill-advised union of Gloucester and Bristol (by the Whigs) in 1836, Ripon was founded, and in 1847, Manchester.   This is all that has been done ; so we have now a population of 21¼ millions spiritually superintended by 28 Bishops, or one to every 760,000 souls, and 700 Clergy.   Can the Bishops be expected to do their work properly ?

If their numbers were *doubled*, they would *then* be *far* from numerous, compared with those of other Churches, ancient and modern.

Each of the 7 Churches (*Rev.* i.–iii.) had its own Bishop, whose charge was comparatively limited.

Ireland has 12 Bishops, or 1 to every 480,000 souls.

Scotland has 7 Bishops, or 1 to every 430,000 souls.

The British Colonies (exclusive of India, whose Episcopate is absurdly inadequate) have 48 Bishops, or 1 to about every 190,000 souls.

The Episcopates of the Romish and Greek Churches are far more numerous than ours; a recent authority assigns to the former 1013 Sees.

The evils arising from the present state of things are manifold; the Clergy are not sufficiently looked after, and thus abuses are apt to creep in, which better supervision would necessarily prevent. The Clergy and Laity alike are unable to avail themselves of the good counsel which Bishops, in general, are well qualified to give. The Bishop of Lincoln once stated that for him to visit each parish in his diocese and spend a Sunday in it, would take 15 years!!

The general discipline of the Church suffers much from the present anomalous state of things; the solemn Rite of Confirmation, instead of being administered annually, is often administered but once in 3 years; consequently many young persons grow up without ever being confirmed at all.

In the Confirmations that are held, everything is of necessity done more or less in a *scramble*; the candidates dealt with by *rails-full* instead of individually, as the Church intends; numerous widely-distant parishes taken together, instead of a *few* contiguous ones, thus putting all parties to needless inconvenience and expense, and some to the risk of positive temptation.

Other drawbacks resulting directly from an inadequate Episcopate must be obvious.

Let all Churchmen then who value Apostolic order and the advantages of Episcopal supervision, combine to demand " More Bishops " as, being with new Church-discipline and building Acts, the most important kind of " Church-Reform " wanted.

If the Ministers of the Crown would only make a beginning (and it is for Churchmen out-of-doors to *compel* them), few practical difficulties would be found to exist. Large available funds are in the hands of the Ecclesiastical Commissioners, which Parliament and private beneficence would readily supplement. There are many fine Churches, easily convertible into Cathedrals, now in existence, and the " Political " difficulty might be got over, *if necessary*, by adopting the plan already in force, whereby the Junior Bishop for the time being has no seat in the House of Lords. [Suffragan Bishops with only 2,000l. a-year and *no* Parliamentary duties (as some have proposed) would create an invidious distinction, and be altogether a very poor expedient.]

The following new dioceses have been proposed as an *instalment*: —

Bristol,	taken out of	Gloucester.	Newcastle,	taken out of	Durham.
Coventry,	„	Worcester.	Southwell,	„	Lincoln.
Cornwall,	„	Exeter.	St. Albans,	„	Rochester.
Jersey,	„	Winchester.	Westminster,	„	London.

The subdivision of the diocese of London is most urgently needed.

Book VI.

Church Rates.

THERE is reason to believe that a good deal of the opposition raised to Church Rates proceeds from ignorance as to their true nature and origin: it is proposed to state in popular language a few historical notes and facts.

The first remark made by an opponent of Church Rates invariably is, *that it is unjust to tax one man against his will to support another man's religion.* If it were a fact that, in the levying of a Church Rate, a man is taxed against his will to pay for another man's religion, Dissenters might oppose Church Rates with some show of reason and equity; but this statement *per se* is a gross (and it is to be feared, too often, a wilful) misrepresentation. A rate to be valid must be voted by a majority of persons registered as ratepayers; but in general, most of those persons who take part in the proceedings in vestry have nothing to do with paying the rate, *so far as their own pockets are concerned.* Church Rate is not a *personal* tax. If a man is a freeholder, he pays it in respect of his *property*; if he is only an occupier, he merely acts as a *middle-man* between his landlord and the rate-collector. *Church Rate is nothing more and nothing less than a charge on land, assessed and collected for convenience sake from the occupier.** No casuistry, however subtle, can explain away this statement. The *occupiers,* who are not freeholders, and who in general comprise nineteen-twentieths of householders of a parish, have nothing whatever to do with the Church Rate, except to act as agents for their landlord. They have therefore no fair pretext for exclaiming against paying these rates on conscientious grounds.

The remarks which follow are condensed from a well-known pamphlet by a well-known Dissenter,† whose clear and candid statement of the legal bearings of the question *has already brought round* many *Nonconformists* actively to *support* Church Rates :—

It is alleged by some that, in opposing Church Rates, they are resisting tyranny and imposture, and State support to an already State-supported

---

* "No man held any species of property, the enjoyment of which was more sacredly guarded by law than the obligation to pay Church Rates. *By the law of England, Church Rates were a charge upon the land.*"—(Lord St. Leonards [ex-Lord Chancellor]. Speech on the Church Rates Abolition Bill, July 2, 1858. Hansard, vol. cli. p. 807.)

† Toulmin Smith, *True Points at Issue on the Church Rate Question.* London, 1856.

Church. The facts are, however, entirely the reverse. A more careful consideration will show that what the opponents of Church Rates are really setting themselves up against are—responsible control, free discussion, the rights of the laity, the requirements of consistency and honesty, and the principles and practice of English self-government. Churchwardens are secular officers chosen annually by every parish to act in its name and in its behalf, both internally and in the external relation of the parish to the State. They have many specific and important duties to perform, the greater part of which have nothing at all to do with the Church. What Church duties they have are simply on behalf of the laity. They are the chief officers of the secular institution of the parish; which institution is itself the recognised and actual basis of all civil government in England. They are accountable to the parishioners in vestry for all their acts and expenditure. To enable them to fulfil their duties, funds are necessary, for no man can reasonably be asked to fulfil public duties and pay the expenses out of his private purse. For many centuries the necessary funds have been provided annually by a Church (or as it would much more accurately be called, a Churchwarden's) Expenses Rate. It being a common law obligation that every parish is to repair its Church, part—in most cases, perhaps the larger part—goes to meet the cost of these repairs (whence the exclusive use of the word Church to describe the rate). None ever goes or ever can go to pay the stipends of the Clergy, but the remainder is appropriated to other and purely secular expenses, the parish clerk, &c. *The maintenance of the churchyard, the public burial ground of the parish, the Church clock—which everybody, be he Churchman or be he Dissenter, profits by—are also amongst the reasonable charges defrayed by the so-called Church Rate.*

The rate made to meet all these expenses incidental to the Churchwarden's office can be made *solely* by the parishioners, whom the law regards as the most fitting judges of what is and what is not wanted : its amount depends *solely* on their will. It has no speciality whatever (as many imagine) as a *Church Rate.* Lord Chief Justice Coke expressly says in a celebrated case, that the inhabitants may "make ordinances or bye-laws for the reparation of the Church, *or* of a highway, *or* of *any such thing* as is for the *general good of the public.*" And all the Judges of the Common Pleas, in another case, declare that the Parish *Church* "is *like* to a *bridge* or a *highway* ; a distringas shall issue against the inhabitants to make them repair it ; but neither the King's Court nor the Justices of the Peace can impose a tax for it." The Churchwardens cannot. None but Parliament can *impose* a tax. But the greater part of a parish can make a bye-law for a rate.* This has always been the law in England ; it is still the law.

There has never been an Act of Parliament for the compulsory levying of Church Rates, except (such is human consistency !) in the time of the Commonwealth, when the Church was down and the Nonconformists in power, who *enforced* Church Rates in parishes whether the inhabitants liked it or no.

Such allegations as tyranny, oppression, and imposition, are not only without meaning : they are *dishonest* [mark well all this ; also that a distinguished *Dissenting* barrister is the writer]. They only serve to mislead the well-meaning, but ill-informed. Those therefore who seek

* Rogers v. Davenant, *Modern Reports*, vol. i. p. 154.

to abolish Church Rates in general are seeking to deprive Englishmen, by *absolute coercion*, of the power and right *of spending their own money according to their own liking*. Those who seek to abolish the Church Rate in their own parish are endeavouring to evade the common law, and dishonestly to embezzle money which does not belong to them. They are doing far more: they are driving Episcopalians to narrow the limits of their communion. What a *part* of the rate helps to do, is simply to sustain the fabric and decent condition of a *place* in every parish in England, to which every man can resort by *right*: that is, the parishioners vote supplies to sustain the ancient and valuable common right of every man to have the *opportunity* of hearing his Bible read without being tacked and ticketed to some sect. *Can Nonconformists reasonably expect Episcopalians to let them retain all these rights and privileges, and many others, such as meeting in public vestry, if they refuse to join in paying the necessary expenses?* So far is the "State" from at present supporting the Church, that every Parish Church in England was founded, *not* by the State, but by *individual donation* in ages past; while the Parson's income is entirely derived, partly from similar sources, and partly from a charge (far heavier than any Church Rate) which has been attached, like any rent-charge, to the ownership of certain classes of property for centuries. The State supports, in the sense of paying, *neither the one nor the other.* To say that it *does*, as many Dissenters do, is either sheer ignorance or wilful misrepresentation. The State is simply a trustee.

It is clear that if the fabric and decent condition of the Church are not maintained by the Church Rate they must be maintained by other means —such as the county rate or the consolidated fund. Every man will thus have an enforced tax to pay, without the chance of a voice in the matter, but there will be an end of responsibility and discussion, and parish control. To expect the State will ever allow the Church to go a-begging on the voluntary system, or to expect that Dissenters are ever going to become powerful enough to coerce Churchmen to put up with *that*, is out of the question. As no one Dissenting body can claim to be numerous enough to be entitled to exclusive use of the Parish Churches, it becomes a simple question between tolerance and intolerance, charity and bigotry; whether because their own doctrines are not preached in them, they would have all Churches closed by withholding funds for keeping them open in the customary manner. Whether, as they cannot have exclusive possession, the *general good* of the public is not in the meantime best served by the Parish Churches being maintained (under the eye and control of *all* parishioners, of *all sects*) in such state that there may be no parish in England without *some place* in it where men can go, as of right, to hear habitually that life and man were made for something more than what is merely work-a-day and worldly. Is it to be declared by a new coercive and restrictive law, that, because individual sects cannot each persuade every man to be of their religious opinions, therefore the common right which Englishmen have inherited through centuries, to have a place maintained in every parish where every man may go up and worship if he pleases—just as they have inherited the right to have the highway maintained, by which they may go to or from that place—shall be taken away? The parishes of England made desolate of any ministry, and void of the necessary presence of some man whose duties are the ever-present words and deeds of Christian charity?

Voters against Church Rates, however they may gloss over the fact, are doing all they can to force on the country a *direct* State support of the Church, at the same time destroying all responsible management and local control over local interests. No man, whatever his creed, can consistently or honestly, or in a spirit of Christian charity or tolerance, refuse his vote to the granting of reasonable and proper supplies to the Churchwardens.

The cause really at stake, then, is the cause of constitutional liberty; of responsible administration; of honest and common right; of religious consistency and charity; of free discussion; of avoidance of *sectarian* domination, and of local interest and share in local affairs. These are the true matters involved. They are indeed matters of true and vital " principle." *Every man* who loves free institutions, civil and religious liberty, responsible management, independent thought, discussion and action, simple manly honesty, and Christian charity, coupled with the assertion and maintenance of the rights of all the laity in the Christian Church (whatever its form of doctrine), *will support the voting of Church Rates,* and resist those who seek their abolition. Those who oppose the voting of Church Rates in any parish are doing all they can to violate the spirit of English institutions.

After this eloquent appeal to Dissenters, *by a Dissenter,* it is certainly needless for a Churchman to say anything more on the general principle of Church Rates. Elsewhere Mr. Smith says :—

"Everyone who knows anything of the history of Nonconformity in England must know that I should be one of the first, from family and traditionary associations, to oppose Church Rates, were such opposition really other than an *ad captandum* cry. But the long and careful study of our institutions, and of the groundwork and mainstay of our liberties, has taught me to see the matter in a very different light; and I rejoice to say that on this occasion [Church Rate contest at Hornsey] *my reasons and arguments have led a large number of previously staunch opponents of Church Rates, and very many Dissenters, to vote for the rate.*"

The following Answers on the subject of Church Rates are all taken from the Minutes of Evidence (Parts i. and ii.) laid before the celebrated Committee of the House of Lords on Church Rates, which sat in 1859-60. A few verbal alterations have been necessary to abbreviate and connect the sense of some of the paragraphs.

Thomas P. BUNTING, Esq. (Wesleyan Methodist).

"Q. 595.—Why are Methodists not hostile to Church Rates, like other Dissenters?—A. I think there is a general feeling that the Church of England is a power of essential importance to the religion of the country, and increasingly so; and we should be very sorry to destroy anything in which we thought there was a blessing."

"Q. 596.—Do you consider the abolition of Church Rates would injure the Church?—A. Decidedly so. . . . I think it would be a heavy blow and great discouragement to the Church; which would have considerable, and it might be permanent, influence. It would be to the disparagement of the Church in the eyes of the common people; and the common people ought not, I think, to be alienated from it."

"A. to Q. 597.—The Church of England is certainly the *only* Church or sect *which makes any permanent and general provision for the poor.*"

"A. to Q. 598.—I believe there would be a great increase of vice and irreligion if any serious damage were done to the Church, such as the abolition of the law of Church Rate would cause."

"A. to Q. 616-7.—*My opinion is, that the present state of things is almost the most perfect which could be devised,* except that greater power is wanted for the recovery of rates, and further provisions for district rates."

Mr. Charles ERWIN (Wesleyan Methodist).

" Q. 247.—Viewing the present state of the law, by which it is left to the majority to vote or refuse a Church Rate, do you consider that satisfactory, or do you wish to see it changed?—A. *I should not wish any change, certainly.*"

" A. to Q. 277.—My experience during these 40 years has been that there is a very close feeling of attachment on the part of the [old] Wesleyan community towards the Church."

Toulmin SMITH, Esq.   (?)

" Q. 458.—The power to make a Church Rate depends upon a power inherent in the parishioners to make it themselves for any purpose?—A. That is precisely the point. It is not that there is anything specially inherent in a Church Rate, as is commonly supposed; but the parishioners have the power to make a rate for any purpose which concerns the common interest of the parish. Attention is particularly called to that. . . The words of the preamble of Sir J. Trelawny's Bill are, 'Whereas it is expedient that the power to make Church Rates should be abolished.' It is put by the promoters of that Bill as if abolishing Church Rates was abolishing an impost, *but it is no such thing ; it is abolishing the power of the parish to do what it likes with its own for the good of the neighbourhood ; it is an attempt to substitute a coercive prohibition in place of the voluntary system which at present exists.*"

Mr. George OSBORN (Wesleyan Methodist Teacher).

" A. to Q. 1763.—It is a patent and notorious fact that no public and collective action against Church Rates has ever been taken by the Methodist body at large."

" A. to Q. 1766.—*As an individual, I should deplore the extinction of the National Church as one of the greatest calamities that could befall my native country.*"

" A. to Q. 1767.—I consider that the Established Church provides instruction and worship of which all may avail themselves if they will, and I look upon it as the greatest Home Missionary Institution of which I have any cognizance."

" Q. 1795.—Supposing it were thrown upon the Ministers of the Church not only to appeal to their congregations for their various charities, but also to undertake the task of obtaining voluntary subscriptions to maintain the fabric, *would not that interfere very much with the pastoral work,* and with their engagements in different directions?—A. *I think so,* and I should regret to see it thrown upon them. I cannot understand why, if a parish is willing to tax itself for the maintenance of the fabric, and the current expenses of the worship, the Legislature should interfere to prevent it from doing so. *The provision which allows it to tax itself appears to me to be a just and reasonable provision* ; and, where it freely imposes a tax, it does appear to me to be quite an inexplicable violation of the principle of religious liberty that it should be forbidden to tax itself, except the object is entirely to overthrow the Established Church. If that is the intention, I can understand the object [of the proposed prohibition]."

" A. to Q. 1801.—I am not aware that any Methodist takes an active or leading part in the affairs of the Liberation Society."

" Q. 1805.—Do you participate in the desire for the separation of Church and State? —A. I differ from it *toto cælo* :" in other words, MOST CERTAINLY NOT.

The Liberation Society is in the habit of putting forth flaring placards, with sensation titles, such as " Churchmen, follow your leaders." A few selections from the published statements of its own political chiefs, comprehending some of the most distinguished members of the " Liberal " party, are here given. Let Dissenters gainsay them if they can.

Earl RUSSELL.

" Certainly I for one cannot assent to the principle put forward by the Protestant Dissenters, that, as a matter of conscience, Church Rates ought to be abolished. That is a somewhat *new* scruple on their part. When it was proposed in former days that Dissenters should not be compelled to attend Church, and that they should not be prevented from having Chapels of their own, it was very properly argued, that it was a principle of religious liberty that they should be allowed to worship God according to their own forms; but it was *not* then contended that they should not be compelled to make any payment to the National Church. *That claim has arisen in more modern times.* . . . . Having sanctioned the abolition of Church Rates without providing a substitute, fresh attacks would be made on the Church; and not being willing to countenance or favour those attacks, I shall oppose the second reading of the Bill."—(Speech in the House of Commons, March 5, 1856. Hansard, vol. cxl. p. 1918.)

" I have only to say that I cannot really understand how we could have a National Church Establishment without some provision or other for repairing its places of worship. They have such a provision both in Scotland and Ireland, and it does seem to me unreasonable that we should have a provision to maintain the minister, but no provision to maintain the Churches. . . . . If we come to the question of an absolute abolition of the rate, I must vote against that, as a violation of the principle of a Church Establishment."—(Speech in the House of Commons, April 27, 1858. Hansard, vol. cxlix. p. 1863.)

The late LORD PALMERSTON, M.P.

"Viewing Churches, therefore, not as emblems of sectarian division, but as national fabrics applicable to the Christian worship of God, it really appears to me that there is no ground for this objection ['conscientious scruples'] against contributing to their maintenance."—(Speech in the House of Commons, May 16, 1855. Hansard, vol. cxxxviii. p. 688.)

The fact that both these noble lords, after giving this testimony, found it politically expedient to record a simple vote in favour of Church Rates abolition, does not lessen the *truth* of their observations.

EARL GREY.

" I cannot concur in the prayer [of some petitions for Church Rate abolition], because I do not consider, now that it has been decided that the minority of a vestry could not make a valid Church Rate, that there is any substantial grievance in the law [for Dissenters to complain of]. . . . . I should deeply regret to find the law so altered as to enable a few malcontent persons to withhold a Church Rate against the will of the majority, nor can there be any injustice in allowing the majority of the vestry to impose a Church Rate."—(Speech in the House of Lords, April 17, 1855. Hansard, vol. cxxxvii. p. 1499.)

The late LORD CHANCELLOR CAMPBELL.

" I confess that the proposal for the total abolition of Church Rates deeply shocks me, and I am surprised that it has met with support in some quarters from which I thought a strong opposition would have been manifested; for I look upon such a measure as neither more nor less than one of SPOLIATION."—(Speech in the House of Lords, April 27, 1855. Hansard, vol. cxxxvii. p. 1849.)

The late Right Hon. SIR ROBERT PEEL, BART., M.P.

" I hope the House will not hastily come to a resolution by which they would discharge members of the Church, being landed proprietors, from obligations to which they are now legally liable. What was the resolution [' that Church Rates ought to be abolished,' Mr. J. S. Trelawny, M.P., Tavistock] in effect, but a resolution that the *land* should be relieved from this burden? If the ground of religious scruples were to be admitted in the case of Church Rates, what security had they that they might not next week have a similar objection urged against the payment of tithes? If you exempted the Dissenter from payment of Church Rates on the ground of religious scruples, why not relieve him from all contributions towards the Church? . . . . Is it fitting, then, that we should exempt the *land* from this charge by a resolution hastily passed by landowners themselves? . . . . I do hope that the gentlemen of England will not consent to relieve themselves from a burden to which their *estates* are now subject, in order to devolve that burden on the Church."—(Speech, March 13, 1849. Hansard, vol. ciii. p. 667.)

VICE-CHANCELLOR SIR WILLIAM PAGE WOOD (Whig ex-M.P.).

"For my own part, as a member of the Church of England, I confess that if I had received property charged with a rate for the maintenance of Baptist, Wesleyan, or Roman Catholic edifices of worship, and if that charge had been made upon the property from the earliest times, I should not have conceived my conscience to have been in the slightest degree affected by the payment of that rate. . . . . I cannot concur in the opinion that we ought to abolish Church Rates altogether."—(Speech in the House of Commons, March 13, 1849. Hansard, vol. ciii. p. 648.)

The late MR. DRUMMOND, M.P. (Irvingite).

"The arguments of the supporters of this Bill [Church Rate Abolition] would tell as much against the monarchy as against Church Rates. By-and-by we should hear of honourable gentlemen getting up in that House to relieve a 'conscientious minority' from the burden of supporting the Throne and the other institutions of the country. All these 'conscientious objections' were always connected with the pocket, somehow or other. You never heard anything about them except when there was something tangible, *something more* than a mere principle or theory, but which the objectors tried to keep in the background. The Bill tends to destroy the Church of England, and on that ground I oppose it."—(Speech in the House of Commons, February 17, 1858. Hansard, vol. cxlviii. p. 1570.)

This declaration, by a Dissenter, is significant.

MR. EDMUND AKROYD (Whig M.P.).

"Certainly, I can never consent to transfer 300,000*l.* a-year from the Church to the *landowners*, who, for the most part, never asked for it, nor desired it. Just reverse the operation—talk of transferring 300,000*l.* a-year from the landowners *to* the Church, and see the outcry that would be made. And was the Church of England so passive that she would tamely submit to such *injustice?*"—(Speech in the House of Commons, June 8, 1858. Hansard, vol. cl. p. 1712.)

The declarations which have been put on record by eminent Dissenters, *condemnatory of those of their brethren who refuse to pay Church Rates*, are so numerous that it is a matter of difficulty to know what to reproduce and what to reject for such a purpose as that which I have now in view; and it is significant to the highest degree that it was not till within the time of the present generation that objections to Church Rates began to be raised at all: thus clearly connecting this anti-Church agitation with the political movements of 1830. The first Dissenting place of worship was raised in the year 1616, and from that epoch down to the year 1830 or thereabouts (a period of 214 years), it may be said that the general body of English Dissenters regularly paid their Church Rates. Only one authority, and that *a Dissenting one*, will be called to prove this. Messrs. Bogue and Bennet write as follows in the year 1833:—"Other Dissenters condemn tithes, but Quakers ALONE *refuse to pay* either them *or what are called Church Rates.*"—(*History of Dissenters*, vol. i. p. 198.)

Of the many Dissenting writers entitled to the patient attention of Nonconformists of the present day, none hold a higher place than Matthew Henry. What said this eminent divine, commenting on *St. Matt.* xvii. 24-7 ?—

He [Christ] did this to set an example (1) "Of rendering to all their due, tribute to whom tribute is due," *Rom.* xiii. 7. . . . (2) Of contributing to the support of the public worship of God in the places where we are. If we reap spiritual things, it is fit we should return carnal things. The temple was now made a den of thieves, and the temple-worship a pretence for the opposition which the chief priests gave to Christ and his doctrine, and yet Christ paid this tribute. Note, CHURCH DUTIES LEGALLY

IMPOSED ARE TO BE PAID, NOTWITHSTANDING CHURCH CORRUPTIONS.
We must 'take heed of using our liberty as a cloke to covetousness or maliciousness,
I. Peter ii. 16. If Christ pay tribute, who can pretend to an exemption?"—(*Exposition
on the Old and New Testaments,* vol. iv. 5th edition. London, 1763.)

Mr. Ebenezer Bailey, of Hull, one of the numerous Dissenting teachers
who have come over to the Church within the last few years (now, I
believe, at Cambridge, preparing to enter the ministry of the Church), in
a celebrated pamphlet, addressed the following powerful exhortation to
his former Congregational (Independent) friends:—

"But against compulsory payments for the support of religion, it is urged that it is
unjust to compel Dissenters to contribute towards the expense of a Church to which they
are conscientiously opposed. I reply, that no man's scruples of conscience can interfere
with the general duty of the Government. If so, of what use are our civil rulers? The
writer just now quoted says, 'If it be right to give up a national Church because some
conscientiously object to an Establishment, it is equally right to give up an army and navy
because some conscientiously object to war. It is no answer to this to say that they who
think an Established Church unlawful are *many*, while they who think war unlawful are
few. The question is, whether it be right in Government to support by national funds an
institution which is beneficial to the nation, although some of the people conscientiously
object to it? And if it be wrong in a Government so to do in one case, it is equally *wrong*,
though it might not excite so much clamour, to do it in another case. If it be wrong—if
it be coercion of conscience—if it be shameful tyranny in the Government to compel 1000
Dissenters to pay taxes, a portion of which shall be devoted to the extension of the national
Church—it is equally wrong—equally coercive of conscience—equally shameful tyranny,
and more disgraceful persecution, because committed against a weaker and more defence-
less body, to compel one single helpless Quaker to pay taxes, a portion of which shall be
devoted to the support or enlargement of the national army.'

"Moreover, I see not how it can be a violation of the rights of conscience, inasmuch as it
is a charge which compels not to conformity in either doctrine or worship, but only to a
pecuniary contribution for the promotion of the public good. I deny that any Dissenter
is compelled to support the religion of the Church of England; he gives to the demands
of the magistrate. It is true the civil ruler, when he receives the taxes, appropriates a
portion of them to the support of the Church, but this is *his* act, and in no way touches
the conscience of the man who pays the tax. The distinction will be seen at once by the
recollection that none could be more opposed to heathen worship than the apostle of the
Gentiles, and yet he exhorts the disciples to pay tribute to Cæsar, though Cæsar, when he
got it, appropriated a portion of it to the support of a false religion. Supposing Dissenters do not in any way profit from an Established Church (which can by no means be
granted), yet it does not follow that the supreme magistrate is to be debarred on that
account from applying a part of the national revenue to what he conceives the most useful
and important of national objects. The public expenditure flows and must flow in various
channels from which the bulk of the people derive no immediate advantage. From the
army, the navy, the customs, the excise, a harbour, a breakwater, a canal, a bridge, and a
thousand other things, this or that person may reap no direct benefit; but it would be
absurd to assert that they cannot be justly called upon to contribute to the expense, even
though they may consider one or all of these objects absolutely unlawful. It cannot be
urged for a moment that every man who pays taxes is responsible for their proper distribution. If those monies which are demanded of an individual are erroneously appropriated, he is not at fault. His cash-box may suffer, but certainly not his conscience.
And in thus arguing I am putting the Church of England on a par with the worship of
Jupiter, and regarding her clergy as no better than the priests of a heathen temple; and
even on that ground I have proved scripturally that it is the duty of Dissenters to pay
tribute. But how is my argument confirmed by the fact, that the *Church* is not evil, but
good, and that her object is to dispense the blessings of salvation all around. It
appears to me that, so long as the support of the Establishment, by legal provisions, shall
be deemed necessary or proper by the constitutional authorities, they have an undoubted
right to tax the community of every description for that purpose, and that a difference of
opinion entertained by individuals as to the fitness of the object is no ground of exemption. The State enjoins me to pay, and by force of the social compact the State has a
right to my obedience, and my paying is the evidence, not of my submission of opinion,
but of my civil obedience to the State; and if the State applies, or orders me to apply, the

money paid to an object which I do not apprehend to be aid-worthy, that is no ground for my refusal to obey, or there is an end to civil obedience at once, and the private opinion of every individual becomes the measure of his submission. The duty of the subject is to render 'tribute to whom tribute is due,' and the reciprocal duty of the ruler is to spend the public money in the way most conducive to the public interest. The Dissenter who conscientiously believes the Church of England to be an evil instead of a good, may use all lawful means to procure a change in the law which legalises the appropriation of public monies to its use; but in the meantime, while the law remains unchanged, we claim the exercise of that Christian forbearance which submits to every ordinance of man for the Lord's sake, and declines to take the law into its own hands.

"It has been necessary thus fully to state the principle for which we contend, but I think it right to say that this principle is seldom called into operation except in the article of Church Rates, which, from the smallness of the amount, ought not to be regarded as burdensome. The endowments and possessions of the English Church are, for the most part, voluntary grants, and have no right to be regarded as a tax imposed by the Government. Much is heard from time to time about the voluntary system. It is trumpeted forth from pulpit, hustings, and platform, in every variety of publication, daily, weekly, and monthly; but let those who catch up the phrase to flourish it in the face of the Church know that to a very great extent the Church of England depends upon the voluntary principle, since nearly all her endowments were at first the willing gifts of wealthy individuals. Pious proprietors of estates did in days gone by erect our Churches for their villagers: and instead of enriching the Church with lands, they entailed on their children the parochial tithes for religious purposes. The building and endowment of a Church by a nobleman, an opulent commoner, or by subscription, is a purely voluntary act; and when years and ages have rolled away, that act does not lose its voluntary character. He who gives a thousand pounds in bequest to a charitable institution, to be paid by equal annual instalments, is as truly a voluntary contributor as though he gave the whole to be expended at once. We, however, affirm, notwithstanding, that the Church of England has a right to legal revenues for her support.

"Seeing, then, that the Church of England is established by the Government of our country (and we have shown that it is lawful, expedient, and imperative for the rulers of a nation thus to advance the best interests of their people), what is the rule of conduct to be observed by those who dissent from it? It is difficult to imagine anything more express and plain than the divine commandment is with respect to submission to the civil power. I must cite the well-known language of the apostles, ' Let every soul be subject unto the higher powers, for there is no power but of God: the powers that be are ordained of God,' &c. (*Romans* xiii.)—(*Conformity to the Church of England*, 2nd ed., 18mo. London, 1864, p. 18 *et seq.*)

I will now direct attention to a few historical facts relating to Church Rates, for the purpose of showing that the obligation on the part of parishes to contribute collectively to the repair of the parish church is a time-honoured one, bound up with the foundations of the civil fabric of the English Constitution.

In 696 A.D., the Anglo-Saxon Legislature of Ina passed a law, that every dwelling was to be valued at Christmas; and the rate so imposed, called "Cyric-Sceat," or Church Scot, was to be paid in produce, money being scarce, at the following Martinmas. Defaulters were to be fined forty shillings, and to pay the Church Scot twelve fold.—(*Leges Inæ*, 4; in Thorpe, *Ancient Laws*, vol. ii. p. 460.)

"This pious care of Divine ministrations may be considered as the legal origin of Church Rates. Thus, earlier than almost any English written laws, appears on record a legislative provision for the due performance of holy offices."—(Soames, *Anglo-Saxon Church*, 3rd Edition, 8vo. London, 1844, p. 92.)

1021 A.D. King Canute and his Legislative Council, held at Winchester, decree that, " In the repair of the Church, all the people ought to assist according to what is right;" or, as we should say, according to their assessment.—(Thorpe, *Ancient Laws*, vol. i. p. 410.)

" The law of Canute places the existence of contribution, on the part of the people, at as early a period as 1030 beyond a doubt. It is mere shuffling to say that our present law of Church Rate derives no support from it, because when the law lays the burden on the people it does not say 'how they were to assist it,' or in what proportions they were to contribute to it. That they were to assist is certain, and that is all any man can be supposed to mean when he says that Church Rates are as old as the time of Canute, and that they have existed for 800 years."—(Archdeacon Hale, *Antiquity of the Church Rate System.* London, 1837, p. 29.).

In 1026, Canute writes a letter urging the regular payment of the Church dues *according to the ancient laws.* Among them is named *the Kirk Scot payable at the Feast of St. Martin to the parish church.* (See the letter in *Florent. Vigorn. anno* 1031.) Not only is the liability affirmed as one of right, but the King says he will set in operation the recognised machinery to enforce the right. We soon meet with the distinction of payment by the parishioners for the nave, and by the rectors or vicars for the chancel.

In 1285 is passed the statute " Circumspecte Agatis " (13 Ed. I.), restraining the Crown from interfering with the Ecclesiastical Courts granting monitions to compel the repairs of churches and churchyards.

" The obligation upon the parishioners to repair, thus recognised and placed beyond all reasonable dispute, is the law of England to this day."—(Denison, *Church Rate, a National Trust,* p. 60.)

Or, in the words of a high legal authority :—

" It is admitted that the parishioners are under an imperative legal obligation to provide for the necessary repair of the Church, and the expenses incidental to public worship."—(Lord Truro ; Judgment in the Braintree case, 4 Clark, H.L.C. 794.)

In 1370, a case came before the Court of Common Pleas, in which the judges admitted the power of parishioners to rate themselves and enforce rates by distraint. (*Year Book,* 44 Ed. III. p. 18. See Archdeacon Hale's account in his *Charge* of 1860, p. 25.) Thus it appears that there were " Church Rate Martyrs " 494 years ago.

For the popular purpose I have in view, it is not requisite to pursue farther this branch of the subject; suffice it, that the great antiquity of Church Rates is proved: and that, moreover, when a Dissenter refuses to pay his Church Rate, duly voted by a majority of the ratepayers in vestry, he is resisting one of the plainest common law obligations anywhere to be met with.

A Dissenter frequently asks the following question : " How would you Churchmen like to have to pay for other people's religious worship ? Why, therefore, should we pay for yours ? " The second question is hastily put in immediate succession to the first, on the gratuitous assumption that a Churchman must object to do as indicated. It may not be generally known (and, to avoid being compelled to ascribe the question to a malicious motive, I desire, in charity, to suppose that it is not generally known), *that Churchmen, whether they like it or not,* do, as a matter of fact, pay a very considerable sum annually to the sustentation of creeds other than their own. A certain gift, called the *Regium Donum,* is paid every year to the Irish Dissenters, to be apportioned into salaries for their ministers ; and, till the year 1851, a similar gift used to be paid out of the Imperial Treasury to the English Dissenters. It is a question of principle, not of amount, and Dissenters should be careful to avoid too nice inquiries into some of these subjects.

To this it may be added that Dissenters do not refuse to pay poor rates or county rates; yet out of the former are paid the clergy who are work-house chaplains, and out of the latter those who are prison chaplains; so that, in point of fact, under a state of things existing for a considerable time past, *Dissenters themselves contribute towards religious worship expenses not their own* and in which they do not concur, *without being consulted*, and more than that, *without grumbling.* To be consistent, if they find fault with Church Rates, they should find fault with poor rates and county rates: *from all three, contributions towards Church worship are derived.*

Again, of 10,367 parishes in England and Wales, Churchmen are re-turned as sole possessors in 1455, and as chief possessors in 7825. On the other hand, the parishes in which the owners are either Dissenters or equally divided, are only 1087. Therefore, on the commonest ground of justice, if Dissenters are entitled to be thought of, much more so are Churchmen, seeing how largely as landowners they outnumber the Dissenters. But more than this, it must be borne in mind that of the ratepayers who take part in the voting in vestry, very few are landowners, and therefore very few really pay the rate, except as deputies, as men-tioned at the beginning of this Book; so that we Churchmen have an-other ground entitling us to appeal to Dissenters to exercise forbearance in reference to parochial matters affecting the Church. Dissenters may depend upon it that this view of the matter has not escaped consideration. A distinguished Whig nobleman, Lord Lyttelton, publicly stated at a meeting in London in 1864, that if any of his tenants persisted in refusing to pay the Church Rate, he should add the amount to their rent, and hand over the difference to the churchwardens.

Granting that the present state of the law is most unsatisfactory—as undoubtedly it is—Dissenters who desire alteration should appeal to Par-liament, but in the interim should pay the dues, and refrain from disturb-ing the peace of parishes. There are plenty of public duties to which their attention might usefully be directed; and it may well be a question whether such a course would not be more in harmony with the practical exemplification of those great principles of charity and brotherly love set forth in Holy Scripture. The churchwardens and ratepayers of every parish are charged, not to renovate the laws, but to administer them; therefore Dissenters having anything to find fault with should go to the Legislature direct and not to the parish vestry, there to raise a tur-moil against those peaceable ratepayers who desire to do their duty as good citizens, by carrying out the provisions of the law, and repair-ing the houses of God by a duly regulated assessment on the parishioners at large.

By the law of England, as now understood, no Church Rate can be levied but by the consent of the majority. This is the principle, and acknowledged to be a sound one, by which all taxes are imposed upon us in Parliament, and all rates in parishes. It is one of the characteristics of Englishmen that they willingly bow to the decision of the majority: a majority levy a highway rate, and demand payment, *whether men use that way or not*; a majority levy a gas rate, and demand payment, *whether men benefit by the light or not*; rates are levied to provide public baths and libraries, and no man is exempted from payment on the ground that *he never avails himself of them.* To exempt Dissenters from payment on the ground that they build their own meeting-houses, &c., is just as conclusive as if a man should object to pay a poor's rate, because he provides for his own family. Church Rates are levied by the majority of the ratepayers for what they believe to be for the good of the whole parish, and Dissenters are required to pay, not because they are Dissenters, but *because they are parishioners.*

No appeal such as the present would be complete without some further allusion, however brief, to a movement now being agitated for " Liberating Religion from State Patronage and Control," as its promoters say, but which would be more accurately described as intended to *liberate the Church from her property.* In self-defence, we are called upon to take note of it. Its openly avowed object is to DESTROY EVERY VESTIGE OF A PUBLIC NATIONAL PROFESSION OF RELIGION. As means to an end, it is busily engaged in assaulting the Established Church, and in promoting legislative aggressions on her civil position and specially on her property. The Society alluded to has a large annual income (4000*l.*), which it spends in stirring up religious strife and dissension in every parish with which it comes in contact. Just now its efforts are mainly directed against Church Rates, regarding them, and justly, as an outwork of the great fortress Church-and-State,—National Religion. It is well known that many Dissenters joined the Society in the belief that it had nothing further in view than to secure relief to Dissenters from Church Rates. That belief, if ever well founded, has long since been a thing of the past, and the Society's recognised leaders have publicly proclaimed a war to the knife against the Church of England. (See *ante*, p. 41 *et seq.*)

Upon those who glory in this ungodly policy, words of expostulation would probably be thrown away ; but we Churchmen do earnestly entreat the many constitutional Dissenters, who have voted against Church Rates without thought or reflection, to consider whether the time has not come for them to declare their convictions in a tangible form. Let all such Dissenters who really regard the Church as the great bulwark of religion in the land, sever themselves from these dangerous revolutionists of whom I have been speaking, now that they clearly know that Church Rate Abolition is *designed to involve*, and *very likely would involve*, something much more serious.

"The Dissenting Leaders openly avowed, in their evidence before the House of Lords in 1859, that the present movement against Church Rates is only a wedge by which they are trying to separate between Church and State. They warned us that even if Church Rates are abolished, Dissent cannot be satisfied and will not rest until all property belonging to the Church of England, as the National Church, shall have been taken from it, and applied, not even to education, but to ordinary Government purposes. And this, whether the property has been originally granted by public law, or, being of private gift, was only secured to the Church by Act of Parliament at the Reformation, or before, or since. They demand that all Parish Churches, Cathedrals, Parsonages, Advowsons, Tythes, Glebes, and Church land, shall be seized by Parliament, and sold to any who may choose to buy, for any use whatever ; and that the proceeds, after satisfying existing interests, shall be thrown into the ordinary Tax Fund for Army, Navy, or other public purposes. What a goodly use to be suggested by professing ministers of the gospel of peace, for property granted at first to spread the kingdom of the Prince of peace ! Every village would then lose its Church and Clergyman, unless the inhabitants chose to subscribe money enough to buy back their own Church, and undertook to provide every year for the Clergyman's necessary income, and also for repairs. Can they be friends of the *poor* who propose such schemes ? How few parishes could raise money for this, even if they consented to do it ! And all this would soon have a wider result. There would no longer be churchwardens, nor vestry ; and after a while, no parishes, and no power of managing their own affairs among themselves alone. Everything would be done by Unions ; and all local business would gradually pass away from villages themselves, and be managed or controlled by some central despotic power in London, like the Poor Law Commissioners. Are Englishmen prepared thus to yield up local self-government, which is in fact the principle of Parliament, and of a Municipality also ? to have nothing to say in their own local affairs? to change their habits and feelings, and lose all that which they are accustomed to reverence, value, and look up to? Would England be happier, more godly, or better off, for losing at once, as a national institution, all her Parish Churches and Clergy? Would the poor, the sick, the aged, the children, be better cared for? The whole plan is only a vast scheme for mere godless robbery of the poor, and of parishes, and of the Church of God. It is easy to say that the scheme is too wild to be worth fearing. But the Dissenting Leaders know better—'Little by little' is their watchword.

"Let us look the Dissenters' plan in the face, and think for a moment what the results would be. This country would be OLD ENGLAND no longer: all would be new and strange, sour and heartless. The effects would be felt in every parish—in some more, in some less. Religion would be turned at once into so much *money's worth*. Three-fourths of the parish churches would be without ministers, for what would they have to live upon? The churches, in far the greater number of parishes, would be sold for barracks, warehouses, barns, or other common uses, or pulled down for the materials, because the parishes would be too poor to buy them. Roman Catholics would buy many, and what then would become of the Protestant poor? Dissenters would buy some; and, probably, fit up part of the church as a dwelling-house for their minister. Rich landowners would buy some and put in ministers, of whatever sort or sect they liked. What an uneasy blank would be everywhere felt! No longer in every village, rich or poor, a minister of God appointed, as a matter of course; maintained and controlled by lawful authority, to uphold the cause and teach the will of God; a bond of union among all classes; a principal inhabitant, spending generally from his own private property much more than he draws from the place. Tythes and rent-charge now go into the hands of a friend to the inhabitants, but then they would be drawn by the tax-gatherer, or by some lay purchaser eager to make the best interest on the money price he had paid. Who could then spare time from making his own daily bread to do the missing minister's *outward* work in a parish? Who would take care—whom would the poor trust to take care—of schools, clothing clubs, and the other benevolent arrangements to alleviate poverty and distress? Who would be leader, year after year, in all the nameless means of good, spiritual and temporal, to the poor? To what sure and faithful friend would the distressed and sorrowful, the sick and needy, go, and claim a right to go, for comfort, help, and advice? Hard and heartless, and unfeeling to the poor, is the whole of this atrocious plan for doing away with the National Church. Let the thinking and foreseeing poor of England answer for themselves whether it would not prove so."—(*The Church, Church Rates, and Dissenters,* p. 10.)

Hear what Dr. Pye Smith said in his controversial correspondence with Professor Lee, of Cambridge :—

"I know, however, that there are some, and those persons of unquestionable moral excellence, and who would abhor any violation of what is strictly just, who recommend the resumption (or rather it would be the assumption, for the State could not resume what it never gave) of the Church property by the Government, as a part of the desired reform. This to my apprehension would be downright robbery. May our country never be dishonoured by it!"

In the opinion of this eminent Dissenter, the Liberators are embarked in a cause which, if crowned with success, will be justly branded as an act of "downright robbery," and "a dishonour to our country."

Attention is invited to the following extract from the well-known Dissenting periodical, the *Eclectic Review.* If the words had been penned for the express purpose of condemning Mr. Miall's mis-statements in his recently published book on Church Property, they could not have been more direct and emphatic :—

"It is, however, equally fallacious to talk of the Church property as being *vested* in the Legislature. Dissenters who hold this language expose themselves to the charge of being either very ignorant, or guilty of wilful and malicious misrepresentation. The tithes are no more vested in the Legislature than are the Irish estates of a London Company, or the endowments of our Dissenting academies and meeting-houses. The manner in which the abolition of tithes by a simple Act of Parliament is sometimes spoken of as a thing quite feasible, legal, and desirable, might have suited a French Constituent Assembly. But that British Christians—nay, ministers of the Gospel—nay, individuals enjoying the

F

benefit of endowments—should be so far misled by party zeal as to join in the unprincipled clamour against Church property raised by the advocates of uncompensated spoliation, forgetful alike of consistency, the decencies of their sacred office, and the plain dictates of common honesty—this, we must avow it, has filled us with amazement and shame. The cause of Dissent is under small obligations to those who have brought down upon it this deep disgrace."—(*E. R.*, February 1832, p. 129.)

The following statistics deserve serious consideration :—

From a Parliamentary return for 15 years preceding 1856, relating to 9676 parishes, it appears that Church Rates were *granted* in 8280 (85·5 per cent.) and *refused* in 408 (4·2 per cent.). The residue possessed endowments, &c., or gave dubious replies. The question inevitably suggests itself : *Are the* 8000 *to be coerced to please the* 400, *or shall the* 400 *yield to the* 8000 ?

Again, another return shows the following results :—

Total parishes giving replies .	9647
Relying on Church Rates alone	5291
„ Church Rates and Endowments .	684
„ Church Rates and Endowments and Voluntary Subscriptions	365
„ Church Rates and Voluntary Subscriptions .	1775
„ Endowments only .	430
„ Endowments and Voluntary Subscriptions .	297
„ Voluntary Subscriptions only .	805

Adding together the first four numbers, we ascertain that Church Rates enter into the financial arrangements of no less than 8115 parishes (84·1 per cent.), but do not do so in 1532 parishes (15.9 per cent.)—a result well in accordance with the previous one, though arrived at by a wholly different process.

WHY IT IS SOUGHT TO ABOLISH CHURCH RATES?

In the summer of 1859, the Duke of Marlborough obtained a Committee of the House of Lords to inquire into the question of Church Rates. That Committee sat on numerous occasions in 1859, and also in the early part of 1860, their Report and the evidence taken before them being laid before Parliament in the month of March in that year. The information they elicited was of great importance, both as regards the designs of the Dissenters, and the consequences which would ensue were those designs permitted to be carried into effect. Churchmen have been so entirely in the dark relative to the real question at issue, that it is most desirable that they should be made clearly acquainted with the demands of the Dissenters, as expressed by their representatives at that Committee. I therefore make no apology for directing attention to the following extracts from the minutes of the evidence, comprehending some of the more important topics touched upon by the two leading Political Dissenting witnesses, Messrs. Morley and Foster.

Mr. Samuel MORLEY.

Question 661. (Lord *Wensleydale.*) You object to a State religion altogether?—Answer: I do.

A. to Q. 662. Distinctly; if you were to relieve Dissenters to-day from any prospective payment in respect of religion, their efforts would remain as vigorous as they have hitherto been, in order to establish the general principle of exemption on the ground of injury to religion. [?]

A. to Q. 696. *I quite believe that the concession of this question of Church Rates will not satisfy the ultimate expectations, or I will say, if you please, the requirements of Dissenters.*

Q. 698. You have alluded to ultimate objects; would you feel it consistent with your position before this Committee to state what those ultimate objects might be?—A. I should be sorry to misrepresent those objects, but I can state only my own impression of what they are. I believe that the *great* object is *to separate religion from the slightest connection with the State.*

Q. 699. Would Dissenters feel that Church Rates being abolished, and, so far, there being by that abolition a line of demarcation drawn between the interests of the Dissenter and the interests of the Churchman, the Churchman should be left in the enjoyment of the endowments which have been provided for the sustentation of the Church?—A. That is a very important question. THAT THE SETTLEMENT OF THE CHURCH RATE QUESTION WOULD MEET THE DIFFICULTIES WHICH DISSENTERS MAKE, I DO NOT BELIEVE. I think you would find that the organisations which at present exist would remain so long as there existed any form of interference by legislation with religion.

A. to Q. 700. I believe that the opinion of Dissenters is, that *Church property is national property*, and that it would have to be dealt with according to the judgment of the nation.

Q. 722. (Lord Bishop of *London.*) I think you have stated that it is the view of certain Nonconformists that they regard Church Establishments altogether as things which are injurious to religion?—A. I do believe so.

Q. 723. And that ultimately they may hope, in the extreme future, to find an opportunity of taking the property which is now appropriated to the Establishment and applying it otherwise?—A. That would certainly be the course of events, if they shape themselves as, no doubt, many sanguine minds are anticipating.

Q. 738. Can you state what proportion of free sittings there are in Dissenting Chapels? —A. *The proportion is very small indeed.* I am bound to make that acknowledgment; *and it is a difficulty.*

A. to Q. 753. I daresay the phrase has sometimes met your lordship, "the separation of Church and State." I believe that is the object which numbers of earnest men have set before themselves: and I venture to say, and I would take the liberty to repeat it, whose object, and only object, is a religious one. [?]

Q. 754. That step is the taking away from the Church its property, and giving it to the State for some general purposes?—A. *That is not the only result that is necessarily involved.*

Q. 756. In fact, this question of Church Rates, as you present it, is but a small point altogether as compared with the great question of the separation of Church and State?— [Answered in the affirmative.]

Q. 763. You have stated that there is a strong opinion on the part of Dissenters that Church Rates ought to be abolished even as applicable to Churchmen?—A. YES, CLEARLY.

Q. 674. Would that apply to all Dissenters?—A. With very few exceptions, probably it would.

Q. 772. (*Chairman.*) Still you do look upon the abolition of Church Rates as taking off one link in the connection of Church and State?—A. UNQUESTIONABLY.

Q. 773. And a step in the direction of that ultimate object which it is desired to attain for the promotion of the interests of religion?—A. I quite think so.

Q. 778. So that I believe that the views entertained by the Dissenters whom you represent [the Independents] would be these: that they do not look upon the question of Church Rates as a grievance which they desire to be removed from them, but that they look upon it as a great religious question which they would wish to see carried out in the country?—A. I quite believe that is the feeling of a large number whom I represent.

Q. 791. In fact, the great principle which you think ought to permeate and to actuate religion in everything is the voluntary principle?—A. I quite believe that.

A. to Q. 797. I have no hesitation in saying, that if a Bill were introduced into the House of Commons to-night, the object of which should be to charge upon *Churchmen* the support of their own places of worship, there would be opposition to it commenced to-morrow which would be fatal to the measure.

Q. 799. (Lord Bishop of *London.*) I do not quite see what the ground of that opposition would be, unless it were with the view of some ulterior measures. Why should any Dissenter object to a Churchman, who conscientiously thinks that the State has a right to charge him, being charged by the State?—A. The object of the Dissenters is to get off of the statute-book all enactments which bring the policeman into operation with a view to enforce payment by anybody. Your lordship may not be able to believe that there is a religious basis for that opinion, but I can assert that there are numbers of men who have that opinion. [?].

Q. 800. (Lord *Wensleydale*.) You would not only object to the compulsory rate for yourselves, the Dissenters, as regards the sustentation of the fabric of the Church, but you would object to Churchmen being compulsorily called upon to support their own Churches?—A. *Quite so.*

Q. 828. Asked by the Lord Bishop of *London*, whether, seeing that out of 12,000 parishes only 500 refuse Church Rates, it is not very unfair to compel the remaining 11,500 to give way to 500, and how a Dissenter would answer this?—A. I am bound to say there is much substantial reason for the difficulty.

A. to Q. 842. (*Chairman*.) I merely meant to refer to the fact that there is in every constituency a representative body of the views which I have put before the Committee. The particular Society to which reference has been made, has correspondents in every constituency, and there is a degree of co-operation with them, not on behalf only, I beg the Committee to believe, of mere noisy talkers, but of earnest, thoughtful persons in every constituency and in every moderately large town; and there is a course of action which candidates understand perfectly well, and which is found to be operative on this particular question.

Q. 844. (Earl of *Romney*.) Does your Society send down individuals into different parishes in the country?—A. Not frequently.*

CHARLES JAMES FOSTER, LL.D.

Q. 1507. (*Chairman*.) May I ask what the objects are which your Society have in view?—A. *We wish to what is commonly called separate the Church from the State. We wish to take away all funds and property with which the State has endowed any religious denomination whatever.* We wish also to free all denominations of persons who may happen to be under special legislation, on religious grounds, from such special legislation.

Q. 1511. Do you include tithes?—A. YES.

Q. 1519. Suppose that persons not conforming to the Church were exempted from the payment of Church Rates, would that satisfy the body of Dissenters?—A. I THINK NOT.

Q. 1522. Do you think it is consistent with the principles of civil and religious liberty, for one part of the community who entertain one view to force that view upon another portion of the community who do not entertain it?—A. No; certainly not.

Q. 1523. Is not that the course taken by your Society?—A. Hardly that. [?] [This question completely trapped the witness, and he was unable to make a straightforward reply.]

Q. 1529. (Lord Bishop of *London*.) In the first place, you object to Church Rates as they are; and, secondly, you object to the connection between Church and State?—A. Yes.

Q. 1530. Is that opinion entertained, do you think, by the great majority of Dissenters in this country?—A. I do not think that the second point in the question would be entertained by the great majority of the Dissenters.

Q. 1531. When you speak of Dissenters, you probably mean not to include Wesleyans?—A. Very slightly so.

Q. 1532. Do not the Wesleyans form a very large portion of the population?—A. Yes. Until recently they had decidedly declined to have any political connection with us.

Q. 1533. Your impression is that the Wesleyans might object to Church Rates, but certainly would not object to the connection between Church and State?—[Answered in the affirmative.]

---

* This statement is, I believe, in substance thoroughly untrue. There are probably very few parishes to which, during the last few years, when a Church Rate contest was going on, a visit has not been paid by "J. Carvell Williams, Esq.," the Secretary of the Liberation Society, to stir up the evil passions of a schismatic and irreligious mob. I can testify to this from personal experience.

Q. 1551. Then, in fact, all endowments for Dissenting meeting-houses are quite as much public property as endowments of the Church of England?—A. Under that condition they would be. [Here the witness was again admirably caught in his own trap.]

Q. 1583. (Lord Bishop of *London.*) Would it be right to say that the objects of the Liberation Society are the application to secular uses, after the equitable satisfaction of existing interests, of all national property now held upon trust by the United Church of England and Ireland, and the Presbyterian Church of Scotland, and concurrently with that, the liberation of those Churches from all State control?—A. Yes; except that it is not quite complete. The *Regium Donum* is also one of the objects of our Society.

Q. 1596. (*Chairman.*) Do not many men pay a Church Rate because it is the law, who do not attend Church, but who, if the law were removed, would not make a voluntary gift for the maintenance of the Church?—A. I think there are such persons.

A. to Q. 1602. Our Society is called one for the Liberation of Religion, and it may naturally be supposed that we are interested in the spread of religion; and we think that the arrangements made by the English Church hamper the means of spreading religion. [?]

Q. 1604. Your object is, as I understand you, the promotion and spread of religion? —A. I hope that is my personal object, and I believe this to be the object of those with whom I act. [?]

Q. 1612. (Lord Bishop of *London.*) The Society has, I think, printed a number of publications pointing out what flaws in Church Rates could be found, and suggesting a mode by which legal difficulties might be thrown in the way of raising a Church Rate?—A. Yes.

Q. 1613. Is it your impression that, in the election of members of Parliament, there was any particular activity in the Parliamentary Committee as to those elections?—A. *Undoubtedly; it is part of our duty.*

Q. 1614. All legitimate and constitutional means to return members who are pledged against Church Rates are, of course, used by the Parliamentary Committee?—A. Yes.

Q. 1632. (Lord Bishop of *Oxford.*) You stated that you could not feel the returns that were referred to by the Bishop of London to be correct. Have you any data or figures which enable you to question their correctness?—A. No, I have not.

Q. 1642. (*Chairman.*) You have spoken of communications that came from villages and from market towns; do those communications come from Dissenters or from Churchmen?—A. *I have no doubt they come from Dissenters.*

Q. 1664. I understand the Society for the Liberation of Religion have formed no definite idea as to what would be the objects to which the property of the Church should be applied?—A. I do not suppose that the Society considers that any part of its business.

Q. 1667. In fact, it is rather an object which is held out as one of the intentions of the Society, than anything that they have substantially made up their minds upon?—A. I do not admit that. . . . . Supposing our Society to continue, the accomplishment of our object will come before long.

Q. 1678. That is to say, you look upon the Episcopalians merely as tenants of the ecclesiastical edifices, without paying rent for them?—A. Yes.

Q. 1679. I believe I am right in saying that the view you entertain of Church Rates is, that a settlement of the Church Rate question would by no means settle the objects you have in view, but that there are ulterior objects which you also wish to see accomplished, even although the question of Church Rates was settled to-morrow?—A. YES.

Q. 1684. (Lord Bishop of *Oxford.*) You are aware that the great Fathers of Evangelical Dissent in England have been opposed to the separation of Church and State?— A. Yes.

Q. 1688. Asked whether the original desire to see the separation of Church and State was likely to have been connected with any political movement?—A. I think it is not at all unlikely.

Q. 1691. I think the Committee understand that you give it quite as your impression, that if the Church Rate question was settled to-morrow, it would not tend to produce what I may call peace between the Established Church and the body of Evangelical Dissenters?—A. It could not be regarded as settling the questions in which we feel that we have an interest.

Q. 1701. (Earl of *Powis.*) With regard to secularisation, do you consider the tithes now held by ecclesiastical bodies to be national property?—A. YES.

THE CONSEQUENCES OF ABOLISHING CHURCH RATES.

We are not left in the dark on this point; the evidence of which I have already quoted so much is full of warning.

The Rev. John C. MILLER, D.D.

"Q. 178. (*Chairman*.) Are you able to state whether there is very great difficulty experienced in providing the sums necessary for the performance of divine worship, as well as for the maintenance of the fabrics?—A. There is in many parishes the greatest possible difficulty. The present system, as carried on in Birmingham, is a perfect millstone round the necks of a great majority of the ministers of the town. I do not speak from theory or opinion; I speak in that respect from my knowledge of facts. I may be allowed to add to that answer, that so strong was my own feeling upon that point, that being called on often to have begging sermons for arrears of congregational expenses, I at last announced to my people, so wearied was I with it, that I never would allow those collections in my church again—that we must cut down our expenses to what we could raise in some other way; and I have never allowed any such collections in my church since; but most of the clergy are obliged to have quarterly collections to pay their wardens' expenses, and some of them put an addition on to the pewage."

" A. to Q. 233. (Lord Bishop of *London*.) *I believe that if the system which is pursued in Birmingham with respect to Church Rates* [viz. the voluntary] *were once extended to the whole of this country, spiritually, it would be the greatest national calamity that could befall us.*"

"Q. 238. (*Chairman*.) Is it not the case at present, that whether for the building of churches or the erection of schools, the clergymen are obliged to make very widely extended appeals, not only to their own people, but to persons very foreign to their parishes? A. *The truth is, that begging is now a chief element in our duties.*"

" Q. 239. Then, if the provision of the funds necessary for repairing the churches were thrown upon the voluntary system, would not it oblige the clergyman to extend his begging operations very largely?—A. He would have to extend them; and as a result of my own observations of Birmingham, I should say he would extend them unsuccessfully, and that the churches would go to decay."

" Q. 240. Would it not very seriously interfere with the time which he ought to give to his parochial duties?—A. *It does now most seriously.*"

"Q. 241. Would it not add very largely to his anxieties?—A. *It does now most heavily.*"

" Q. 242. And in those ways very seriously prejudice his spiritual work.—A. We all feel in Birmingham that we are becoming secularised more and more every day; we get on by constant begging."

" Q. 342. (*Chairman*.) Have you not sometimes had promises of voluntary contributions for the repair of churches which you have not afterwards had fulfilled?—A. When I first went to Birmingham, the churchwarden in office as the people's warden, who, like other people's wardens, had gone into office pledged against the rate, told me that he had had very fair promises that if they did not insist on the rate one would give a 5l. note and another would give a 5l. note, and soon; but he gave me to understand that after the rate had been refused many of them left him in the lurch."

The Ven. Archdeacon SANDFORD.

" Q. 1043. (*Chairman*.) What is the general state of repair of the Churches in your archdeaconry?—A. The Churches in Birmingham itself are going into decay, and I consider that the state of the Birmingham Churches is conclusive against the theory of the honourable member for Birmingham, Mr. Bright, as to the efficiency of the voluntary system, because Birmingham enjoys the advantages of very exemplary and energetic clergy, who, if any men could uphold their fabrics by the voluntary system, would do so. . . ."

Dr. Miller's opinion is confirmed by—

The Right Hon. W. E. GLADSTONE, M.P.

" I think the practical result of the simple abolition of Church Rates would be to throw in the rural parishes upon the clergy—who are already in many respects overburdened, with but limited stipends, with their, I must say, generally unbounded liberality, and the absence in many cases of aid derived from other resources—a charge which it would be most unjust to them to impose on their shoulders, and which would have the effect of making a fresh demand for secular objects on time which ought to be at the disposal of their parishioners for spiritual purposes."—(Speech in the House of Commons, March 7, 1866. Hansard, vol. cxxxi.)

Enough : if anything I have written shall lead to the more correct understanding of the true points at issue in the Church Rate question— which are something more than who is to pay for washing Mr. A.'s surplice, or repairing Mr. B.'s gown—my labours will not have been altogether in vain. To put the matter in a few words, those who vote for a Church Rate vote *not simply in favour of a twopenny-halfpenny tax of mere local concern, but publicly declare their solemn belief that an Established faith is a blessing to a nation, and ought to be strenuously upheld.*

APPENDIX TO BOOK VI.

SUGGESTED SETTLEMENTS OF THE CHURCH RATE QUESTION.

As it may be expected that the Church Rate question will at no distant period come before the country for fair common-sense discussion in anticipation of a settlement, it may be convenient to lay before the reader abstracts of some of the more rational schemes which have been more or less formally propounded. The abstracts are taken from papers circulated by the Church Institution. I leave out of consideration 2 proposals which are both equally bad: total abolition, and letting the present law remain, in its essential points, untouched.

I. The Duke of Marlborough.—" Bill to amend the law relating to the Assessment and Levying of Church Rates."

Jurisdiction of Ecclesiastical Courts as to Church Rates to cease, and that of the Temporal Courts to be substituted.

Whenever a majority refuse a rate in a parish where no rate has been voted for two years last preceding, the Churchwardens annually to cause inquiry to be made of every parishioner whether he is desirous that his name should be omitted from the registry of persons entitled to vote at Vestry meetings for making a rate and electing Churchwardens; and the Churchwardens to enter in a " Church Register Book" the names of all who shall not within a certain time have signified such desire, and only such persons are to be entitled to be present and vote, and the rate is to be laid upon such persons only.

For the purpose of a Church Rate, the word " parish" is to include every ecclesiastical district.

Church Rates to be assessed and collected after the manner of Poor Rates.

II. Mr. Hubbard, M.P.—" Bill to amend the law of Church Rates."

Every parish or district to hold a Church vestry to transact business connected with Church Rates only, to consist of ratepayers not disqualified under this Act, and of such owners (or their agents) qualified by this Act.

Church Rates to be assessed on the same valuation as the Poor Rates, and for each assessment not exceeding 6*l.*, the owner, unless he claims exemption, to be rated at not less than three-fourths of assessment, and to possess the right of voting at vestry in lieu of tenant, exercising one vote for every such property to the extent of 6 votes.

Jurisdiction of Ecclesiastical Courts for recovery of Church Rates to cease; but the visitation of the ordinary, or his officer on his authority, not to be affected. All persons not conforming to the Church of England who may choose to claim exemption by giving the necessary notice to the Churchwardens before January 8 in each year to be exempted, in which case the owner to be rated unless he also claims exemption before January 29. Such owner, without prejudice to his own right, also to possess the right of voting at vestry in respect of such property.

Persons while exempt to be precluded from attending the Church vestry, to be deprived of seats in Church, and not to act as Churchwardens in any matter relating to the Church. Rates to be levied as at present, where money has been raised on security of the same.

III. Mr. Cross, ex-M.P.—" Bill to amend the law of Church Rates."

Any person may exempt himself from the rate by notifying to Churchwardens, between January 1 and March 1, his desire not to be rated; but no person, during the period of his exemption, is to be entitled to vote on the appointment of churchwardens or the making of rates, or to have any seat in the Church to the exclusion of those who pay rates.

Jurisdiction of Ecclesiastical Courts as to Church Rates to be abolished.

Church Rates to be assessed and collected after the manner of Poor Rates.

The Small Tenements Act to be applicable to Church Rates, so as to render the owners of tenements under yearly value of 6*l.* liable instead of the occupiers.

IV. Mr. Estcourt, ex-M.P.—;" Bill to abolish the Jurisdiction of Ecclesiastical Courts in respect of Church Rates, and to alter and amend the Law relating to Church Rates."

Jurisdiction of Ecclesiastical Courts as to Church Rates to be transferred to the tribunals which deal with Poor Rates.

Each Ecclesiastical District to be a separate parish for the purposes of this Act.

Churchwardens once in each year to publish on the Church door for three successive Sundays, and to levy and collect an owner's Church Rate, not exceeding 1*d.* in the pound upon all property which has been assessed to a Church Rate within the last 5 years, such rate to be solely applied to the repairs of the Church, Church clock, bells, and belfry, the maintenance of the churchyard, the providing of registers, the performance of Divine worship; insurance; and the payment of fees. This rate to be payable by tenants, who are to deduct it from rent due to the landlord.

Church vestry to levy an occupier's Church Rate for any purpose connected with Divine worship, to be collected only from occupiers who are members of the Church vestry.

The Church vestry to consist solely of owners rated as aforesaid, and of all occupiers who shall during the preceding 12 months have paid any Church Rate, or, being ratepayers, shall have contributed to any subscription in lieu thereof, and who shall not decline to be members of such Church vestry by delivering a notice to that effect to the Churchwardens before Easter in each year.

Church vestry to control the audit of Churchwardens' accounts; furniture and fittings of the Church; salary of officers; appropriation of seats; and all expenditure incurred for the benefit of the congregation.

Small Tenements Acts to be applicable to occupiers' rates under this Act.

Church Rates to be assessed after the manner of Poor Rates.

V. Mr. Alcock, ex-M.P.—" Bill for the voluntary Commutation of Church Rates."

The Charity Commissioners to be a Corporation, under the title of Church Rate Commutation Commissioners.

Such Commission, on having a yearly sum secured to them, either in Consols or in rent-charge, sufficient to defray the expenses properly payable out of Church Rates in any parish, to award that no Church Rate shall thenceforth be raised.

Commissioners to release such rent-charges on having transferred to them an equivalent sum in dividends from Consols, and to release portions of land from liability where the residue affords sufficient security.

VI.

The rate to be levied only for expenses connected with the fabric, conceding expenses connected with the services in return for improved facilities for enforcement.

District parishes to be exempted from paying Church Rates to the parish out of which they were taken, and to levy Church Rates for themselves.

The Churchwardens to possess the power to excuse from the payment of Church Rates.

Landowners (including tenants for life) to possess the power, by deed or will, to charge their land with the Church Rate.

VII.

The average rate of the preceding 25 years to be the amount on which the parish shall be for the future assessed, such amount to be considered due on January 1 in each year.

Property which under the present law would be liable to Church Rates, to be liable to this commuted payment.

Remedies for recovery to be the same as those given for tithes, under the Tithe Commutation Act.

District parishes to share in such commutation, the amount assessed being according to the rateable value of the property within such district parish. Chapels of ease to be treated as one with the mother church.

If any exemption be conceded, anyone exempting himself by a written notice, on or before January 8 in each year, to relinquish his rights in Church vestry, or parochial matters connected with the Church.

VIII.

The direct charge of Church Rates, and all powers of imposing and levying the same, to be transferred from the tenants to the owners of property, and such owners to have conferred upon them the further powers of exercising their votes by means of voting papers; also, of commuting their liability to the rate.

The present jurisdiction of the Ecclesiastical Courts to be abolished, and the mode of assessing and recovering Church Rates to be assimilated to the law now in force with respect to Poor Rates.

A tribunal of appeal from owners' vestries, either for or against the rate, to be provided. Every ecclesiastical district to be a separate parish for Church Rate purposes.

IX.

The general incidence of the existing law to remain untouched.

The jurisdiction of the Ecclesiastical Courts to cease in matters of a strictly temporal nature—that is to say, in matters not having reference to the objects for which the rate is made.

Churchwardens to be protected when collecting rates by providing that in no case shall allegations of invalidity justify a refusal to pay, or be a defence when payment is sought to be enforced.

The following machinery for deciding upon questions of validity is suggested:—Previous to collecting, Churchwardens to submit their rate to the justices of Petty Sessions, who shall confirm, quash, or amend the same in any way that they shall deem proper, and their determination to be final unless any persons who consider themselves aggrieved shall appeal to a higher tribunal.

The Small Tenements Act to apply to Church Rates, and vestries to have power to excuse from payment.

The Justices to have power to audit Church Rates, analogous to the power given them by 5 & 6 Will. IV. c. 50, as to Highway Rates. At such audit any parishioner may object to any item of disbursement, that it was made for a purpose not authorised by law; such objection not to be gone into by the Justices, but machinery to be provided by which it will, under their authority, be sent up to the Spiritual Courts.

The Bill to be framed with especial reference to existing Acts of Parliament, and their actual words made use of when practicable, so that the duties imposed upon Justices would be such as they are constantly called upon to perform in other matters.

A Bill embodying the proposals of No. IX. has been prepared by Mr. J. G. N. Darby, of the Church Institution, and has received considerable attention. Should a convenient opportunity offer, it is probable that it will be brought before Parliament.

Book VII.

Inconsistency and Church Defence.

The inconsistency of many professors of what is right and proper in the present day is truly deplorable. Many Christians go to Church, Sunday after Sunday, and would not wish to be absent themselves on any account, who think nothing of habitually requiring their servants to desecrate the Lord's Day by using carriages and horses, &c. (and thus in many cases hindering their attendants from joining in public worship), without the slightest occasion for it. If they are *bonâ fide* invalids, it is another thing; but what proportion do the invalids who ride in carriages on Sunday bear to the non-invalids?

The Post Office is another field for an extensive display of Christian inconsistency. Many who will not work themselves by writing letters on Sunday, will make Post Office servants work by posting letters on Saturday and Sunday, which in nine cases out of ten would well keep till Monday. Thoughtlessness is probably at the root of much of this.

Equally as marked as the preceding is the inconsistency of professing Churchmen in certain ecclesiastical matters. How many who dislike Dissent of all kinds, both in theory and practice, and who would be unwilling to have anything to do with the ministrations of Schism, or attend the meeting-houses of the Sects, think nothing of indirectly countenancing Dissent with their money. How many deal with Dissenting tradesmen and not with Church ditto, for no better reason than that a little trouble is saved thereby? The former are nearer their residences; to go to the latter would involve a little longer walk, a little more trouble, forgetting all the while that by patronising Dissent in small things, they encourage Dissent in large matters. The whole strength of Dissent in England lies with the small tradesmen. Everybody knows there are few Dissenters among the upper and lower classes of the community.

What interest the lower classes have in religion (alas, that it is so little!) is exclusively given to the Church, as the affair at Bedford, in July 1862, proves. How when a mean-spirited sectary began to burn a Prayer Book in the public street, he was set upon by a mob, who taught him and his a lesson which they will be slow to forget.

But I am digressing. So long as professing Church folks patronise Dissenting shopkeepers,* so long and no longer will Dissent upraise itself

---

* Dissenting shopkeepers are in general much more independent, not to say impudent, than their Church brethren. Churchmen have many annoyances to put up with in consequence.

like a hydra-headed monster in England. I have before me a recent number of the *Liberator*, and the large number of half-crown and five-shilling subscriptions is an undoubted confirmation of the accuracy of this reasoning. Dissenters do not display the same inconsistency as Churchmen. You will not find Dissenters dealing with Church-people, and passing over their own brethren of Ebenezer and Bethel. No; they are too keenly alive to the consequences that the Church would flourish and Dissent pine away. I am not insisting too much on this trade question, but simply offer it as one of the ways in which Dissent could be brought low, and ought to be brought low, if the Church of England as a religious *establishment* is to be preserved. The toleration of Dissent is one thing, the encouragement of it another. Churchmen ought to see that they cannot *encourage* Dissent and preserve the Church at the same time.

All that I have said above applies, *mutatis mutandis*, to professing Churchmen as Conservative* politicians; though these have, as it were, a special way of their own of trumpeting forth their inconsistencies, in the resolute refusal of large numbers of them to support their own newspapers. They seem unable to recognise the mighty power of the newspaper press for good or for evil, as the case may be.

How many thousands of *professing* Conservative Churchmen, *Clergymen* included, read nothing but the miserable trash doled out by the (Democratic) *Daily Telegraph*, or the (Dissenting) *Morning Star?* By so acting, they not only throw discouragement on the organs of their own party, but complacently suffer themselves to be victimized, often by the most extravagant falsehoods and misrepresentation, on the part of their "Liberal" protégés; but this serves them right.

The following facts are worthy of attention :—(1) Conservative Opinions are held by a large proportion of the people of England : (2) They are supported by very nearly one-half the members of the House of Commons : and (3) there is an *overwhelming* preponderance of Whig and Radical newspapers daily instilling the most mischievous ideas into all (but more particularly the working) classes. Can we doubt that the large circulation now enjoyed by many Whig-Radical papers, both London and Provincial, (the former especially,) is due to any other cause than that in too many instances Conservatives *habitually purchase these journals, to the exclusion of their own?* Our opponents do not act in this short-sighted and unprincipled manner. I think it may be asserted without fear of contradiction that no Radical supports the *Morning Herald*; that no Dissenter subscribes to the *Tablet*: and that no Romanist relies on the *Protestant Layman* for news. Oh, that Conservative Churchmen would take a little lesson of consistency from their opponents !

If Conservatives generally would only give a hearty support to their own newspapers, all cause for complaint would speedily vanish ; seeing that the *Developement of QUALITY and INFLUENCE depend on INCREASE of CIRCULATION.* The *Standard* and the *Times* are instances of the never-failing truth of this Rule: time was when both papers charged for 4 pages 7d. Now we can get 8 pages for 1d.—and 16 pages for 3d. respectively ; all because the daily circulation of each has increased from 5,000 to 50,000 or thereabouts.

---

* Perhaps this word is rather an equivocal one for use here. I desire to designate that large class of Englishmen who are in *theory* firm constitutionalists, opposers of democracy and organic change, not always exactly Tories, not always exactly Whigs.

The following extract admirably sets forth this point:—

" In proportion to their numbers, their means, and their position, neither the clergy nor the laity of the Church, by their subscriptions or their communications, afford that constant and substantial support to Church newspapers which Dissenters give to their organs. The consequence of this is, that beyond the affairs of their own parish, and in all the controversies and movements which affect the Church as a body, the majority of the members of the Church are much less informed, and less prepared to do their duty in such matters, than the majority of the Dissenters are in what concerns the special interest of their sect. It is the few, comparatively, who support Church newspapers and help them fight the Church's battles. The others take in *Punch,* or some other no-Church or anti-Church publication, and they occasionally *borrow* their neighbour's ·Church newspaper."

Conservative Churchmen in general, and Clergymen in particular, often betray great want of principle in their publishing arrangements. How many good sound works on political and religious matters have first seen light at the hands of Radical, Dissenting, and Infidel printers and publishers?

Not long since, a clergyman who wanted to publish a Reply to the *Essays and Reviews,* actually entrusted it to the publisher of that miserable book, instead of going to some orthodox Church bookseller. Another clerical work which lately came under my notice was issued by one of the Liberation Society's Agents.

Closely akin to, and equally to be reprehended with the foregoing, is the conduct of many Conservative Churchmen at Parochial and Parliamentary Elections. How many Church Rates have been lost,—how many seats have been lost, solely by the base and discreditable indolence of electors professing sound opinions, who were too lazy to walk across the road to put them in force, by recording their votes in the good cause?

Some again, in answer to remonstrance, say, " Oh! what good is my *one* vote?" wholly overlooking the fact that everything in the universe is made up of " one votes," of atoms, that is to say. History records many instances of the good and the harm done by these " one votes." It was " one vote " which led to Lord Melville's impeachment in 1805. It was " one vote " which paved the way for the advent to power of Sir Robert Peel, in 1841. Last, but not least, it was " one vote " which saved the Church her Church Rates for the session of 1862. If 30 more " one votes " had been forthcoming at the polling booths during the General Election of 1859, Lord Derby would not have been driven from office, and the Church might have been spared some at least of the assaults of the Dissenters, connived at by the Whigs, to which she has since been subjected in the House of Commons.

In the Registration Courts, Conservative Churchmen seldom appear to advantage; frequently, figure apart, do not appear at all. There are hundreds and thousands of Conservative Churchmen, possessing the requisite qualifications for Parliamentary votes in boroughs and counties, who are utterly heedless of the fact that the franchise is a sacred trust, to be exercised for the good of the community, and not simply a worthless privilege to be sought for and exercised, or the contrary, according as their *legs* dispose them. Sir R. Peel it was who said that the battle of the constitution must be fought in the Registration Courts, if it was to be fought properly or at all—words of solemn import.

The question of money is another on which great numbers of professing Churchmen seem all astray. They appear quite above the commonplace idea that the possession of wealth confers responsibility on its possessor. They have hundreds and thousands of pounds for spending in useless luxuries, but can only afford 1*l.* 1*s.* for this or that charitable object. Many Churchmen, however, who are inclined to spend their money, see no inconsistency, as they draw a cheque of 500*l.* for the new Church, in drawing at the same time another for perhaps 50*l.* for the new Meeting-house, the first sermon in which is more than likely to be in abuse of the Church or her Clergy, or both.

The instances which are too often met with of Churchmen subscribing to the funds of Dissenting Meeting-houses, are humiliating examples of the personal inconsistency of some professors. *Dissenters do not subscribe to build Churches*; very, very, very seldom at least, I suspect. Conservative Churchmen, as a body, are very backward in diving into their pockets for political objects. For the hundreds Churchmen subscribe for Church Defence purposes, the Dissenters put down thousands for Church Destruction purposes. Thus, the Liberation Society for destroying the Church as an Establishment, has an income more than three times as great as that of the Church Institution for defending the same (Office, 4 Trafalgar Square). *Some have spare time, but not spare funds; others have spare funds, but not spare time: if the latter did their duty, they would come forward ungrudgingly with their money, and then plenty of active and diligent workers, who would make good use of it, would be sure to offer themselves.*

Now for a few practical observations on organisation for Church Defence, as arising out of what has just been said.

The Church is now assailed by three classes of enemies : (1.) The Infidels who, disliking religion, dislike the Church because she is religious : (2.) The Voluntaries who disapprove of her connexion with State; and (3.) Those who are envious of her wealth and position. This latter class is more numerous than is commonly supposed. The Church is rich in worldly possessions (*given* to her by her pious and attached sons and daughters), but their own sects are poor and much in want of the same, and therefore they are jealous and wish to appropriate (steal) her property. However, these three classes of Englishmen, comprehending— (*Liberator*, Aug. 1862, p. 143)—" Independents, Baptists, United Presbyterians, Quakers, Unitarians, Wesleyan Methodists, Methodist Free Churchmen, and Primitive Methodists," have formed themselves into an Association whose grandiloquent title is, " The Society for the Liberation of Religion from State Patronage and Control," whose aim may be thus curtly expressed, TO DEPRIVE THE CHURCH OF ALL HER PROPERTY, AND TO DEGRADE HER TO THE POSITION OF A SECT.

The object of the Church Defence Movement is simply to counteract and defeat the revolutionary intrigues of the Dissenters, and their guiding star, the Liberation Society. This is the plainest way of stating what we are doing, and we ask help with *money,* and, if possible, with *influence* and *time.* Our opponents have at their disposal vast sums of money, no inconsiderable portion of the newspaper press, lecturers, paid and unpaid— in fact, a gigantic machinery for the dissemination of their opinions. If a seat in Parliament becomes vacant, the Liberation Society sets to work to try and secure the return of an anti-Church candidate ; if a Church-rate contest is impending in a parish, the Society supplies the enemies of the Church with tracts and bills, &c., to carry on the warfare : not unfrequently they send down lecturers to descant on the (supposed) hardships of having to pay these rates, and generally to abuse the Church and her system, setting forth at the same time the distinctive principles of their

Society. What I now insist upon in the most emphatic language possible is, that the attainment of these unconstitutional ends can only be prevented by Churchmen steadily resolving to meet the Dissenters with their own weapons, man for man, money for money, tract for tract, &c.

Let it not be for one moment fancied that these assaults on the Church of which I am speaking come from a small knot of insignificant politicians, destitute of anything but impudence. Such an idea is wholly the reverse of the truth. There are in England alone, hundreds of thousands of persons (comprising nearly all sectaries but Wesleyans) pledged by their teachers and preachers, and representatives in Parliament, to the total and unconditional subversion of the Established Church. Add to these, the numerous Irish Romanists hostile to the Irish branch of the United Church, and we get a large sum-total of enemies.

We have already seen that the Church is assaulted by the Dissenters not only with their money and influence, but with their pens and tongues.

I ask any rational Churchman possessing a particle of self-respect for himself or his Church, whether a limit of forbearance has not already been reached, beyond which it is not goodwill, but reprobation, which we may fairly pour down upon the Dissenters,—beyond which forbearance ceases to be laudable, and becomes culpable and cowardly?

The foregoing observations must have pointed out the propriety, nay, the necessity, of a Church Defence movement, such as that conducted by the Church Institution. The expense of carrying on adequately this movement is very great, and its promoters are most inconveniently crippled by want of funds. What they have they spend in the following, amongst other ways :—

(1.) The preparation and presentation of petitions to Parliament. N.B. The 20,000 Church Defence petitions sent up since 1860 have contributed in a large degree to the pleasing fact that hardly a single measure in the least hostile to the Church has passed into law since the movement was begun. (2.) The whipping up of friendly members, and the canvassing of doubtful and hostile members, in relation to impending divisions in Parliament. (3.) The publication of circulars and handbills calculated to explain aggressive proposals, and so warn friends. (4.) The holding of public meetings, setting forth to the ignorant and apathetic the dangers which menace the Church, &c. &c.

It is not easy to define in so many words what is required to be done, but any person at all conversant with the working of an organised system of public agency will readily comprehend that money, in greater or less abundance, is absolutely and indispensably necessary for duly carrying on the same. Half-an-hour spent at the office in Trafalgar Square during the height of the Parliamentary session will do more to enlighten a stranger than many pages of written explanation. During a particular week in February 1861, 80,000 circulars (chiefly on the Church Rates Abolition Bill) were sent out from the office, which there is every reason to believe contributed largely to the ultimate rejection of the Bill; and we may say, *ex uno disce omnes*. Up to the end of 1865, it had issued 520,000 publications — a fact alone proving that it has not been idle.

Unless Churchmen put their hands into their pockets and pull out plenty of money, the *temporalities* of the Church are irretrievably lost; nothing but a bountiful supply of the "sinews of war" will enable us to withstand the combined attacks of Dissenters, Romanists, Secularists, *et hoc genus omne.* It is a matter for great thankfulness that so much good has already been done; but the work done bears a very small proportion to that in store for us. The separation of Church and State is the *great* question which is *coming.*

Let me entreat every reader of this forthwith to constitute *himself* (or herself) a local Church Institution, and diligently to canvass his friends for money, asking for five shillings here, one shilling there, ten shillings here, half-a-crown there, according as he thinks the parties he is addressing can afford to give. It is hardly to be credited what large sums may be obtained in a short time by unflagging energy and determination in collecting isolated small sums. INDIVIDUAL EXERTIONS is the point I wish to enforce on all.

Work! work! work! ought to be the golden rule of every loyal and consistent Churchman. Nothing short of extraordinary exertion will suffice to meet an extraordinary danger. Above all, let it be remembered that 1*l. now* is worth 3*l.* paid three years hence.

It is a grave reproach to our professing friends that they are so indifferent about this money question. How little sovereigns are grudged for luxury and finery on the part of many who "cannot afford" more than a shilling (sometimes nothing at all) for the preservation of that for which, if once lost, a substitute could never be found,—the National Church of England! The enemy are clamouring at the gates: take warning, O ye English Churchmen and English Churchwomen, ere it is too late, and they get within the fortress!

Always distrust persons who wish you every success, &c. &c., but who, when pointedly asked to give their time or their money to a good cause, begin to make excuses. The principles of such persons are not worth much.

As a concluding remark, I would say that so long as PROFESSORS are not ACTORS, neither the Church nor the cause of Constitutional Conservatism can flourish as they ought in England.

APPENDIX TO BOOK VII.

A protest against certain current misnomers may not be inappropriate here. "Why not call things by their right names?" is a very necessary question just now. In the good old days of our forefathers, there used to be Meeting-houses, Conventicles, Sectaries, Schisms, and Schismatics, Now, matters are changed for the worse, thanks chiefly to callous Churchmen. Meeting-houses have risen into "Chapels" and "Churches;" Sectaries into "Dissenters" and "Free Churchmen;" a Teacher and Preacher of Schism into "Dissenting Minister" and a "Dissenting *Clergyman.*" John Stiggins's *Ana*baptist meeting-house has become the "Baptist *Church*; Minister, the *Rev.* John Stiggins." It now rests with Churchmen to repudiate these cool assumptions of the Clerical style, that love of aping the Church which characterises all forms of Dissent in the present day, but a special repudiation should be bestowed on that insulting gimcrack toast, "The Bishop and Clergy of all denominations." Catholic and Protestant are two words excessively misused; English Churchmen are all Catholics and ought always to be Protestants in the sense of *protesting* against the errors of Rome *and schism,* but the fashion of dubbing all Romanists "Catholics," and all Anglicans "Protestants," is a very misleading and objectionable one.

Book VIII.

The Roman Catholic Question.

Part I.—WHAT SAITH HOLY SCRIPTURE?

It is here proposed simply to place in juxta-position certain texts of the Bible and certain doctrines of the Romish Church for the purpose of showing the antagonism existing between the latter and the former.

1.—*Celibacy of the Clergy.*

St. Matthew viii. 14.—"And when Jesus was come into Peter's house, he saw his wife's mother laid and sick of a fever."

We learn from this passage that St. Peter, reputed to have been the first bishop of Rome, had a wife. If there is one man more than another whom Roman Catholics profess to revere, it is the Apostle Peter, yet his example if followed would countenance the marriage of the clergy.

I. *Corinthians* ix. 5.—"Have we not power to lead about a sister, a wife, as well as other apostles, and as the brethren of the Lord and Cephas?"

Some subtle Romanists attempt to get over this passage by saying that "wife" in the A.V. is a perversion, the original word signifying no more than "woman." That the Greek word bears this meaning is quite true, but it is a *suppressio veri* not to say that "wife" is one of its usual meanings. Not the least noticeable feature about this quotation is the writer's allusion to St. Peter's wife, previously spoken of by St. Matthew.

I. *Timothy* iii. 2.—"A bishop then must be blameless, the husband of one wife."
Hebrews xiii. 4.—"Marriage is honourable *in all*."

It may therefore be asserted in the most decided manner that the compulsory celibacy of the clergy is one of the most unscriptural of all the dogmas of the Church of Rome. From *Acts* xxi. 9, we learn that St. Philip the Evangelist had a wife, and St. Ambrose tells us that all the Apostles save SS. John and Paul had wives. In *Acts* xviii. it is expressly stated that Aquila, a well known Apostolic preacher, had a wife.

"Siricius, who according to Dufresnoy died in the year 399, was the first pope that forbade the marriage of the clergy; but it is probable that this prohibition was but little regarded, as the celibacy of the clergy seems not to have been completely established till the papacy of Gregory

VII. at the end of the eleventh century; and even then it was loudly complained of by many writers. The history of the following centuries abundantly proves the bad effects of this abuse of Church power."— (*Bp. Tomline.*)

2.—*Public Worship in an unknown tongue.*

1. *Corinthians* xiv. 2-19.—"He that speaketh in an unknown tongue *speaketh not unto men,* but unto God; for no man understandeth him . . . In the church I had rather speak five words with my understanding, that by my voice I might teach others also, than ten thousand words in an unknown tongue."

If ever words had any meaning attached to them these have, in condemnation of the Prayers of the Romish Church being in Latin. As Burkitt well remarks, the Apostle pleads in particularly strong terms the necessity of all public offices of religion being performed in a language known and understood by all the congregation, and the impiety and absurdity of the contrary practice is very manifest.

3.—*Worship of the Virgin Mary.*

St. Matthew iv. 10.—"It is written, thou shalt worship the Lord thy God, and *him only* shalt thou serve."

It is difficult to conceive how any Christian with a Bible in his hands can reconcile this, and the numerous texts akin to it, with adoration of the Virgin Mary. A well-educated Romanist once endeavoured to make me believe that they only worshipped the Blessed Virgin in the same sense that the word is used in our marriage service and elsewhere, that of *respect* or esteem; but this was an obvious falsehood. That there is no special warning against this error to be found in the New Testament may well be explained on the assumption that such Divine adoration as Romanists uphold is too palpably a violation of the whole spirit of both Testaments to require special notice. And much the same holds good with another *modern* Romish blasphemy, the Immaculate Conception of the Virgin Mary. It is for Romanists to prove the affirmative rather than for us to prove the negative. The best way of meeting a Romanist is to challenge him—"What saith the Scripture?" and then he must be silenced. The doctrine of the immaculate conception was not invented till the middle of the *twelfth* century, hence it is that a general condemnation of it is all that is provided, *e.g.* "All have sinned and come short of the glory of God." Our Saviour Christ *alone* had an immaculate conception. No Romanist can prove the contrary, that is, that any one else that ever lived was conceived without sin.

3.—*The Assumption of the Virgin Mary.*

This is one of the numerous fables of the Romish Church concerning which Holy Scripture and Church History alike are silent. The story goes (and the story seems fabricated to extenuate her worship) that she was miraculously carried up into heaven, to which some apocryphal accounts add, that she had previously risen from the dead.

4.—*The doctrine of Seven Sacraments.*

In common with all branches of the Catholic Church, the Church of Rome recognises the two Sacraments of Baptism and the Lord's Supper; but to these she adds, *without any Scriptural authority,* five others (so-called)—viz. Confirmation, Matrimony, Holy Orders, Penance, and Extreme Unction.   The Anglican Church recognises in the first three, solemn ordinances agreeable to Holy Scripture, but she rightly refuses to place them on the same level as Baptism and the Lord's Supper.   The other two are mere ceremonies, of which the latter is absolutely unscriptural.

Romanists found their doctrine of Extreme Unction on *St. Mark* vi. 13, and *James* v. 14, but a little reflection will show the weakness of such a basis of argument. " In both cases the anointing with oil is expressly connected with the *healing* of those anointed.   Extreme Unction, on the contrary, is an anointing administered to a *dying* person when there is no hope of his recovery.   This discrepancy between the anointing of the apostolic times and the anointing practised by the Church of Rome is so glaring that some of the ablest Romish controversialists have been obliged to acknowledge that Extreme Unction is founded on Church authority, and not on the authority of Scripture."—(*Ryle.*)

5.—*Refusal of the Cup to the Laity.*

I. *Corinthians* xi. 25-6.—Jesus "took the cup, when he had supped, saying, This cup is the new testament in my blood: this do ye, as oft as ye drink it, in remembrance of me.   For as often as ye eat this bread, and drink this cup, ye do shew the Lord's death till he come."

It is important to observe that the apostle is addressing the whole Corinthian Church, clergy as well as laity, and beyond any question the cup was intended for both alike ; or had it been otherwise the restriction would have been expressed, not left to be inferred.

"It appears from the unanimous testimony of the Fathers, and from all the ancient rituals and liturgies, that the Sacrament of the Lord's Supper was, in the early ages of the Church, administered in both kinds as well to the laity as to the clergy.   The practice of denying the cup to the laity arose out of the doctrine of Transubstantiation.   The belief that the sacramental bread and wine were actually converted into the body and blood of Christ naturally produced, in a weak and superstitious age, an anxious fear lest any part of them should be lost or wasted.   To prevent anything of this kind in the bread, small wafers were used, which were put at once into the mouths of the communicants by the officiating ministers ; but no expedient could be devised to guard against the occasional spilling of the wine in administering it to large congregations.   The bread was sopped in the wine, and the wine was conveyed by tubes into the mouth, but all in vain ; accidents still happened, and therefore it was determined that the priests should entirely withhold the cup from the laity.   It is to be supposed that a change of this sort in so important an ordinance as that of the Lord's Supper could not be effected at once.   The first attempt seems to have been made in the 12th century ; it was gradually submitted to, and was at last established by the authority of the Council of Constance in 1414 ; but in their decree they acknowledged that ' Christ did institute this sacrament of both kinds, and that the faithful in the primitive Church did receive both kinds ; yet a practice being reasonably introduced to avoid some dangers and scandals, they appoint the custom to continue of consecrating in both kinds, and of giving to the laity only in one kind,'—thus presuming to depart from the positive command of our Lord respecting the manner of administering the sign of the covenant between himself and mankind.   From that time it has been the invariable practice of the Church of Rome to confine the cup to the priests. And it was again admitted at the Council of Trent that the Lord's Supper was formerly administered in both kinds to all communicants, but it was openly contended that the Church had power to make the alteration, and that they had done it for weighty and just causes."—(*Bishop Tomline.*)

" There is not any one of all the controversies that we have with the Church of Rome in which the decision seems more easy and shorter than this. And as there is not any one in which she has acted more visibly contrary to the Gospel than in this; so there is not any one that has raised higher prejudices against her, that has made more forsake her, and has possessed mankind more against her, than this. This has cost her dearer than any other."—(*Bishop Burnet.*)

6.—*The Books of the Apocrypha not Canonical.*

By no section of the Apostolic Church were the books of the Apocrypha regarded as a portion of the canonical Scriptures or employed (to quote St. Jerome's words) " to confirm the authority of the Church's doctrines." They were properly looked upon as human compositions, from which, however, some good might be got. They are neither cited nor mentioned by any of the inspired writers of the New Testament. Neither do Philo or Josephus make any allusion to them at all, much less to their being genuine "oracles of God." Yet, in spite of all this, the Council of Trent boldly and unblushingly affirmed them to be of equal authority with the inspired books always received by the Church without dispute.

7.—*Justification by Meritorious Works.*

Romans iii. 28.—" Therefore we conclude that a man is justified by faith."
St. James ii. 17.—" Even so faith, if it hath not works, is dead, being alone."

Faith and works go hand in hand, the latter arising out of the former ; but the Church of Rome has decreed that good works " are truly meritorious towards obtaining eternal life." "As this doctrine of the merit of good works is one of the most arrogant and scandalous of the corruptions of the Romish Church, so it is one of the most modern, having never been generally in that Church itself before it was settled by the Council of Trent (in 1546)."—(*Dr. Nicholls.*)

8.—*Works of Supererogation.*

St. Luke xvii. 10.—"So likewise ye, when ye have done all those things which are commanded you, say, We are unprofitable servants: we have done that which was our duty to do."

In the face of this, the Church of Rome asserts that there are such things as " good works not commanded by Christ," but recommended to the consideration of the faithful. The Church of England speaks thus in her XIVth Article :—" Voluntary works besides over and above God's commandments, which they call works of supererogation, cannot be taught without arrogancy and impiety, for by them do men declare that they not only render unto God as much as they are bound to do, but that they do more for his sake than of bounden duty is required." Bishop Tomline justly characterises the above cited text as so clear and decisive that it is unnecessary to explain or enforce it.

9.—*Mortal and Venial Sins.*

St. James ii. 10.—"Whosoever shall keep the whole law, and yet offend in one point, is guilty of all."
Romans vi. 23.—"The wages of sin is death."

"The error of the Romanist is this—that he makes the two classes of sin ['mortal' and 'venial'] to differ not only in enormity and degree, which we admit to be the case, *but also in their nature and kind*. No amount of venial sins, according to Bellarmine, would ever make a mortal sin."—(*Dean Hook.*)

In point of fact, the Church of Rome says that 'some sins are mistakenly so called; they are not really sins, and in nowise endanger the salvation of souls.' The glaring antagonism between this notion and St. James's statement requires not to be pointed out.

10.—*Purgatory.*

Ecclesiastes ix. 5-6.—"The dead know not any thing, neither have they any more a reward; for the memory of them is forgotten. Also their love, and their hatred, and their envy, is now perished; neither have they any more a portion for ever in anything done under the sun."

Cardinal Bellarmine thus explains what Purgatory is:—"Purgatory is a certain place in which, as in a prison, the souls are purged *after* this life, which were not fully purged *in* this life; to wit, so that they may be able to enter into heaven, where no unclean thing is." In other words, there is no pressing necessity for repentance on earth! The Council of Trent declared that—"There is a purgatory, and that the souls detained there are helped by the suffrages of the faithful, but principally by the sacrifices of the acceptable altar."

St. John v. 24 is a striking refutation of Bellarmine's words. See also Bishop Beveridge's able reasoning, cited in Hook's *Church Dictionary*, art. "Purgatory."

11.—*Indulgences.*

Indulgences are (so-called) pardons for sin invented by Pope Urban II., as incentives to persons to join the Crusades for the recovery of Palestine; subsequently they became *purchaseable* at certain prices, proportioned to the enormity of the special sin requiring pardon, *as estimated by the Romish authorities*. Many of these can only be obtained from the Pope himself, at Rome. A pardon for having been a heretic costs 36*l.* 9*s.* of our money; but a Romanist murdering a man will be let off for 7*s.* 6*d.* A pardon for perjury is sold for 9*s.*; one for robbery for 12*s.* Of all the blasphemous assumptions of the Church of Rome, few surpass in iniquity this one of pretending to power to forgive sins, which rests in God alone. In I. *St. John* i. 9, we are told that it is God who "cleanseth us from all unrighteousness," emphatically disproving the existence of any human power of efficacious absolution. The decisive passage in *Isaiah* lv. 1 can hardly fail to come into the mind—"Ho, every one that thirsteth, come ye to the waters, and *he that hath no money*; come ye, buy, and, eat; yea, come, buy wine and milk *without money* and without price." The most obtuse mind could scarcely venture to say that this does not refer to spiritual things—salvation for endangered souls. The case of Simon Magus (*Acts* viii. 18) ought to be till the end of time a decisive refutation of the very idea of *buying* remission of sin.

12.—*Image Worship.*

Exodus xx. 4–5.—"Thou shalt not make unto thee any graven image. . . . Thou shalt not bow down thyself to them."

In this matter the Romish Church has thoroughly paganised herself; and we may regard image worship as one of her most flagrant breaches of Divine law. The apologists of images commonly shelter themselves under the plea that they do not really adore the images, but merely employ them as reminders of duty. This, whether true or false, is anyhow repugnant to the aphorism of St. John—" Little children, keep yourselves from idols" (I. *St. John* v. 21). A thing of this kind, set on foot with the best of motives, frequently lays the foundation for grievous abuse, as in fact has been the case in this matter. Images were not authoritatively adopted into the Romish Church till the second Council of Nice, 787 A.D.

13.—*Relics.*

The worship of relics, now an article of faith in the Romish Church, is a corruption closely akin to that condemned in the previous section, though if anything it is a trifle more absurd, revolting, and idolatrous. It is a further exemplification of what may arise from a lawful thing unlawfully indulged in. About the 4th century, we find beginning to spring up an excessive love and veneration for things which had belonged to distinguished professors of the Christian faith; especially such things as their garments, and even their hair, bones, &c. Gradually these relics came to be regarded as something more than curious and interesting remains of bygone times. Monks carried them about for show and pecuniary gain, and thence the successive steps of reverence and absolute worship were not long postponed. This climax was consummated by the Council of Trent, 1562, recording a solemn curse against all who impugned the doctrine of relic worship.

14.—*Invocation of Saints.*

I. *Timothy* ii. 5.—"For there is . . . one mediator between God and men, the man Christ Jesus."

Ephesians ii. 18.—"Through him we both have access by one Spirit unto the Father."

Colossians ii. 18.—"Let no man beguile you of your reward in a voluntary humility and worshipping of angels."

The Invocation of Saints is an error which arose in the Church of Rome, almost contemporaneously with that of veneration of relics. The early Christians instituted commemorations of saints, which were harmless enough in themselves, but after the lapse of time it became customary to deliver public orations to celebrate their virtues; then they were addressed in formal apostrophes, and urged to use their influence with God in heaven; till finally, their intercession was directly prayed for. This stage was reached about the 5th century, and the Council of Trent confirmed the custom as a proper one by decreeing that "all men are to be condemned who do not own that the saints reigning with Christ offer their prayers to God for men; and that it is useful to invoke them, to procure their assistance in asking God for blessings through Christ." In the present day, the impiety is carried to extreme lengths. Not long since there appeared in some of the newspapers a long litany imploring a number of saints (so called), whose names were given, to intercede with God for the perversion of England to the Romish Faith ! !

15.—*Transubstantiation.*

Perhaps the most erroneous of all the errors of the Church of Rome is that with which I conclude this section—Transubstantiation. "The idea of Christ's bodily presence in the Eucharist was first started in the beginning of the 8th century, and it owed its rise to the indiscretion of preachers and writers of warm imaginations, who, instead of explaining judiciously the lofty figures of Scripture language upon this subject, understood and urged them in the literal sense. Thus the true meaning of these expressions was grossly perverted; but as this conceit seemed to exalt the nature of the Holy Sacrament, it was eagerly received in that ignorant and superstitious age; and was by degrees carried farther and farther by persons still less guarded in their application of these metaphorical phrases. This has always been a favourite doctrine of the Church of Rome, as it impressed the common people with higher notions of the power of the clergy, and therefore seemed to increase their influence."—(*Bp. Tomline.*)

In arguing against this doctrine, we may first observe that it is utterly repugnant to our physical senses, since we see and taste the bread and the wine after the consecration, and know that they are still only bread and wine. Again, the circumstances of the institution, if the Gospel narratives convey a just account of it (which of course they do), forbid any such supposition as that the Apostles were presented with material flesh and blood, to say nothing of the fact that they were forbidden to drink blood by the Mosaic law, which regulated at that time not only their actions but those of their Divine Master. Romanists, not great adepts at quoting Scripture, profess to base their doctrine on the well-known "Hoc est corpus meum" (*St. Matt.* xxvi. 26—"This is my body"), wilfully blind to the obvious necessity of interpreting this and other kindred expressions figuratively and typically: but with those who profess such reverence for authority and traditions, it surely ought to suffice that this doctrine was never broached till the pontificate of Gregory III. Its final confirmation was as late as the Lateran Council of 1215 A.D. That the figurative interpretation was the only one accepted by the primitive Church we learn from the writings of more than twenty fathers, without a single testimony on the other side.

Two Scripture passages may be noted as disproving any such doctrine as Transubstantiation. In *St. Matt.* xxvi. 29, our Saviour, *after the consecration* of the elements, speaks of "this *fruit of the vine*": on the Romish view he ought to have said *this blood*. Again, St. Paul, in I. *Cor.* xi. 26, says: "As often as ye eat this *bread* and drink this cup, ye do show [or commemorate] the Lord's death till he come." The Roman Catholic ceremonies of elevating and adoring the Host are entirely human figments, and the fact that the whole doctrine did not rise up till nearly 700 years after Christ's departure from the earth, ought to prove to every rational being that it is a human fabrication, wholly destitute of the slightest foundation in apostolic authority.

The foregoing will serve to point out some of the worst departures of the Romish Church from the pure Christian Faith and Word of God, and may be found useful for impressing on one's mind a feeling of thankfulness for the purity of the Church of England.

PART II.—REFLECTIONS ON THE POLITICAL ASPECTS OF ROMANISM IN ENGLAND.

THE Reformed Church numbers among its assailants few so active and uncompromising as the Romanists, of whom I now propose to speak, in the hopes of persuading some at least of my readers, that fraternisation with Popery on the part of English Churchmen is the height of folly.

The following Romish opinions are sufficiently candid to be worth an extended circulation :—

"If ever there was a land in which work is to be done, and perhaps much to suffer, it is here. I shall not say too much, if I say that we have to subjugate and subdue, to conquer and rule, an imperial race; we have to do with a will which reigns throughout the world as the will of old Rome reigned once: we have to bend or break that will which nations and kingdoms have found invincible and inflexible. . . . . Were heresy [*i.e.* Protestantism] conquered in England, it would be conquered throughout the world. All its lines meet here, and therefore in England the Church of God must be gathered in its strength."—(Rev. Dr. MANNING in the *Tablet,* August 6, 1859.)

" The [Roman] Catholic Church is getting to feel its true dignity and right position in this country. What we of course aim at, in God's good time and way, is to be, as we have once been, *the dominant Church of England.* We had gradually, under the pressure of the penal laws, forgotten our place in the world as God's only Church; we had been snubbed so successfully, that we thought it gain even to make common cause with the sects of yesterday [Dissenters], and, pinning ourselves to their sleeve to get, if it might be, a share in the poor pickings of concession which, with mighty professions and small fruit, were from time to time vouchsafed to us. What can have led [Roman] Catholics to detach themselves from *this ignoble, though profitable, alliance,* except a growing consciousness of their true strength and nobility?"—(Rev. F. OAKELEY in the *Tablet,* May 14, 1859.)

" You ask, if the Roman Catholic were lord in the land, and you were in a minority, if not in numbers yet in power, what would he do to you? That, we say, would entirely depend upon circumstances. If it would benefit the cause of Catholicism, he would tolerate you; if expedient, he would imprison you, banish you, fine you; possibly he might even hang you. But be assured of one thing—he would never tolerate you for the sake of the 'glorious principles of civil and religious liberty.' . . . .

" Shall I hold out hopes to the Protestant that I will not meddle with his creed, if he will not meddle with mine? Shall I lead him to think that religion is a matter for private opinion, and tempt him to think that he has no more right to his religious views than he has to my purse, or my house, or my life-blood? No! [Roman] Catholicism is the most intolerant of creeds. It is intolerance itself, for it is truth itself. We might as rationally maintain that a sane man has a right to believe that two and two do not make four, as this theory of religious liberty. Its impiety is only equalled by its absurdity."—(*Rambler* [Romish magazine], September 1851.)

Pure and unadulterated treason is freely indulged in by many Romanists, both in this country and in Ireland. Let one specimen suffice. When it was generally expected that the Emperor of the French contemplated an invasion of England, the *Tablet,* in a leading article, wrote :—

"It will be the most popular act of his life. He will have every Frenchman on his side, with the unconcealed sympathies of every nation in the world. When he sets out upon his campaign on English soil, he need fear no secret societies or insurrections at home; he will be hailed as the avenger of nations, and as the scourge of a race that is unpopular wherever it is known. We have the great honour of uniting against ourselves the good wishes of all people, and that will be no pleasant recollection when the French are seen upon our soil."—(July 16, 1859.)

There are probably few newspaper readers who cannot call to mind analogous instances, in the shape of altar denunciations, &c.; and the tampering with the law continually practised by the Romish Clergy in Ireland at elections and elsewhere, is a matter of too common notoriety to require further allusion here. Since these pages were prepared for the press, no less a man than Mr. J. A. Roebuck, M.P., has publicly declared in his place in the House of Commons (February 17, 1866), and amidst the applause of the assembled members, that the Irish Roman Catholic priests "have taught the people to hate the English name, and that for years they have been preaching sedition." The kidnapping of children may also be included under this head.

Admitting these evils, we may go on to ask, *What is the cause,* and *what is the remedy?*

The cause is to be found in the unfaithfulness of English Churchmen in days gone by. The Emancipation Act of 1829, and the Maynooth and " Godless " Colleges' Acts of 1845, were three of the most mischievous enactments which were ever placed on the statute-book. The evils resulting from the Emancipation Act are thus graphically expressed by one of its avowed *supporters* : —

" It is only due to the memory of men who underwent much obloquy for the time, and were even treated with a peculiar and galling kind of contempt not usual in English political warfare, to ask ourselves, after an experience of just thirty years—Which side was in the right? Have the results been in accordance with the sanguine anticipation of Canning, of Mackintosh, of Grey, and of Brougham? or has the measure turned out as was predicted by Lord Eldon— 'that hater of all that was liberal and pleasant'—and by Lord Winchelsea, at whose tirades we have all laughed so heartily? There is, unhappily, no doubt about it; the genius, the liberality, and the eloquence were wrong; the narrowness, the bigotry, and the prejudice were right. Ever since the day of deliverance, the conduct of the Roman Catholics has more and more confirmed the predictions of their enemies, more and more disappointed the anticipations of their friends. On abstract grounds it was right to give them political power; but it would be childish to deny that we have raised up among ourselves a party which is neither Liberal nor Conservative, neither English nor Irish, which holds its allegiance to a foreign Power paramount to its allegiance to its domestic Sovereign ; which is the decided, if not the declared enemy of knowledge and enlightenment; which seeks to widen and render more intense its isolation from the rest of the community, and to make the divisions of society and the common intercourse of life strictly co-extensive with its religious belief. . . . . Where, but in a Roman Catholic meeting, presided over by a Bishop, and harangued by Deans and Canons, could the name of the Queen be received with a burst of disapprobation which rendered the speaker inaudible, from the very voices which yelled out a determination to fight for the Pope?

. . . . " There is no divided allegiance, as was apprehended. The allegiance is wholly given to one person, and nothing is left for the Queen but yells of disapprobation, and the accusation of having starved two millions of her subjects. . . . . They [the Roman Catholics] must be content to accept the most desponding predictions of Lord Eldon as less than true, and to be regarded by the world as holding their liberties, in spite of their own slavish tenets, by the free will and grace of the people and the Sovereign whom they libel, as the only friends of despotism in the land of freedom, and the only partisans of ignorance in an age of enlightened progress."—(*Times,* Dec. 13, 1859.)

The injurious influence of this Act and the Maynooth Act is still being felt by the Reformed Faith generally, and the English Church in particular. So far from satisfying the Romish party, they have only been stimulated to greater demands, which successive Whig Ministries, anxious to catch a few Romish votes in Parliament, have unhesitatingly, though, perhaps, reluctantly, given in to. The progress made by the Romish party in England and Scotland is hardly to be conceived without the aid of statistics ; thus : —

	1829.	1860.	1861.	1865.
Clergy	447	1342	1388	1521
Chapels, &c.	449	993	1019	1132
Monasteries	0	47	50	58
Convents	0	155	162	201
Colleges	2	12	12	12

Between 1853 and 1860 the number of Romish Army Chaplains was increased from 85 to 160, and the salaries from 2702*l.* to 8093*l.*

The amount annually paid out of the Imperial Exchequer towards the sustentation of the most intolerant Church on earth, and one of the Church of England's bitterest foes, amounts to the enormous sum of 385,462*l.*, according to the return for 1864. Can it then be wondered at that Popery is making the rapid strides it is ? that the throne, and all that civil and religious liberty which every Englishman holds to be his birthright, is endangered ? Romanism upraises itself everywhere ; even our most gracious Sovereign's household is infested with it : its numerical strength in high places is considerable, and, under Lord Palmerston's auspices, increased rapidly. Romish Bishops arrogate to themselves territorial titles, in open defiance of the Ecclesiastical Titles Act, and members of the Government look on silently and complacently, and in many matters actually encourage the party. Thus, in 1859 an order was issued by the Poor-law Board [its Secretary being a Dissenter !] giving, in effect, to the Romish Clergy power to enter at all times into our workhouses. The good feeling of the country was successfully aroused, prompt organisation was resorted to, and in consequence of the vigorous opposition the order met with, the Government gave way, by admitting that it was only to be held permissory. Great vigilance is necessary, as the Romish party are as warm about the matter as ever.

A few sessions ago a Bill was introduced into the House of Commons by a professing member of the Church of England (and a Whig), to throw open to Romanists several high offices of State from which they are now debarred. This, and several others of a similarly aggressive character, was defeated ; but further efforts are certain to be made when a favourable moment offers itself. A Bill carried by Sir G. Grey, on behalf of the Government, for the appointment of salaried Romish Chaplains for prisons is one of the latest innovations we have witnessed ; and it was followed up by something almost as objectionable—the elevation to the English Bench of Mr. Serjeant Shee, the well-known Romish barrister.

I have thus pointed out certain evils, and the *cause* is the flagrant inconsistency of English Churchmen in patronising Popery individually, and collectively, through the Government. The *remedy* is :—The unconditional repeal of all statutes conferring on Roman Catholics anything more than the right to worship God according to their own forms, uninterfered with by any body, beginning with the *Maynooth Grant*. A great many Churchmen, Members of Parliament, and others, oppose the repeal of this iniquitous endowment, believing that by so doing they should be violating a compact. If this were really the case, it *might* be unfair to meddle with it. A compact *was* made, it is true, but only for 20 years after the union of Ireland with England in 1801. That time expired in 1821 ; from that year till 1845 the money was paid by an annual vote of the House of Commons as a voluntary gift from England to Ireland. Then, in 1845, an unprincipled Minister carried a Bill for the permanent endowment of the college with some 26,000*l.* a-year. These are the simple historical facts of the question. The Maynooth Grant was originally instituted with this idea—that Irish Romanists would have Romish Clergy ; Romish Clergy would be educated. If they were not educated at home, they would be abroad, and many bad foreign ideas would be superadded to their education ; therefore (argued expediency statesmen), it is better for us English Churchmen to pay the expenses, as the lesser evil. In point of fact, however, the Roman Catholic population of Ireland has so largely fallen off that Maynooth educates not only Clergy for Ireland, but for many of the Colonies. The mischief brought about by St. Patrick's College is thus cosmopolitan, not local. A State professing the Reformed Catholic Faith is a party to the wholesale propagation of "damnable heresy." Roman Catholics are not conciliated by it, and Reformed Catholics cannot reasonably be expected to desist from agitation till the political blot is removed.

It is impossible to set forth in a small compass a tithe of the evils arising from the latitudinarian spirit of the age in reference to Popery. Some cannot see, and others will not see, and so the mischief increases. There ever will exist real antagonism between the Anglican and Roman Churches so long as the latter presents itself as it now does in Christendom; and what is wanted more than anything else in the present day is high-principled, consistent recognition of the fact that Popery is in its essence a sworn enemy to most things that Englishmen hold dear.

APPENDIX TO BOOK VIII.

PROTEST AGAINST THE MAYNOOTH BILL.

The following admirable Protest from the late Archbishop (Sumner) of Canterbury and other members of the House of Peers was recorded twenty years ago against the third reading of the Maynooth Bill. It has lost none of its truth and logical power since; and can more forcible arguments than it contains be now wanted for the continuance of opposition to the Endowment of Maynooth, and for protests and petitions against the national iniquity and dishonour which are involved in the maintenance, out of the public purse, of that seminary of Jesuit propagandism:—

"DISSENTIENT:

"1. Because I hold it to be contradictory to the first principles of the Reformation to provide for the establishment of an order of men to be educated for the express purpose of resisting and defeating that Reformation—men whose office and main duty it will be to disseminate and perpetuate those very corruptions of the Christian faith which the Church of England has solemnly abjured, and some of which the whole legislature of England has declared to be superstitious and idolatrous.

"2. Because the most unbounded toleration of religious error does not require us to provide for the maintenance and growth of that error, but rather imposes upon us a strong obligation to prevent by all just and peaceful means its increase, and to discourage its continuance.

"3. Because this measure has a tendency to raise in the public mind a belief that religious truth is a matter of indifference to the State; and by consequence to subvert that principle of succession to the throne which is the title of the present dynasty, and which forms an integral and essential part of the constitution of this kingdom."

The signatures appended were those of the Bishops of Cashel, Chester, Llandaff, London, and Winchester, and of the Earls of Cadogan, Clancarty, and Winchelsea.—(*Times*, June 19, 1845.)

PAPAL AVERSION TO THE BIBLE.

The following remarkable "*Extract from a despatch addressed by Mr. Odo Russell to the Earl of Clarendon, dated Rome, Feb. 8, 1866,*" has been lately issued from the Foreign Office:—

"Travellers visiting the Pope's dominions should be very careful not to bring forbidden books or Colt's revolvers with them, the Custom House officers having strict orders to confiscate them. . . . Forbidden books are those condemned by the Congregation of the Index. . . . But, above all, travellers should be careful *not to bring English, Italian, or other Bibles with them,* THE BIBLE BEING STRICTLY PROHIBITED."

Here we see Popery in its true colours, as the bitter, uncompromising, malevolent foe to God's Word.

Book IX

Brief Notes on the Prophetical Portions of the Books of Daniel and the Apocalypse.

The following notes are in no sense whatever original: they are derived from the concurrent testimony of the Christian Church in all ages, and are designed more to suggest reflection and encourage inquiry, than to do over again what has already been often done—unfold an elaborate train of argument. To save space, the scriptural quotations will not be set out at length, and no references to authorities will be given; it must suffice, therefore, to say that they are chiefly the following:—Newton, Elliott, Bickersteth, Wordsworth, Mant, and Barnes. The reader is, in all cases, supposed to have read the verses before perusing the notes, otherwise the latter may appear involved, and, at times, ungrammatical.

Daniel vii. 3. These represent 4 powerful kingdoms which were to arise in succession on the earth.

Verse 4. The union of the attributes of the lion and of the eagle denotes the combination of great power with great activity: the plucking of the wings points to a curtailment of the power; and finally, the human transformation foreshadows a civilising or taming result.

Commentators are very generally agreed that this beast signifies the Chaldæan monarchy, and the changes it underwent under a succession of weak rulers.

Verse 5. The bear typifies cunning and ferocity; and "devouring much flesh" means conquering many nations.

The Medo-Persian monarchy is here referred to. The Medes and Persians were a fierce and unpolished race, and the bear is an apt symbol for them. The 3 ribs may incidentally refer to the constituent kingdoms—Media, Persia, and Lydia—which formed Cyrus's empire 544 B.C.

Verse 6. Fierceness and strength are symbolised. The 4 wings point to a large and rapid range: the 4 heads specify its being a power, which was afterwards to become severed into 4 smaller powers.

The Macedonian empire is spoken of. The extent and grandeur of Alexander the Great's conquests are well known: it is equally well known that at his death, his dominions underwent a quadripartite division amongst 4 of his generals. The spots on the leopard *may* have some reference to the great number of the nations who owned Alexander's sway.

Verse 7. General expressions of power, foreshadowing an empire of extreme territorial rapacity.

The application is to the Roman empire, celebrated for its mighty power. The 10 horns point to 10 smaller kingdoms which were to arise out of it when it was destroyed.

Verse 8. The language here points to the developement at some future period, after the beast acquired its 10-horned form, of a new feature which should gradually rise into a new power, absorbing 3 of the existing ones. The eyes denote intelligence, intellectual ability. The concluding clause explains itself; arrogance, &c.

Verse 11. The final overthrow of the 4th beast, on account of the blasphemies of the 11th horn, is here described.

Verse 12. The general notion which this verse would seem intended to convey is, that the 3 first beasts would be superseded without any general convulsion, and would escape that ruthless destruction with which the 4th beast would be *consumed when its 11th-horn phase became matured.* It did in fact happen that the Babylonian, Medo-Persian, and Macedonian monarchies disappeared quietly from the page of history.

Verses 19–21. It need merely be mentioned further that the "look more stout than his fellows" (20) denotes that the authority typified by this horn which absorbed 3 of the 10 horns would become the most conspicuous and important of all the 11. The "war against the saints" naturally prefigures that the 11th horn would persecute the chosen people of God.

Verse 23. The Roman empire, as above, verse 7.

Verses 24–5. The 10 kingdoms seem to have been as follows :—

1*Ostrogoths.	4 Vandals.	7*Heruli.	9 Huns.
2 Visigoths.	5 Franks.	8 Saxons.	10*Lombards.
3 Sueves.	6 Burgundians.		

Commentators are very generally agreed upon 7 of the above, but concerning the other 3 there have been some slight differences of opinion. The names with asterisks denote, according to the best evidence, the 3 nations which soon became absorbed. It remains to be added that various eminent Romanists (Calmet, Bossuet, Machiavelli, Dupin, &c.) concur in this decem-partite division of the old Roman empire.

Finally, that the little or 11th horn represents the PAPACY there can be no substantial doubt.

"Speaking great words against the Most High" aptly represents that race of men who arrogate to themselves the title of Vicars of Christ,—and who claim to receive or have sanctioned the bestowal on themselves of names and prerogatives which can belong only to God, such as "His Holiness" and many others.

"Wearing out the saints" eminently prefigures those multitudinous persecutions with the record of which every student of history is familiar. What thrilling scenes will not the mind instinctively recal in thinking of the expressions, 'Inquisition,' 'Waldenses,' 'Queen Mary' ("the bloody Mary") of England,' 'The Massacre of St. Bartholomew's Day,' &c.

"Changing times and laws" at once reminds us of the Gregorian Calendar, Saints' days, Celibacy of the Clergy, Transubstantiation, &c. &c. The last clause of verse 25 states the duration of this little horn.

According to prophetical language, "time and times and the dividing of time," (or half a time) are 3½ years; and the ancient Jewish year, consisting of 12 months of 30 days each, "a time and times and half a time," are reckoned in the Apocalypse as equivalent to "forty and two months," "or a thousand two hundred and three-score days;" and a day in the language of the prophets being used for a year (*Ezek.* iv. 6), we have the duration of the little horn set down at 1260 years.

The most natural period from whence to start this computation* is 606 A.D., when the Emperor Phocas conferred on the Pope the title of "Universal Bishop;" thus we have it that the Papacy will be destroyed in 1866 A.D.

The remainder of the book of Daniel, with perhaps two exceptions, deals with events more or less connected with the Jewish polity up to and inclusive of the death of Christ, and has no special connection with the events now to be discussed as revealed in the Apocalypse. The possible exceptions alluded to are the prophetical periods given in chaps. viii. 14, and xii. 11-12. Many think that these are to be taken as literal years, and run on to our own times. All that can be said is that no clue to the real interpretation has *in this case* been vouchsafed to us.

The Opening of the Seven Seals.

Revelation vi. 2. The white horse, the bow, and the crown, all obviously symbolise a period of victorious triumph and general national prosperity.

The application is to the state of the Roman empire between 96 and 180 A.D.—an era remarkable for the position to which this empire attained during it. (See a striking passage in *Gibbon*, vol i. p. 137 and p. 216, an unintentional but most efficient commentator on the Apocalypse.) White horses were generally used by the Romans for all purposes of State display and pageantry. The introduction of the bow into the symbol has been thought to have reference to the fact that Nerva, one of the emperors of this epoch, was by birth a Cretan, and the Cretans were distinguished for their skill as archers. The javelin was the usual Roman imperial badge, and the substitution of the bow for the javelin can hardly fail to have some special meaning. The crown (στέφανος) was in use now, but was superseded in the 3rd century by the διάδημα.

Verse 4. Obviously a symbol of bloodshed and extensive warfare generally.

The Roman empire onwards from 180 A.D. Bloodshed of every kind characterised this period. An emperor came to the throne usually by foul means: jealousy led to his assassination: his murderers then fought amongst themselves about the succession. Often it happened that em-

---

* Some commentators prefer 533 A.D., when Justinian promulgated an edict declaring the Bishop of Rome to be the head of the Church. The duration would thus have run out about 1793 A.D. The least that can be said is that the discredit and damage brought on the Papal power at this period by the French revolution furnishes a singular coincidence.

perors were put to death by some one fresh on the scene, who seized the imperial purple for himself, but only kept it perhaps for a few months, when retribution overtook him, and some other wretch stepped into his shoes.   Thirty-two emperors and 27 pretenders passed across the stage in 92 years ! ! !

Verses 5–6.   The expressions here point to oppressive taxation and scarcity of food.

The Roman empire, *circa* 200.   For some remarkable proofs of the financial hardships under which the Roman people laboured about this time, see Gibbon, *Decline and Fall*, i. 293, (Ed. of 1854) and the authorities there cited.

Verse 8.   Whilst this seal is in the fullest sense self-expressive, we have not to seek far for its historical representation—viz., the events which happened between 235 and 284 A.D.   Gibbon must again be referred to for particulars; suffice it to say, that he estimates that *one half the human race* were cut off by war, pestilence, and famine, "in a few years." —(Vol. i. p. 415.)

Verse 9.   A clear allusion to a period when there was a great on-slaught on the upholders of the Christian faith; and though there were many such, the last under Pagan Rome—Diocletian's, 303 A.D.—is the one here prefigured.—(See Gibbon, vol. ii. p. 269.)

Verses 12–17.   These verses point to the destruction of the Roman empire.   The emperors had become feeble and powerless.   All martial prowess seemed to have fled from the people, and the whole face of the empire was in a word revolutionised, when affairs came to a climax with the siege, capture, and sacking of the imperial city by the Goths under Alaric, 410 A.D.   When the reader is reminded that it was during this period of decline that Christianity finally triumphed over Paganism, the metaphor of " a great earthquake " may be said to have been abundantly fulfilled both politically and ecclesiastically.   In Gibbon will be found ample illustration of the circumstances foreshadowed in these verses, many of them spoken of to the very letter—*e.g.*, that the year 365 was signalised by an appalling earthquake along all the coasts of the Mediterranean, whereby thousands upon thousands of lives were lost. (*Decline*, vol. iii. p. 293.)   There is nothing unreasonable in accepting a twofold fulfilment in such cases as these—a literal as well as a figurative.

Revelation viii. 1.   The seventh and last seal differs from the pre-vious ones in being subdivided into seven periods, each heralded by a trumpet.   The series of events prefigured are of course continuous and successive.   Whilst no certain explanation can be given as to the meaning of the half hour's silence, it seems not unlikely that it may signify that there would be a pause in the occurrence of events after the sixth seal and before the first trumpet.

The Sounding of the Seven Trumpets.

Verse 7.   These expressions symbolise a very widespread desolation, and the reference is to the extent of the ravages of Alaric over Europe subsequent to his capture of Rome.

Verses 8–9. The language would be that which would apply to devastation carried on through the agency of a marine force. And there is no difficulty in finding the required parallel—viz., the incursions of Genseric and his Vandals on the seaboard of the Mediterranean, between 428 and 468 A.D.

For graphic details of the ravages effected by the piratical fleets of this great conqueror, see Gibbon, vol. iv. p. 276.

Verses 10–11. The great star represents some mighty leader, and the other expressions describe the baneful results of his career.

Expositors are very generally agreed that Attila, King of the Huns, is here referred to. Whilst the brilliancy of his exploits fitly entitled him to be compared to a star, he who was called the "Scourge of God" might also aptly be further designated as "wormwood."—(See Gibbon, vol. iv. p. 194.)

Verse 12. Likewise symbolic of important mundane calamities.

Here is represented the advent into Italy of Odoacer, King of the Heruli, 476 A.D., who extinguished the name of the western Roman empire, and became himself King of Italy.

Revelation ix. 1. From the 13th verse of the preceding chapter, it may be inferred that there was some kind of a pause to be expected between the fourth and the fifth trumpets. The "star" is again some distinguished leader to whom great powers for doing mischief were granted.

Verse 2. The "smoke" is some false doctrine which was to spread very widely over the earth.

Verse 3. Voraciousness may be regarded as the ruling notion here.

Verse 4. There is a command in the Koran to this effect. This is a singular coincidence, in view of the interpretation to be offered below.

Verse 5. Five months = 150 days = 150 years prophetically. What it is intended should be conveyed here (and in verse 6) is an intimation of much suffering and oppression, rather than excessive destruction of life.

Verse 7. The turbaned cavalry of the East might well be prefigured here.

Verse 8. The bloodthirsty and bearded oriental furnishes an apt type of the ideal creature thus pourtrayed, whose powers of offence and defence would be further described by the figurative language of verses 9 and 10.

The reader will be prepared to learn that it is generally agreed that Mahomet and the Saracen hosts form the subject of the preceding imagery. As regards the period mentioned in verse 5, it will be found, by examining the pages of Gibbon (the *infidel* Gibbon), that proceeding onwards from 622 A.D., the date of the celebrated flight of Mahomet, by the year 772, or thereabouts, a marked change had come over the Saracens :

they had been generally checked, had relaxed their efforts at conquest in consequence, and had begun to settle down into something like a peaceful and refined community. Astronomy is particularly indebted to the Arabians, as is well known.

Verses 13-14. It is a natural inference that the power about to be alluded to would have some local connection with the River Euphrates, and be a confederated power of four distinct members.

Verse 15. The time here mentioned is a prophetic indication of the period during which this woe would continue ; and on the principles already discussed (1 day = 1 year), modified by the necessary substitution of Julian for Jewish reckoning (365¼ days to the year, instead of 360), re-presents 365¼ + 30 + 1 + an hour ($\frac{1}{24}$th of a year, = 15 days), or 396 years 106 days.

The description is that of the modern Turkish power—an amalgamation more or less of the four dynasties which arose on the death of Malek Shah, Sultan of Persia.—(Gibbon, vol. vii. p. 168.)

Now, the termination of the Turkish woe must undoubtedly be taken as 1453 A.D., the year of the capture of Constantinople (the exact day being May 29), and the fall of the eastern Roman empire, at which period the Turks are considered to have reached the zenith of their fame and power. Now, reckoning backwards, 396 years 106 days takes us to 1057 A.D. ; and the next matter for inquiry is, can we obtain from the page of history any well-defined epoch at or about 1057 which would reasonably serve as a *terminus a quo* for the present trumpet. We can. In 1055 the Turks captured Bagdad, and overthrew the empire of the Caliphs. In February 1057 the Turkish Sultan, Togrul, having embraced Islamism, set forth from Bagdad at the head of an immense horde to conquer and ravage the habitable globe, and from the day of his departure to the fall of Constantinople there elapsed 396 years 130 days—an interval of 24 days (an insignificant quantity) only in excess of the assumed prophetical interval.* Who will presume to say that there is not in this coincidence to be seen the finger of God ?

Verses 16-19, especially 17. It is well known that artillery was first used on a large scale for purposes of warfare at the siege of Constantinople, and we have here a prophetical description of it.—(See Gibbon, vol viii. p. 160.)

Verses 20-1. " Even the western Christians, under the influence of Rome, and the Roman Catholic Governments, who had seen the Eastern and Greek Churches thus punished and quite destroyed, for their su-perstitious and vicious practices, yet even they still persevered in the practice of idolatry, saint-worship, and image-worship ; nay, would not so much as reform that cruel spirit of persecution, nor of putting cheats, delusions, and impositions on the understandings and properties of man-kind."—*Pyle.*

---

* Bishop Newton used the old 360-day reckoning, making up a period of 391 y. 15 d., and he considered this began to run from 1281 A.D., the date of the first recorded Ottoman victory over the Christians to 1672, the date of the capture of Cameniec, the last of the said victories. This may be ; but what is given in the text is preferable for several reasons.

Revelation x. 1-3. The Reformation is here announced: the "little book" is the Bible, now rendered accessible to the people, the universality of its range being typified by the position of the angel's feet. It need hardly be mentioned that the seven thunders refer to the Papal denunciations of the Reformation, but a critical proof of this will come more conveniently under a later chapter.

Verses 5-8. It is important to point out that there is a very recognised mis-translation here: It should be "the time shall not be yet;" that is to say, the end would not be directly after the appearance of the second angel, as the A. V. seems to have it, but in the future, when the seventh trumpet should sound.

Verse 9. The consequence of eating—*i.e.* reading the little book—might either arise, internally as it were, from the unpalatable or rebuking character of its contents; or externally, from the results which would flow from the being known to have perused it. Either interpretation would be good grammatically; but no doubt the second is the true one, for it harmonises with the historical facts, Bible-reading by the masses being, as is well known, altogether proscribed by the Papal authorities, with what concomitants it is needless to particularise.

Revelation xi. 1-2. In reference to the omission here enjoined in regard to the court of the Gentiles, Barnes says:—"Though near the Temple, and included in the general range of building, yet it does not pertain to those who worship there, but to those who are regarded as heathen and strangers. . . They occupied it, not as the people of God, but as those who were *without* the true Church, and who did not appertain to its real communion. . . The interpretation would demand that they should sustain *some* relation to the Church, or that they would *seem* to belong to it—as the court did to the Temple; but still, that this was in appearance only, and that in estimating the true Church it was necessary to leave them out altogether. Of course, this would not imply that there might not be some sincere worshippers among them as individuals . . . but what is here said relates to them as a mass or body—that they did not belong to the true Church, but to the Gentiles."

"Forty and two months" is 1260 days (as above)—that is, 1260 years; and this is merely another method of indicating the time mentioned in *Dan.* vii. 25. And therefore in this view of the matter the treading under foot of the Holy City by the Gentiles for 42 months alludes for the second time to the duration of the supremacy of the Papacy under the collective name of "the Gentiles." The inference, then, has been drawn that in *its corporate capacity* the Church of Rome is not a part of the true Church of Christ. I refrain from expressing any opinion.*

Verse 3. No significance need be attached to the number "two;" it probably means nothing more than that there would be preserved from apostacy a sufficient amount of testimony to keep up the evidence of truth, two being, under the Law, the number of witnesses necessary to decide a cause (*Deut.* xix. 15). The period here, it will be observed, is the same as in the previous verse; but it will presently appear why it

---

* "If it be possible to be then where the true Church is not, then it is at Rome."— *Homily for Whitsunday.*

H

seems preferable to understand 1260 literal days or 3½ literal years (of 360 days each) to be meant.

Verses 7-11. The opening sentence of this passage we are ·to understand as meaning that after such an interval as the Almighty considered proper, the beast would institute an aggressive movement against all the faithful witnesses to truth. Accordingly, we find this fulfilled in the persecutions raised by successive Popes of Rome against all who protested against their man-made dogmas. It has been computed, and on satisfactory grounds, that since the rise of the Papacy 50 millions of persons have been put to death in Europe for their religious opinions.

From the language employed we should be led to expect an apparent triumph over the witnesses, to be followed after a short interval (3½ days = 3½ years) by their resuming their functions.

The period when the Papacy held most absolute sway is universally allowed to be the beginning of the 16th century. On May 5, 1514, there was held a sitting of the Lateran Council, at which an official member made, amid loud demonstrations of applause, the following memorable and momentous announcement in reference to the Roman faith :—"*Jam nemo reclamat, nullus obsistit;*" which may be freely translated—"There is an end to resistance to the Papal supremacy." Let us take this date— May 5, 1514—and reckon onwards 3½ years (3 y. 180 d.), and see to what we are brought. Three years onwards makes May 5, 1517. Then 180 days will be—

May 5-31	.	.	.	.	.	.	.	.	. 27
June	.	.	.	.	.	.	.	.	. 30
July	.	.	.	.	.	.	.	.	. 31
August	.	.	.	.	.	.	.	.	. 31
September	.	.	.	.	.	.	.	.	. 30
October	.	.	.	.	.	.	.	.	. 31
									–––
									180

So that the 180th day from May 5, 1517, was October 31, 1517. Now, if a reference be made to any suitable book of history, we shall find that it was on this precise day—October 31, 1517—that *Luther inaugurated the Reformation, by posting up his renowned theses on the doors of the Church at Wittemberg.* Can this be described as an accidental coincidence ? Certainly not. "The great city which is spiritually called Sodom and Egypt, where also our Lord was crucified," is therefore the city of Rome. It has been objected "this cannot be," for our Lord was not crucified there. To this there is the unanswerable retort, "all the phraseology here is figurative, and there is no impropriety in saying that our Lord has been figuratively crucified at Rome as often as his people have been murdered by decrees emanating from Rome."

Verse 13. To liken the Reformation to an earthquake is no unreasonable simile. Many have supposed that the fall of the "tenth part of the city" alludes to the complete severance that was effected between Great Britain and Rome at the epoch now under review. This may be so, or merely a slight general falling away may be prefigured. It must never be forgotten that at no time was the connection between our country and the See of Rome more than one of acquiesced-in alliance. England never acknowledged nationally the Papal supremacy, even to the slight extent that Sardinia does in the present day.

Verse 15. Introducing the closing scene in the world's history, which we shall presently see bears several subdivisions.

Revelation xii. 1-2. The Church about to be increased. The imagery here is not uncommon in different parts of Holy Scripture. The original of ' wonder ' is σημεῖον, a sign, which is more expressive.

Verse 3. Bishop Newton remarks: The dragon is the well-known sign or symbol of the Devil or Satan, and of his agents or instruments. In this case the agent is Rome. Concerning the seven heads and ten horns, see *post,* on *Rev.* xvii. 9-10. It may be added that in the 3rd century A.D., the eagle, as a Roman national ensign, was superseded by the dragon.

The remainder of this chapter offers no features of particular difficulty. The periods mentioned in verses 6 and 14 are identical *in every sense* with those found in *Dan.* vii. 25, and *Rev.* xi. 2, which see.

Revelation xiii. 1. Here commences an enlarged description of the beast, which was simply mentioned in chap. xi. 7. The beast is Rome in its several forms. It will be more convenient to postpone the proof of this till we come to chap. xvii., where the whole question is again gone into ; meanwhile, let it be remembered that Romanists admit that the beast typifies Rome, but they say it is Rome Pagan. St. John himself refutes them : "I saw a beast rise," not ' I saw a beast which had risen.' Rome Pagan had risen in St. John's time ; therefore Rome Pagan is not alluded to here, whatever may be.

Verse 5. Forty-two months, equal to 1260 days (years). See note to *Rev.* xii. 3, and the references there given.

Verse 11. This is called another beast, in the sense that it superseded the first, had many of the attributes of the first, and others super-added peculiar to itself. Rome in its spiritual character is here alluded to ; what we understand by the one word " Papacy."

Verse 12-13. Nothing could possibly be more descriptive of the Papacy than this. It has maintained its sway by deception and delusion, by its pretended miracles, down to the present day.

Verse 18. The Greek word ΛΑΤΕΙΝΟΣ, *Lateinos, the Latin* [man] was remarked by Irenæus, who died *circa* 200 A.D., as fulfilling according to the Greek system of expressing numbers by alphabetic letters the requisite conditions, and the resulting opinion is now pretty generally received by members of the Reformed Church, British and Foreign. In the Church of Rome " they Latinise everything : mass, prayers, hymns, litanies, canons, decretals, bulls, are conceived in Latin. The Papal Councils speak in Latin. Women themselves pray in Latin. The Scriptures are read [when read!!!] in no other language under the Papacy than Latin. In short, all things are Latin."

Revelation xiv. 8. Not the literal Babylon, because that had long ago fallen, whereas the vision had reference to something future, as from St. John's time. " By Babylon is here meant, Rome, as all authors of all ages and countries agree."—*Bishop Newton.* Compare 1. *Peter* v. 13.

Cardinal Bellarmine relies on this text to prove that the apostle was at Rome at least once in his life. He says, "that Peter was at one time at Rome, we show first from the testimony of Peter himself, who thus speaks at the end of his 1st Epistle," &c. &c.

The Pouring-out of the Seven Vials.

Revelation xvi. 2   The French revolution of 1789, a truly "grievous sore," is here prefigured.

Verse 3.   Pourtrays the great naval warfare carried on by England against Europe, which did not end till there were no more ships for her to capture.

Verse 4.   The Napoleonic wars in Northern Italy—pre-eminently a country of rivers.

Verse 8.   The great European wars, 1804–15.

Verse 10.   The overthrow of the Pope's authority and his expulsion from Rome, 1799, which continued for some years.

Verse 12.   The curtailment of the Turkish power. This began in 1820 with the commencement of the Greek insurrection, and has continued to the present day, being even now in progress.

Verse 13.   The common interpretation of this verse is that it fore-shadows the attacks made on the Church by Infidelity, Popery, and Mahometanism. There is less certainty on this point than on most others arising in the course of the present enquiry.

Verses 17-21.   A lively image of the fall of Babylon, or Papal Rome, involving in her fall the ruin of all the nations in league with her. The concluding sentence prefigures an awful destiny.

Revelation xvii 3-7.   A very noticeable feature in these visions of St. John here forces itself very prominently on our attention—namely, the variety of the imagery employed to designate things in themselves identical. The beast, the scarlet woman, and Babylon, are figurative representations of one and the same object, and that object is none other than the CHURCH OF ROME, according to almost universal belief.

Verse 6.   Let us now look a little into this. The partiality of Popery for scarlet is notorious; it is the recognised colour of popes and cardinals. Equally notorious is her love of excess of ornaments, of gaudy pageantry and of theatrical display, generally in public worship (which, alas! some professing English Churchmen are imitating, to the entire destruction of real genuine piety).

In reference to the characteristic mentioned in verse 6, who will presume to say that the Church of Rome is not in an eminent degree "drunken with the blood of the martyrs of Jesus?"

Verses 8-9.   Rome, it is well known, is built on seven hills, and the Latin equivalent, *septicollis*, is met with in the classics.

Verses 10-11.   The seven kings here are seven forms of Roman government: five had passed away when St. John wrote—viz. 1, Kings; 2, Consuls; 3, Dictators; 4, Decemvirs; 5, Military Tribunes, (Livy, Tacitus.) The one existing in the Apostle's time was the Imperial; and the seventh, *then* future, was the Ducal, which lasted from 568 to 727 A.D.; the eighth, the Papal, followed.

Verses 12–14. See on *Daniel* vii. 24–5. "One hour" means simply a short time. That whilst there would ever be ten kingdoms during the existence of the beast, any given set of constituent members would only remain intact for a brief space, as has truly been the case according to history. There were no symptoms of a decempartite division of the Roman empire in St. John's time.

Verses 15–17. The events described in these verses are of course in the main still future, but things are happening now day by day, eminently calculated to pave the way for them. The foreign correspondence of our newspaper press teems with evidence that the hold of the Papacy over Romanists, in professedly Roman Catholic countries, is growing gradually but steadily weaker: as witness the state of ecclesiastical politics in France, in Belgium, in Sardinia, in Naples, in Italy generally. We may deplore the seeming alternative, infidelity; but it is none the less true that Roman Christianity is thoroughly undermined over the greater part of the continent of Europe.

Verse 18. As if to avoid every trace of doubt as to what is really the subject of these visions, verse 18 is added for the vindication of philosophic Christians, for the silencing of scoffers generally. "The woman which thou sawest is that great city, which *reigneth* over the kings of the earth." Observe the word "reigneth;" it is in the present tense: present, therefore, as regards St. John's epoch. And what was the great city which reigned over the kings of the earth in St. John's time? Can any mortal man doubt that it was of ROME alone that such words could be true?

Revelation xviii. 12–13. I pause over chapter xviii. only to draw attention to the last three words in verse 13. I ask boldly and unflinchingly, *Is it not a literal truth that the Church of Rome makes a merchandise of the souls of men?* Let history and the reader's conscience answer.

Lack of space hinders me from saying anything about I. *Thessalonians*, ii. 3–12, and I. *Timothy* iv. 1–3, as I had designed; suffice it to remark, that there again, I think, we have Popery pourtrayed. Verses 2 and 3 of the passage cited from the *Epistle to Timothy* are a life-like picture of the Church of Rome.

I have finished my recital. If any ask "*Cui bono?*" I say simply that whilst history may serve to illustrate the inspiration of Daniel and St. John, Churchmen and Statesmen may be constrained to fulfil their national duties in England, imbued with a belief that Roman Catholicism has a destiny foreshadowed for it in Holy Writ, namely, its destruction in a few years. Further, that it is still, as it ever was, a mighty engine of tyranny—a mighty power of darkness not to be trifled with, much less to be petted. If these points were thoroughly appreciated, Popery would receive different treatment at the hands of our rulers to what it does.

BOOK X.

Miscellaneous.

LIST OF USEFUL BOOKS AND PUBLICATIONS.

In the following list are given the names of a variety of works which will be found useful in carrying out a systematic Church and State policy. All are new or recent, and, it is presumed, still in print : —

THE SUNDAY QUESTION.

BAYLEE, Rev. J. T.—*History of the Sabbath.* (Seeley & Co. 3s. 6d.)
BILEY, Rev. E.—*The Perpetual Obligation of a Sabbath.* (Seeley & Co. 1s.)
GILFILLAN, J.—*The Sabbath.* (Edinburgh : A. Elliott. 6s.)
HILL, M.—*The Sabbath made for Man*: a Prize Essay. (J. F. Shaw. 8s.)
STEVENS, Rev. H.—*Forty-nine Opinions of Eminent Men.*
STEVENS, Rev. H.—*The Sabbath and the Decalogue*; a reply to Dr. Macleod. (Seeley & Co. 1s.)
WORDSWORTH, Ven. Archdeacon—*The Perpetual Obligation of the Lord's Day.* (Rivingtons. 6d.)

ENGLISH CHURCH HISTORY.

HARVEY, Rev. F. B.—*Historical Sketch of English Nonconformity.* (Church Institution, 4 Trafalgar Square.)
SHORT, Bishop T. V.—*History of the Church of England.* (Longmans. 10s. 6d.)
SMITH, Rev. E.—*The Church of England before the Reformation.* (S.P.C.K., 243. 3d.)
SOAMES, Rev. W. A.—*History of the Anglo-Saxon Church.* (Parker & Son. 7s. 6d.)
VENABLES, Rev. G.—*Our Church and our Country.* (Macintosh. 6d.)

CHURCH AND STATE.

BARDSLEY, Rev. J.—*The Scriptural Connection between Church and State.* Manchester, C.D.A., No. 7. (Rivingtons. 1d.)
BAYLEE, Rev. J., and E. MIALL—*Discussion on Church Establishments.* (Macintosh. 6d.)
CHAPMAN, Rev. D. F.—*Questions and Answers on an Established Church.* (Herald Office, Preston. 1d)
EDDOWES, Rev. J.—*What does the Bible say About It?* Bradford C.D.A., No. 4. (Macintosh. 1d.)
LYTTLETON, Hon. and Rev. W. H.—*Church Establishments.* (S.P.C.K. 4d.)
MASSINGHAM, Rev. J. D.—*The Scriptural Connection between Church and State.* (Macintosh. 2d.)
Essays on the Church. By a Layman. (Seeley & Co. 5s.)

THE BICENTENARY OF 1662.

CLIFFORD, Rev. J. B.—*Lecture on the Bicentenary.* Bristol C.D.A. (Macintosh. 3d.)
VENABLES, Rev. G.—*How did They Get There?* (Macintosh. 2d.)
WALKER, Rev. J.—*The Sufferings of the Clergy.* (J. H. Parker. 5s.)

DEFENSIVE ORGANISATION.

CHURCH INSTITUTION Publications—I., III., X., XII., and XIII. (Office, 4 Trafalgar Square. Gratis.)

HALE, Ven. Archdeacon—*Designs of the Liberation Society.* (Rivingtons. 6*d.*)

MASHEDER, R.—*Dissent and Democracy.* (Macintosh. 3*s.* 6*d.*)

MOLESWORTH, Rev. I. E. N., D.D.—*The Necessity and Design of Church Defence Associations.* Manchester C.D.A., No. 6. (Rivingtons. 1*d.*)

CHURCH RATES AND ENDOWMENTS.

DENISON, Ven. Archdeacon—*Church Rate a National Trust.* (Saunders, Otley, & Co. 5*s.*)

HALE, Ven. Archdeacon—*Charge on Church Rates.* 1859. (Rivingtons. 1*s.*)

HALE, Ven. Archdeacon—*Charge on Church Rates.* 1860. (Rivingtons. 1*s.* 6*d.*)

HARVEY, Rev. F. B.—*Opposition to Church Rates.* (Church Institution, 4 Trafalgar Square.)

MAGEE, Very Rev. Dr.—*The Voluntary System : can it Supply the place of the Established Church ?* (Bath: R. E. Peach.)

O'CONNOR, Rev. W. A.—*Church Establishments and Church Rates.* Manchester C.D.A., No. 4. (Rivingtons. 1*d.*)

TOTTENHAM, Rev. E.—*The Established Church and Church Rates.* (Macintosh. 1*d.*)

VENABLES, Rev. G.—*Tithes and Offerings.* (Macintosh. 1*d.*)

The Church and its Endowment. (Macintosh. 1*d.*)

CHURCH PRINCIPLES.

BAILEY, E.—*Conformity to the Church of England.* (Hamilton, Adams, & Co. 4*d.*)

CAUDWELL, E.—*The Church of England the best Church ; or Reasons for being a Churchman.* (Masters. 2*d.*)

STORR, Rev. F.—*A Threefold Cord that binds Me to My Church.* (Macintosh. 1*d.*)

STOWELL, Rev. Canon—*I am a Churchman.* (Macintosh. 1*d.*)

STOWELL, Rev. Canon—*The Moderation of the Church of England.* Bristol C.D.A. (Macintosh. 1*d*)

TAYLOR, Rev. T. G.—*Why I am a Churchman.* (S.P.C.K., 184. 2*d.*)

THE ROMAN CONTROVERSY.

BARNES, A.—*Notes on Daniel and the Revelation.* (3 vols. Routledge. 12*s.*)

WORDSWORTH, Ven. Archdeacon—*Babylon ; or the Question Considered 'Is the Church of Rome the Babylon of the Apocalypse ?'* (Rivingtons. 1*s.*)

WORDSWORTH, Ven. Archdeacon—*Lectures on the Apocalypse.* (Rivingtons. 10*s.* 6*d.*)

THE IRISH CHURCH.

HUME, Rev. A., D.D.—*Results of the Irish Census of 1861 with reference to the Church in Ireland.* (Rivingtons. 1*s.* 6*d.*)

LEE, Rev. A. T.—*Facts respecting the Present State of the Church in Ireland.* (Rivingtons. 2*d.*)

MISCELLANEOUS.

CLABON, J. M.—*Church and Party : Remarks on the Duty of Churchmen in and out of Parliament.* (Rivingtons.)

CREE, Rev. E. D.—*Lay Preaching.* (J. H. Parker. 2*d.*)

HOOK, Very Rev. Dr.—*Church Dictionary.* (Murray. 12*s.*)

HUME, Rev. A., D.D.—*Various Statistics.* Birmingham C.D.A., Nos. 3, 4. (J. H. Parker. 4*d.*)

MILLER, Rev. Canon—*Churchmen and Dissenters.* Birmingham C.D.A., No. 2. (J. H. Parker. 1*d.*)

PULMAN, JOHN—*The Anti-State Church Association Unmasked.* (Macintosh. 8*s.* 6*d.*)

WORDSWORTH, Ven. Archdeacon—*The Episcopate.* (Rivingtons.)

LIST OF IMPORTANT PARLIAMENTARY PAPERS ON CHURCH QUESTIONS OF RECENT DATE.

THE names within parentheses are those of the members who moved for the committee or the return, or who brought in the Bill, as the case may be. Where a publication bears no "sessional number," it is because it was

" presented to both Houses of Parliament by command of Her Majesty."
An asterisk denotes House of Lords' returns. The titles have been
abbreviated somewhat in most cases : —

ARCHDEACONRIES : Return of the Offices held by each Archdeacon, with Incomes attached
to each (Mr. *Hadfield*). [1860: No. 613. 4*d.*]

BIBLE PRINTING PATENT : Report and Evidence, &c., from the Select Committee on (Mr.
Baines). [1860 : 162. 1*s.*]

BURIALS BILL : Minutes of Proceedings of the Select Committee on (Sir *S. M. Peto*).
[1862 : 306. 1*d.*]

BURIALS : Returns of the Burials in Cemeteries formed under the Burial Acts, distinguish-
ing the number of Interments in Consecrated and Unconsecrated ground (Mr. *Hadfield*). [1860 : 560. 2*d.*]

CAMBRIDGE UNIVERSITY : Report and Evidence, &c., from the Commissioners on the State,
Discipline, Studies, and Revenues of the University and Colleges of Cambridge, &c.
[1852. 8*s.*]

CATHEDRAL COMMISSION : Reports of the Commissioners on the State and Condition of the
Cathedral and Collegiate Churches in England and Wales. [1854-5. 10*s.* 6*d.*]

CHARITIES : Return of the number of Informations, Petitions, Proceedings at Law, and
Probable Amount of Income of Charities in Chancery. [1852 : 94. 3*s.*]

Ditto   Supplementary Return (Mr. *Pellatt*). [1856 : 177. 1*s.* 3*d.*]

Ditto   Supplementary Return (Mr. *Copeland*.) [1861 : 298. 4*s.* 2*d.*]

CHURCH BUILDING ACTS : Return of Parishes Divided and Districts Assigned to Churches
under the Provisions of the Church Building Acts, and the Parish of Manchester Division Act (Mr. *Deedes*). [1861 : 557. 10*d.*]

CHURCH RATES REFUSED : Names of all Parishes in which (during the last fifteen years)
Church Rates have been refused, and since that refusal have ceased altogether to be
collected (Lord *R. Cecil*). [1856 : 319. 2*s.*]

CHURCH RATES : Report and Evidence, &c., from the Select Committee on the Assessment
and Levy of Church Rates. [1851 : 541. 4*s.* 2*d.*]

CHURCH RATES : Report and Evidence, &c., from the Select Committee of the House of Lords
on the Present Operation of the Law and Practice respecting Assessment and Levy of
Church Rates (Duke of *Marlborough*). [1859, 2nd Sess.: 24.* 3*s.* 6*d.*]

Ditto   Ditto   [Part II. 1860: 154. 1*s.*]

CHURCH RATES : Return from each Parish, setting forth the Gross Amount expended during the last seven years for Church purposes, with Supplemental Return. (Commonly
called Mr. *Walpole's* Returns). [1859. 5*s.*]

CHURCH RATES : Return of all Moneys received and expended by Churchwardens from
Easter 1853 to Easter 1854 (Sir *W. Clay*). [1856 : 323. 2*s.* 6*d.*]

CHURCH RATES : Return of the Number of Rates refused, 1833—51. [1852 : 346. 8*d.*]

CHURCH RATES : Return of the several Bills introduced into Parliament in relation to
Church Rates during the last twenty years, together with the Names of the authors
(Mr. *Bristow*). [1861 : 47. ½*d.*]

COMMON PRAYER BOOK : Return for Copy of the Alterations in the Book of Common
Prayer, prepared by the Royal Commissioners for the Revision of the Liturgy in 1689.
[1854 : 332.*]

ECCLESIASTICAL COMMISSION : Report and Evidence, &c., from the Select Committee on
(Mr. *H. Seymour*). [1862 : 470. 5*s.* 6*d.*]

Ditto   Supplementary Report, &c. (Mr. *H. Seymour.*) [1863 : 457. 4*s.*]

EDUCATION (DISSENTING SCHOOLS) : Report to the Education Commissioners by the Committee appointed by them in reference to Dissenters' Schools (Mr. *Dillwyn*). [1861 :
410. 3½*d.*]

EDUCATION GRANTS : Return of the Amount paid to each Parish or Place in the years 1859
and 1860 (Mr. *Henley*). [1862 : 101. 1*s.*]

EDUCATION (POPULAR) : Report of the Commissioners on. [1861. 18*s.* 3*d.*]

EDUCATION (DESTITUTE CHILDREN) : Report and Evidence, &c., from the Select Committee
on. [1861 : 460. 3*s.*]

ESTABLISHED CHURCH : Reports (5) of Commissioners on the State of the Established Church
with reference to Ecclesiastical Duties and Revenues, with Maps. [1835-7. 6*s.*]

LOCAL TAXATION RETURNS (transmitted annually to the Home Office. [1862 : 437. 4*s.* 2*d.*]

   Ditto [1863 : 496. 4*s.* 10*d.*]
   Ditto [1864 : 524. 4*s.* 10*d.*]
   Ditto [1865: 447. 4*s.* 4*d.*]

MAYNOOTH COLLEGE : Report from the Commissioners on. [1855. 7*s.* 6*d.*]

OXFORD UNIVERSITY: Report and Evidence, &c., from the Commissioners on the State, Discipline, Studies, and Revenues of the University and Colleges of Oxford. [1852. 8s.]

PLURALITIES: Returns of all Clergymen holding more than one Church or Chapel, showing the full Income derived from each. [1861: 517. 6d.]

PRISONERS, DENOMINATION OF: Return showing, in each Prison in the United Kingdom, on January 1, 1862, the number of Prisoners of each Religious Denomination. [1862: 233. 10d.]

PUBLIC SCHOOLS: Report and Evidence, &c., from the Commissioners on. [1864. 4 parts, 1l.]

RELIGIOUS WORSHIP: Mr. Horace Mann's Report and Tables. [1853. 2s. 6d.]

SABBATH: Report and Evidence, &c., from the Select Committee on the Laws and Practices relating to the Observance of the Sabbath. [1832. 2s. 6d.]

SPIRITUAL DESTITUTION: Report and Evidence, &c., from the Select Committee of the House of Lords on the Deficiency of Means of Spiritual Instruction in populous districts, and to consider the fittest means of meeting the difficulties of the case (Bishop of Exeter). [1858: 387. 7s.]

SUNDAY RAILWAY AND CANAL TRAFFIC: Report and Evidence, &c., from the Select Committee of the House of Lords on the expediency of restraining the practice of Carrying Goods on Railways and Canals on Sundays. [1841: 354. 2s. 4d.]

SUNDAY TRADING: Report and Evidence, &c., from the Select Committee of the House of Commons on the prevalence of. [1847: 666. 2s.]

TITHES: Return of all Tithes commuted and apportioned. [1848: 298. 3s. 3d.]

A FEW FACTS BEARING ON THE BICENTENARY MOVEMENT;

OR, 1862, 1662, AND 1642.

A.D. 1640–1650.—A period of much civil and religious discord, culminating in open rebellion, and the murder of England's lawful king. Puritanism, under the twofold form of Presbyterianism and Independency successively, gains the ascendant. The Church, with her Bishops and Clergy, is set at defiance, spitefully entreated, dis-established, and for a short time crushed. In the place of monarchy, that most bitter of despotisms, democracy, is set up, first in the garb of Presbyterianism, and afterwards in that of Independency. Its *ultimate* characteristics under both are hatred of the King, the Bishops, and the Clergy, and all who differ from it, Nonconformists as well as Churchmen, if the former do not belong to the dominant sect. Toleration is not thought of, except for one's own clique. Bishop Jeremy Taylor writes a book on Liberty of Conscience, and a Puritan answers it by another, in which Toleration is denounced as a damnable sin. Another says, "If the Devil were to ask a courtesie of a State, he would ask no more than a Universal Toleration, and an uncontrolled libertie in every one to preach and expound the Scripture," whence we are to infer that Toleration is devilish! Now for a few details :—

1641, Dec.—Ten Bishops imprisoned in the Tower.

1642, Feb.—Bill passed turning all the Bishops out of the House of Lords. Committees appointed by the Commons to inquire into the "scandalous immoralities" of the Parochial Clergy. They deprive of their Benefices, in the most cruel manner, at least 7,000, whose "immorality," in most cases, consists only in their having Episcopal Ordination, and supporting the King. Many are forcibly expelled by the Puritan soldiers of the Parliamentary armies, and many sell off their property and escape to the Royal armies for refuge. Of those on whom the Puritans can lay hands, great numbers are imprisoned, some in hulks in the Thames. The brutal atrocities and inhuman cruelties perpetrated by these odious persecuting fanatics, would have done credit to the most bigoted Papist of the preceding century. The Church Livings thus rendered vacant are filled up by the appointment of Presbyterians, Independents, Anabaptists, and other Nonconformist Ministers, and not a few *lay* sectaries. As a compensation, the ejected Clergy are promised a fifth of their tithes annually; but, as might have been expected, the promise is seldom kept.

1643, July.—The Westminster Assembly of Divines decree the "Directory for Public Worship," the "Confession of Faith," and two Catechisms. [N.B. These are in substance still adopted by the Scotch Presbyterians, all of whose Ministers are, I believe, pledged to the extirpation of " black Prelacy," or the Episcopal form of Church Government.] Ordinance passed for defacing and destroying all ornaments in Churches of a Popish character. Many Puritans forthwith take hammers and chisels and commence business on their own account, and the marks of their sacrilegious hands remain in many Churches to the present day.

1645, Jan.—Ordinance passed displacing in Public Worship the Prayer Book, by the Directory. Laud, Archbishop of Canterbury, murdered on the scaffold. Aug. 23.—Ordinance passed utterly prohibiting the use of the Prayer Book *even by private individuals.* Penalty: first and second offences, a money fine; third offence, one year's imprisonment.

1646.—Presbyterianism established *pro tem.*, and in 1649 permanently.

1649, Jan.—The King murdered on the scaffold. Feb.—The House of Lords abolished. The office of king abolished. [Thus we see that the prosperity of the civil power is intimately bound up with that of the Church: the latter goes, and, by consequence, the former soon follows.]

1650–1660. —Presbyterianism wanes; Independency supplants it. Persecution carried on by both against all who differ from them. The Quakers, particularly, suffer much at the hands of their Puritan tyrants, and nearly 2000 are thrown into prison.

1656, Dec.—*By order of Parliament*, James Naylor is set in the pillory, whipped from Westminster to the Exchange, his tongue bored with a hot iron, his forehead branded with the letter B, also with a hot iron, sent to Bristol and publicly whipped, imprisoned in the London Bridewell for two years, condemned to hard labour, and all for what? BECAUSE HE IS A QUAKER! We are told that "he put out his tongue very willingly, but shrinked a little when the iron came upon his forehead."

Voila ! Dissent and Democratic liberty [?] in 1656.

1660, May.—The Monarchy and Church restored. The ejected Clergy of 1643 are restored to their Benefices by Act of Parliament, but only a few hundreds out of the 7,000 are in a position to avail themselves of the offer.

1661, May.—Bishops re-admitted to the House of Lords.

1662.—The Act of Uniformity passed. By the Act of 1660 a few hundreds out of the 7,000 Clergy ejected in 1643 came back to their Cures, but as most of them (that is to say, 6,000 or more) were either dead or unwilling to claim their own just rights, it follows that a similar number of Nonconformists are still in possession of Livings *not their own.* By the Act of Uniformity now passed, these 6,000 are offered permission to retain *what they had unjustly acquired possession of*, on the following conditions:—That they would receive Episcopal Ordination, renounce the League and Covenant, declare their assent to the Prayer Book, and sign

a declaration of conformity to it. Three months, ending on St. Bartholomew's Day, are allowed for them to make up their minds, and when that
day arrives it is found that the great majority of these Dissenters have
conformed ; those who have not, said to be in number about 2000 (though
it is believed to have been much less), of course retire from Livings
which never belonged to them, and it was to commemorate the ejection
of these 2000 intruders that the Dissenters of 1862 proposed to
celebrate

"THE BI-CENTENARY OF 'BLACK BARTHOLOMEW,' 1662."

This is the case stated, I believe, with perfect impartiality. The Dissenters of 1862 proposed commemorating a body of men with whom they
could have had no legitimate sympathy whatever. The ejected Ministers
were friendly to an Established Church and a National Liturgy, only they
preferred the Presbyterian to the Episcopalian form of Church Government, both of which the Bi-centenarians hate with a bitter hatred.

The Bi-centenarians speak of the ejected Dissenters of 1662 as their
religious ancestors, concealing the fact that of the 300 Meeting-houses
founded by the ejected Ministers, only a few remain which are not in
the hands of Unitarian infidels.

The plain fact is that, under cover of a great religious movement, the
Political Dissenters sought to palm off on Englishmen a gross political
swindle. The Liberation clique threw their influence into the scale, and
the whole business gradually assumed the form of a great political demonstration of anti-Church enmity and spite. On the Dissenters the blow
recoiled ; and on them, and not on Churchmen, rested the blame of all the
ill-feeling and bickerings which sprung up.

ULTRA-RITUALISM.

I have not hitherto taken much part in the discussions which have been
going on lately concerning Ritualism ; but really things are now being
said which render it incumbent on all sober-minded Churchmen to exert
themselves to curb that lawless spirit which, because it is one of the signs
of the times in the world at large, would have been eschewed, one would
have thought, by all professing Churchmen.*

As a sincere member of the Anglican Church, yielding to none in the
firmness of my allegiance to her, I must confess to having perused with
great disgust many of the recent literary effusions of the Ultra-Ritual party.
If it were only going to end in the secession of the mass of them to their
natural sphere—the Church of Rome—regrets might be spared. It is,
however, their professed desire to remain in the English Church that I
regret, for I am fearful of our beholding ere long the peace and prosperity
of the Church imperilled—at a period, too, when she possesses a greater
amount of popularity and substantial hold on the affection of the nation
than she has possessed for many generations.

---

* The perusal of any casual number of the *Church Times* newspaper will furnish a
striking example of the manner in which the party seeking to Papalise the Church of
England will repudiate, if necessary for their own ends, things which, in their calmer
moments, they profess to regard as of great importance. These people appear to be Episcopalians only by tradition ; for when their Episcopal overseers venture on remonstrance,
all they meet with is scornful defiance ; (see the Rev. E. Stuart's letter in the *Guardian*,
August 9, 1865.)

As regards the law of the matter, if the letter is uncertain the spirit is not ; and if the result of the present Romanising agitation should be an attempt on the part of persons rightly regarded as not very safe custodians of the Church's interests to make the letter conform to the spirit—in other words, to prohibit as illegal, once and for all, incense, vestments, and the thousand and one follies daily perpetrated by the Ultra-Ritual clergy—whilst I should so far rejoice, I should further hold these said individuals directly responsible for all inconveniences which might follow in the wake of legislative action of the character announced to be imminent, though not at first sight connected with a Romanising Ritual Abolition Bill. The Ritual party are now as surely doing the work of the Eburyites as is possible, could they but see it. I have no sympathy with the Prayer-Book Revision movement, and it is precisely on that account that I wish the Ultra-Ritualists could be made to see the nearly certain results of their courting an effort against themselves, which it seems to me they are now doing. In contending, as they do, for so many antiquated un-Anglican ceremonies, the Ultra-Ritualists are fighting, not over the kernel, but over the husk of religion ; they are diverting their minds and those of their congregations from vital practical Christianity to empty theatrical and mechanical forms.

The Ultra-Ritual party are not consistent. They profess to take their stand on the Prayer-Book of 1549, yet they use a variety of articles of dress not included in those mentioned in that book. The Canons of 1603, the latest promulgated, it may further be remarked, are at variance in the matter of vestments with the Prayer-Book of 1549, and the revisers of 1662 jumbled the two together in a most unfortunate way. However, it is beyond dispute that till within quite a recent period the ministers of the Church of England modelled their dress and the accessories of their worship far more on the Canons of 1603 than on the Edwardian Prayer-Book of 1549, and with these (less ornate, it may be) usages, which have now the acceptance of a couple of centuries to back them, Churchmen would do wisely in resting content. As a Churchman who values a moderate ritual calculated to secure decent and orderly worship, free alike from Puritan coldness and Romish mummery, I must confess that I should be glad to see wholly prohibited all that sensuous paraphernalia with which it is attempted to weigh down the Reformed Church of England— theatrical millinery, incense, excess of genuflections, prostrations, auricular confession, *et hoc genus omne.* When we find " advanced " Ritualists beginning to talk of the desirability of having "high mass " in our churches, surely it is time for moderate men to act. I have little doubt that Ultra-Ritualism will ere long be checked. I wish there were a prospect of its being checked by the forbearance, self-denial, and moderation of its supporters rather than by the strong arm of a hastily improvised Parliamentary enactment, the very preliminary discussion of which may be fraught with consequences calculated to engender new and bitter party strife—a result which would be deplorable after the *rapprochements* of recent years.

Mr. Gresley (no Puritan, be it remembered), in his *Short Treatise on the English Church* (1844), expressed in vivid terms his regrets that there existed such slight willingness amongst Churchmen to conciliate one another. An excellent passage, too long to quote, begins with—" It is surprising how much evil is done, how much ill-will excited, by obstinacy in non-essential points. Members of the same Church ought to be ready to yield to each other in things of no decided importance." If applicable to Low Churchmen 22 years ago, how much more applicable to the extreme Ritualists of the present day! Will the warmest of the latter venture to assert that he can only guarantee the fervour of his prayers when he is vested in "alb, amice, and chasuble?" If not, why persist in childish displays, eminently calculated to bring odium on our Church, and drive her worshipping members to the meeting-houses of the Sects?

CHRISTIAN UNITY.

Few things are more to be deplored than the divisions subsisting in Christendom, but in giving way to this regret many English Churchmen are in the habit of making light of the Errors of the Roman and Greek Catholic Churches, and of sacrificing leading principles of the Reformation: under these circumstances, the following able but anonymous appeal, issued in 1865, sounds a much-needed warning:—

" BROTHER CHURCHMEN,

"You are asked to give money to an 'ASSOCIATION FOR PROMOTING THE UNITY OF CHRISTENDOM.' Unity is a good thing; but unity obtained by the sacrifice of truth is a very bad thing. We must 'speak the *truth* in love,' for true wisdom is '*first* pure, then peaceable.' (*St. James* iii. 17.)

"The prospectus of the Association says that 'the daily use of a short form of prayer, together with *one* 'Our Father,' for the intention of the Association, is the only obligation incurred by those who join it; to which is added, in the case of priests, the offering, at least once in three months, of the Holy Sacrifice for the same intention.'

"In this single sentence several Romish errors are quietly insinuated. That the efficacy of the Lord's Prayer depends upon the frequency of its repetition (so that, for example, six Pater-Nosters are better than one 'Our Father'), or that the meaning of the Lord's Prayer is determined, *not* by His own words, but by our narrow, one-sided 'intentions,' is surely a mischievous superstition, tending to drag down our Lord's teaching to our level, instead of raising us up to His.

"Again, the notion that there is a propitiatory sacrifice capable of being offered 'at least once in three months' for any object which a priest may 'intend,' is purely Romish: a source of power, and of fees to the sacrificing priest, but widely different from the sacrament 'which the Lord hath commanded to be *received*.' The doctrine of 'Intention' was never heard of until the 12th century, when ignorance and vice had overspread the whole of Christendom. Consider the consequences which this doctrine involves. If the efficacy and the application of sacramental grace is dependent upon the 'intention' of priests, we can never feel sure of the validity either of the priest's own orders or of the sacrament which we receive from him, because we can know nothing of the secret 'intentions' of ecclesiastics. The conduct of many priests at the French Revolution, the autobiography of the celebrated Blanco White (for many years a Spanish priest, and afterwards a graduate of an English University), the history of Jansenism, the example of Hoadley, Colenso, and many others, prove that it is no rare thing for priests to disbelieve utterly in the rites which they celebrate. If, then, the doctrine of 'Intention' be true, we can never know whether there be any *really* ordained clergy, or *really* baptised laity to constitute the hypothetical 'Christendom' for which we are to 'pray.'

"At any rate, as members of the Church of England we are *already* members of an 'Association' which has provided ample opportunities of *authorised* intercessory prayer in the Litany, in the prayer for 'all sorts and conditions of men,' in the Collect for Good Friday, and in the beautiful 'Prayer for Unity' in the Accession Service. The Pope (at the instigation of the schismatical 'Archbishop' Manning) has already condemned the new 'Association,' which under pretence of uniting Christendom (!) is alienating and estranging from one another the children of our dear mother, the Church of England."

Fraternisation with Greek Catholics is week by week prated about in one London newspaper (The *Churchman*) in a way that is simply nauseous, puerile, and ridiculous, to the exclusion of matters vitally important to the best interests of the Anglican Church.

CHURCHWARDENS AND PEWS.

Considerable misapprehension appears to exist in the present day as to the exact state of the law governing churchwardens in the allotment of seats in parish churches, and that, too, on the part of persons who, from their position, might be expected to know fully all about it ; so I will state briefly some of the chief points as laid down by the leading authorities. The references appended will enable those interested in pursuing the matter farther to do so.

Sir John Nicholl, in a well-known case, speaks as follows:—"The general law with respect to pews and sittings in churches is little understood. Erroneous notions on this subject are current at least in many parts of the country, and have led to much practical inconvenience. By the general law, and of common right, all the pews in the parish church are the common property of the parish ; they are for the use in common of the parishioners, who are all entitled to be seated orderly and conveniently, so as best to provide for the accommodation of all. *The distribution of seats rests with the churchwardens* as the officers, and subject to the control of the ordinary [the Bishop]. *Neither the minister nor the vestry have any right whatever to interfere with the churchwardens in seating and arranging the parishioners, as often erroneously supposed ;* at the same time, the advice of the minister, and even sometimes the opinions and wishes of the vestry, may be fitly invoked by the churchwardens, and to a certain extent may be reasonably deferred to in this matter."—(Fuller *v.* Lane ; 2 Addams, 425.)

Special attention should be directed to the sentence above which is italicised, as it frequently happens that a good deal hinges upon it, where attempts are made to interfere with the exclusive rights of the churchwardens.

Another very eminent lawyer writes as follows :—" All the pews in a church are *primâ facie* at the disposal of the churchwardens as the parochial officers of the ordinary, except the chief seat in the chancel, which custom appropriates to the rector, whether lay or ecclesiastical, and sometimes to the vicar ; for with regard to the other seats in the chancel, it seems the better opinion that their power extends to them also."— (Rogers ; *Ecclesiastical Law*, p. 164.)

On this extract Prideaux writes :—" The summary of the law upon the subject by the late Mr. Rogers is so able, that no apology, it is confidently felt, will be required for setting it out in this place."—(*Churchwarden's Guide*, 311.) Prideaux himself says the same thing elsewhere, and I may also refer to Burn's *Ecclesiastical Law*, Cripps's *Laws of the Clergy*, and Stephen's *Laws of the Clergy*, all works of the highest authority, as stating the matter in perfectly similar terms.

Nothing, I take it, can be clearer than that the churchwardens are the sole judges of what arrangements it is fit should be made, *subject only* to the Bishop of the diocese as a judge of appeal for dissatisfied parties to resort to. The minister has no power *as of right.*

I make one more citation of considerable importance :—" It should be farther mentioned, that although every parishioner has a right to be seated, he has not a right to a pew, and that persons not being parishioners have no right to a pew or sitting."—(In re *St. Columb's Church, Londonderry* ; 8 *L. T.*, N.S., 861.)

In churches for which commissioners of competent authority have fixed a scale of pew-rents, and in which the pews are accordingly let, the power of the Churchwardens is in some measure restrained by the provisions of the Church Building Acts; and in certain cases the actual *selling* of pews is legalised, although the preferential claims of parishioners over non-parishioners are carefully protected (3 George IV., cap. 72, § 24.)

In the case of parishes cut up into new districts (now very numerous), all inhabitants of such new districts must be treated as parishioners in regard to their claims to seats in the mother-church, until the districts become "new parishes," "distinct and separate parishes," or "district parishes." In "new parishes," persons who shall have claimed and shall have had assigned to them sittings in the church of such new parish, thereby surrender a corresponding number of sittings in the old church (19 & 20 Vict. cap. 104, § 5). There is no similar provision in the case of "distinct and separate," or "district" parishes; but as these are *parishes* for all ecclesiastical purposes, it is apprehended that the inhabitants cease to have a right to occupy sittings in the old church, at all events to the exclusion of inhabitants in the district remaining connected with the said old church.

Churchwardens, especially in populous parishes, would often do well to break in upon the vicious practice still very prevalent, of allowing small families to monopolise large pews. In all cases, however, re-arrangements involving considerable change should be negotiated with tact and discretion, so that long-established uses should not be violently interfered with; nor should these monopolies be touched without strong cause, or the remedy may work greater evils than did the original disease. Finally, churchwardens should pay full attention to the needful wants of the poor, the more so as they are less able to take care of themselves; and neglect on the part of churchwardens often drives them altogether away from church, or even to the meeting-house.

ARE "LIBERATION" DISSENTING MINISTERS HABITUAL LIARS?

The following extract from a lecture delivered by the Rev. J. D. Massingham, M.A., the lecturer of the Church Institution at Huddersfield, on Feb. 24, 1866, will furnish some material for answering the above inquiry:—

"I remember that one of the supporters of the Liberation Society told in my hearing of a poor woman—of course a poor widow woman, to make the case more pitiable—who had the clothes taken from off her clothes line and sold to pay the church rate of our bloated national church. I was very impudent, I am sometimes, the Liberation Society think so— (laughter)—and I wish them to think so. (Laughter.) I inquired the name of the woman who had her clothes taken, and could not learn that; then the name of the parish, but could not learn that; but the only thing the 'rev.' speaker could tell me was vouched for was that it was in Ireland, and he was sure of it. (Laughter.) *Of course that was quite enough for me, for in Ireland there is no such thing as a church rate, so it mattered little where the parish was.* (Laughter). The whole tale was an audacious mendacity. (Applause.) Another advocate of the society, Mr. Charles Williams, stated in my presence some of the most daring assertions I ever heard. For instance, he said that Sir Robert Harry Inglis, in his speech, July 19, 1836, held that Church property was public property. I knew he was rather more of a Tory than I wished him to be, consequently I did not fancy that he would join the Liberation Society, or that he would say anything of the kind, and without looking at his words I felt sure that the representative of our University of Oxford never uttered such a sentence. (Hear, hear.) I could not test it at the time, but went down to London and consulted Hansard, and on page 344 of vol. xxxv. I found these words:— Sir R. H. Inglis rose to oppose the Bill ' because it gave a vantage ground to those who sought the overthrow of the whole system of the Church. For the first time in respect to England, by an Act of the Legislature, unsanctioned by the Church itself, it recognised the principle that Church property was public property. He was himself very unwilling to occupy the attention of the House, but he was still more unwilling to admit such a Bill to pass without recording his opposition to its principles and provisions. The Church of England had not been endowed by the State. The State, at the Reformation, did no more than confirm the measures which the Church, individually and collectively, had previously adopted. The State therefore had no right to interfere with the property, which the State had not given to the Church. Adam de Beke, the great Bishop of Durham, six centuries ago left his estate to that see: had he left it to the corporation of Durham that could not be alienated to a poorer corporation.' Mr. Williams admitted the truth of my quotation, but said Sir Harry Inglis had made use of the words uttered by him. *So Mr. Williams just picked out the words he wanted, and made Sir R. H. Inglis to approve of what he rose to protest against. I need not ask, is not this shamefully dishonest?* Why, Mr. Williams might as well say that the Bible teaches atheism : 'There is no God,' leaving out the previous words that the fool said so: or that the Bible teaches suicide—' He went out and hanged himself,'—'Go thou and do likewise.' *By selecting such words as we want for a purpose, apart from the fair connexion, we may utterly misrepresent any book or speech.* A cause must be very desperate when it requires such a shameful line of advocacy. *I say that a man, or body of men calling themselves Dissenting ministers— ministers of the gospel of Christ, who will write in books or state in speeches things of this kind, which are positively untrue, merely to bring a stigma on the Church of England, I say they ought to be hooted from the land.* (Loud applause.) And then it is attempted to be made out that the clergy of the Church of England are maintained by taxes levied on the people. Why, in a Huddersfield paper I find that at Longwood, the 'Rev.' J. Parker (of Salendine Nook)—Parker seems a famous name, by-the-by, just now—said 'he believed the union between Church and State was unnecessary, *and yet it cost the Government of this country* 7,000,000*l. sterling a-year.*' Fancy the impudence of a man getting up to state that! I only ask him to prove it, and I will give him 20*l.* for his proof—(hear, and applause)—and, if he cannot prove it, call upon him to retract his falsehood (Loud cheers.) The fact is, it is quite untrue."—(*Huddersfield Chronicle,* Feb. 28, 1866.)

AN ELECTIONEERING EPISODE.

The following is abridged from the *Standard* of July 19, 1865. It confirms what I said on p. 79 about rents as affected by Church Rates, and it is a testimony (Dissenting, withal) to the accuracy of my reasoning on the incidence of Church Rate (*ante* p. 69):—

" At a meeting at the Hertford Corn Exchange, on the 7th instant, Mr. Garratt got on a stand and said :—' I wish to ask Mr. Cowper, who is contesting the county and going for the abolition of Church Rates, whether there is not a gentleman on his committee who has had a clause inserted in his tenants' agreements that when Church Rates are abolished their rents should be raised 10*l.* a year?' (Cheers from the Conservatives.) 'I am not afraid to mention him—Mr. Bosanquet—there!' (There was no attempt to answer this, except by shouting.) 'And yet Mr. Cowper comes forward as a Liberal, and for the abolition of Church Rates, having on his committee a gentleman whose tenants' rents are to be raised 10*l.* a year when Church Rates are abolished! Is that liberal? You say I have turned, but I always was a Liberal, and am proud to be a Liberal, although a True Blue! You are like the cuckoo—liberal, but only in song. I never have turned; it is you who have turned; but, if you had been knocked about as I have, you would have resisted. Mr. Cowper I respect as a man ; but tell me the company a man keeps, and I will tell you his character.' (Cheers and uproar.) 'You say you are Liberal. I say you are il-liberal. There is not a Conservative at the present time who has put such a clause in his tenants' agreements.' (A voice: 'Sir E. Lytton !') 'Prove it ! Although a Dissenter, last year I had the honour of paying Church Rates in seven different parishes. It is just like tithe ; a man bargains to pay it when he takes the land, and knows he has to pay it. Suppose there were two pieces of land, exactly similar, for sale, one paying tithe and one tithe free, for which would you give the most ? Why, of course, for the tithe free. Then why try to shirk it ? It is disgraceful and dishonest. I have hitherto supported the Dissenters' cause, and will always support it till they try to crush Church Rates, and then I will desert them.' (Cheers and hisses.)"

SPOTTISWOODE AND CO., PRINTERS, NEW-STREET SQUARE, LONDON.

www.ingramcontent.com/pod-product-compliance
Lightning Source LLC
Chambersburg PA
CBHW032011010726
47493CB00007B/2358